Rachel's Legacy

JULIE THOMAS

Rachel's Legacy

HarperCollins*Publishers*

HarperCollins_Publishers_

First published in 2016
This edition published in 2020
by HarperCollins_Publishers_ (New Zealand) Limited
Unit D1, 63 Apollo Drive, Rosedale, Auckland 0632, New Zealand
harpercollins.co.nz

Copyright © Julie Thomas 2016

HarperCollins_Publishers_
Level 13, 201 Elizabeth Street, Sydney NSW 2000, Australia
Unit D1, 63 Apollo Drive, Rosedale, Auckland 0632, New Zealand
A 53, Sector 57, Noida, UP, India
1 London Bridge Street, London SE1 9GF, United Kingdom
Bay Adelaide Centre, East Tower, 22 Adelaide Street West, 41st floor, Toronto,
  Ontario M5H 4E3, Canada
195 Broadway, New York NY 10007, USA

National Library of New Zealand Cataloguing-in-Publication Data

Thomas, Julie, 1959-
  Rachel's legacy / Julie Thomas.
  ISBN 978-1-46075-848-9 (pbk.)
  I. Title.
NZ823.3—dc 23

Cover design by Amy Daoud, HarperCollins Design Studio
Cover images: Woman © Magdalena Żyźniewska / Trevillion Images;
  Street scene © Lee Avison / Trevillion Images
Typeset in Sabon LT by Kirby Jones
Author photograph by Victoria-p.com

*To Rosa, Bella and all of the other Holocaust survivors
who generously shared their stories with me,
and in the memory of those who died resisting the Nazi regime,
I am in awe of your courage and resilience.*

AUTHOR'S NOTE

This book is a work of fiction. Any references to historical events, real people or real locales are fictitious. Other names, characters, places and incidents are all products of the author's imagination, and any resemblance to actual events or locales or persons, living or dead, is entirely coincidental.

However, all of the characters in the Red Orchestra are real people, and I have used their real names when they are revealed to Kobi Voight. They did do all of the things that my story credits them with, and they died as martyrs to their cause. There is no record of Harro Schulze-Boysen fathering a child, although he and his wife, Libertas, did have an open marriage and so the idea of him having a relationship with someone in their circle is not at all far-fetched. The Horowitzs, Rafael Gomez, the Voights and Maria Weiss are all completely fictional.

Even if we should die, we know this much:
The seed continues to sprout.
Heads may roll, but the Spirit still masters the State.
The final argument
Won't be left to the gallows and the guillotine
And today's judges don't represent the judgement
of the world.

A poem written by First Lieutenant Harro Schulze-Boysen, Luftwaffe,
in his own handwriting and recovered from his cell
after his execution on 22 December 1942.

CHARACTERS

The Voights
Elizabeth Voight   German-born, Melbourne-raised
Karl Voight   Australian-born, her husband
Andrew Voight   their elder son
Lisle Spencer   their daughter
Dr Kobi Voight   their younger son
Sabine Gunther   Elizabeth's mother
Peter Gunther   Elizabeth's father
Mathias Gunther   Elizabeth's brother
Greta Voight   Karl's mother
Karl Voight Snr   Karl's father

The Horowitzs
Benjamin Horowitz   a banker, interred in Dachau
Elizabeth Horowitz   his wife
Levi Horowitz   their eldest son
Simon Horowitz   their middle son
Rachel Horowitz   their twin daughter, a Resistance fighter,
   interred in Auschwitz
David Horowitz   their twin son, interred in Dachau
David Horowitz   Simon's son
Cindy Horowitz   David's wife
Daniel Horowitz   David and Cindy's son, Simon's grandson

Others
Rafael Santamaria Gomez   a conductor
Maria Weiss   a Resistance fighter
Harro Schulze-Boysen   a Resistance fighter
Libertas Schulze-Boysen   a Resistance fighter
George Ross   an investment banker
Professor Dr Mikel Kribbler   Kobi's boss in Berlin
Dr Boris Meyer   Galerie Bassenge, Berlin

CHAPTER ONE

Berlin
June 1942

My dearest darling baby
My hand trembles as I start this, my first letter to you. I
shall try not to cry, because then the ink will be stained
and the words might run together and you won't be
able to read it. My heart is in such a state that it is hard
to know what to write. I am hoping that one day you
and I will sit down and read this together and I can
explain what I cannot write down.

But there is, lurking in the back of my mind, the
fear that I will not be there and you will read them
by yourself. Maybe you will be a young woman, and
my heart flies when I think of how beautiful you will
be. There is so much I want to tell you, so much you
MUST know. If I consider that maybe you will never
know, it feels as if my body will break in two and all
my tears will run out and flood this room. You cannot
possibly know how much I love you, how much my
heart beats in time with yours even though you are
not here with me anymore. But I am getting ahead of
myself. I will try my hardest, my darling, to rein in the
flood of emotion that fills my brain and write you a
sensible letter.

I'm hoping that your name is still the same, because you are named after my mama, your grandmother. She is the bravest and most wonderful woman, and it is my daily prayer that one day I will be able to introduce you to her. I know she will adore you, as I do. The nickname your papa and I gave you the day that you were born was Ebee, a shortened version of her name and yours. Whenever I say it, I think of Mama.

Why did I start writing the letters today? Because I got stopped. I had to take the rickety old bicycle out and deliver some food to the family who are hiding Herr H. Herr H was my brother's violin teacher, and I remember I was always scared of him because he was a very stern man and he was tough on my brother. But I understand now that he was hard because my darling brother was so good at the violin. Today he is not stern or tough, now he cries a lot and wants to know what is happening outside of the tiny windowless room in which he lives.

On my way home a German soldier stopped me and demanded to see my papers. This happens sometimes if we are unlucky, but he was brighter than many of the stupid men with their uniforms and their guns, and he looked at me closely. Then, suddenly, he accused me of being Jewish. I suppose he thought that if I was frightened by him, I might simply admit it. I acted shocked and horrified and told him that Jews are dirty rats and that I most certainly am not! I told him my cover story. That my father is German but my mother was born in Milan, that my name is Francesca Albrecht and I was born here. My father is fighting at the front and I am a good Catholic. I've said it so many times it's almost second nature now, it doesn't feel like a lie.

His tiny piggy eyes narrowed with suspicion, so I

started to recite the Prayer for the Intercession of the Blessed Virgin Mary ... 'Hail Mary, full of grace. The Lord is with thee. Blessed art thou amongst women, and blessed is the fruit of thy womb, Jesus.' Although I don't believe it as I say it, I do find it gives me comfort in times of fear.

He asked me how many disciples Jesus had and I told him that there were twelve, and then he asked me how many days was Jesus in the tomb and I told him it was three, and then he asked me what the third Beatitude was and I panicked. I said I wasn't sure, something about being pure and going to Heaven? He nodded and smiled at me and said it was 'Blessed are the meek for they shall inherit the earth.'

Because I couldn't answer all of his questions, he seemed to think that it meant I really was a Catholic and not a Jew pretending to be a true believer. He told me to go on my way quickly and be careful, as the streets are full of robbers and starving people who might try to hurt me. I pedalled as fast as I could all the way home.

That was close. I was one wrong answer away from disaster. We live with the whims of these soldiers all of the time, and I have seen them shoot people in the street for insubordination or being too terrified to answer a question. I hate disavowing my Judaism, my community and my heritage, it feels like a betrayal of everything I was taught to believe, but if he hadn't believed me, if he'd arrested me and taken me straight to the train station and loaded me into one of those dreadful trains, you would never know who I was and that I didn't give you away. That the fact you are not here with me breaks my heart and rips into my soul every single day.

So, I am sitting in the cellar of my home in Charlottenburg, with a blank piece of precious paper in front of me, and I have decided to write on it and hide it in a safe place in the wall. There are loose bricks all over this room with holes behind them, and I will keep my letters in separate places so that it is less likely that they will all be found. And I shall write them in the language of my faith, the tongue I learned as a small child, so that they can only be read by those who will understand my actions.

When I have finished them, I will take them to Meme and ask her to give them to the couple who are looking after you. It's too dangerous to have you here with us, so they are being your pretend mama and papa until all this hell is over. I think about you all the time and imagine you living in a safe place with animals and fresh food and sunshine. When the evil Führer is defeated, your papa and I will come and get you. We will have a lovely house by a lake and we will sail and swim and live together in peace, far from this frightening city, and with lots of laughter, and we will bring you up in my faith.

So who am I? I am Ruby. I long to tell you my real name, but if this letter is discovered it might get us all killed, so for the moment, nicknames will have to do. I am your mama. Four months ago I gave birth to you in a bedroom upstairs, with my best friend acting as a midwife, and with a doctor and a dentist — both part of our group — helping. Your papa paced up and down in the sitting room and waited; he is very impatient, so that was hard for him. But we both fell in love with you instantly, and you were such a good baby.

I want to tell you so much about your papa. He is brilliant and funny and gentle and kind. When you

*were very small he would rock you in his arms and
sing traditional Prussian folksongs to you. He has
strong hands and little curls that sit flat on his neck
and wonderful blue eyes. He is the love of my life, and
he makes me feel safe when the whole world seems to
be tearing itself apart. Without him I would have just
died of loneliness and the pain of missing my family so
much. But before I tell you more about him, and our
life, I must tell you about my family — your family —
and all of the wonderful people I grew up with.*

Dr Kobi Voight let the letter drop onto his stomach and stared
up at the ceiling. So this is what the funny piece of paper, with
its indecipherable writing and lovely pencil sketches, actually
said. The author, 'Ruby', was German, like his mother, alive
during World War II, like his mother. It appeared she had
made a huge sacrifice, given up her newborn daughter. Why?
If she was delivering food to Jews in hiding, then maybe she
was working for the Resistance. A hero, a brave young woman
who stood up to the Nazi regime. What fate had befallen her?

And why were these letters in his grandmother's, and then
his mother's, possession? His mother thought that Grandma
Gunther had bought them in a market because of the beautiful
sketches; she couldn't read them, because they were written in
Hebrew.

His mother had been born in Berlin, but the family had come
to Melbourne when she was eight; his father's parents were
originally from Munich, and he had felt 'German' on occasions
when he was young. But more lately he had begun to feel as
though a whole part of his being was missing. The Voight side
of his family had died with his paternal grandparents, but
the memories were strong. Now here he was in Berlin, and
somehow it felt as though he was spying on someone else's
family. He picked up the letter again.

My earliest memory is of a drawing lesson. My drawing teacher was called Madame St Claire. Mama told me she was a Frenchwoman who had married a German before the Great War, and he had been killed fighting the French and the British at the Battle of the Somme. She lived with his parents in Berlin and looked after them while she waited for him to come home, and when he didn't, she stayed with them. I didn't understand then how hard it must have been to be French and living in Berlin during that war. Back then I took everything for granted, believed that people would always be nice, and it never occurred to me that we were 'different'.

I remember wanting to have our lessons in the drawing room; the boys had their music lessons in the music room, so why couldn't I have mine in the drawing room? But Mama said I might spill something on her lovely rug, so I sat at the big wooden table in the kitchen. Madame St Claire always wore perfume, and she smelt like the flowers in our garden in the summer. Her hair was red and she wore it wound up in a bun on top of her head. Her hands were rough, and I think she must have had to clean the house for her parents-in-law, but she could draw wonderful people. She taught me how to draw circles and then where to put the features on their faces, and she made me copy out handwriting so that I could make beautiful letters. She will never know how useful that skill has been over the past two years!

One day I made her a present. I drew her eyes. She had the saddest eyes I had ever seen, and I tried to capture what they looked like. When I gave it to her, she cried and hugged me and called me her 'Jolie petite chose', but she told me she cried because my drawing made her so happy. I believed that then and I want you to believe it now.

The only thing I loved more than drawing were the stars at night. Sometimes I would get out of bed and sneak out the back door to stand in the garden and look up at the sky. Once Papa found me and brought me a blanket and we stood together. He pointed out where the different constellations were, and told me how far away they were. And he said that no matter where I was when I was grown up, I could look up at the sky and know that he was looking at it, too, and we would be together. He is a sentimental man, Papa, with a big heart, and I often look up at the stars now and wonder if he's looking at them, too.

So where did we live? In a very big house not far from the Brandenburger Tor. It had lots of bedrooms and bathrooms upstairs, and some wonderful formal rooms downstairs. My bedroom had my bed and my wardrobe and dressing table, and a desk at which to do my homework.

Mama embroidered a silk quilt for my bed with a Star of David in the centre and a dreidel and a menorah and a Torah and my name in Hebrew. All of my dolls sat or stood on the big window ledge, and I dressed them in different sets of clothes that hung in a little wooden wardrobe that my uncle had made for me.

He had made one for Dee, too, to keep his dreidels in. Dee was very proud of his collection of spinning tops. Sometimes I forget that you won't know what these things mean. A dreidel is a top with four sides and four Hebrew letters on it, and you play a game with it at Hanukkah. Dee liked to play for a pot of money, but Papa usually made him play for sweets. It's a game of chance and, depending on what letter it comes to rest on when you spin it, you get nothing, or you get the whole pot in the middle of the table, or half the pot, or you have to add something to the pot.

Papa visited art galleries when he was in other cities in Germany, and he brought me home prints of famous paintings to hang on my wall. My favourites were the da Vinci Portrait of a Musician, the Raphael Portrait of a Young Lady with a Unicorn, and the Albrecht Dürer works, especially the hare and a large piece of turf. We had an original Dürer painting in our entrance hall; he was an ancestor of Mama's and he looked like her. He had curls that came to his shoulders and hazel eyes that were almost green, like Mama. Dee said he was very proud and looking down his nose at us, but I thought he was kind and his clothing was beautiful — he had been very rich.

The best room in the house was the formal sitting room. We sat in the drawing room as a family, but the formal sitting room was for guests. Mama had all her best treasures on display there, the ruby-red Venetian glass bowls and her two Fabergé eggs. Oh, how I loved those eggs! They were covered in enamel that was the colour of the sea and the grass, and had tiny little diamonds around the middle, and one had a big emerald on the top! If I had been good, Mama would take one down from its display box and let me touch it and open it to look at the tiny gold-and-diamond carriage inside.

I used a peacock feather to tickle the small porcelain statues of people, because they were stuck in their fancy poses and couldn't scratch the itch! And the ivory carvings were so cold under my fingers in the winter. There was a marble pedestal with the bust of a Greek politician on it; one day I danced into it and knocked it over, but the bust was so heavy it didn't break.

The long dining-room table had huge silver centrepieces with lots of engraved bunches of shiny grapes which Dee and I used to pretend to eat. We had so many exquisite things and I was so used to seeing them I stopped noticing how wonderful they were.

Most of all we had paintings! In the drawing room there was a Madonna painted by Sandro Botticelli. She had very pale skin and long golden hair, and she was wearing a cloak of bright blue. You couldn't see the colour of her eyes because she was looking down at the fat pink baby in her arms. Papa used to say that she didn't look very Middle Eastern, or even very Italian, but I thought she was gorgeous.

Mama told me that one of the reasons she was glad she had a girl was because she could show off her jewellery. When I had done my homework, and the boys were busy with their music, I would follow her into her dressing room. We would sit on her chaise longue and she would bring out her silver jewellery box.

Oh, how I adored that box! It was heavy, a sort of oval, with fluted sides, and engraved with bold, swirly patterns. Right in the centre of the top were her initials: she was ERH and I was REH, so I'd decided that it didn't matter if the letters were around the wrong way when it came to my turn. When she lifted the lid it was like opening a box of pirate treasure! The first thing I always took out were her pearls, a double string of creamy balls of light, with a tiny knot between each one. Then the diamond brooch in the shape of a violin that twinkled back at me; her lovely sapphire ring; the tiara she wore with her wedding veil; and a ruby-and-diamond bracelet that had been a wedding present from her mother-in-law.

I would put on every piece I could fit and dance
around the room, twirling like a ballerina, until she
made me stop in case something flew off and got lost
amongst the silks and organza of her clothing. She
made me feel like a princess, and I believed one day it
would all be mine. Little did I know. I wonder where it
is now? Worn by the fat wife of some Nazi general?

The question made Kobi smile. He could imagine how bitter these people might have become, so many glorious possessions now in the hands of Nazi thugs. And what about the paintings? He was an artist himself, and an art history lecturer at the University of Melbourne. His passion was the work of Albrecht Dürer, and this family had had an original Dürer in their house! Never in his wildest dreams could he have thought that these funny old letters, which he'd had translated out of sheer curiosity, would talk about an original Dürer painting. Sure, they were a wealthy German family and Dürer was a German artist, but still! It was like a gift from God, a sign of approval of Kobi's intended project.

He didn't recognise the actual painting from the girl's description, and he strongly suspected that it had been lost to the Nazi looters, or to the Red Army that took so much artistic treasure back to Moscow as war loot ... But even so, a Dürer!

The Berlin of my childhood was a gorgeous place. I
remember majestic concrete buildings and monuments
and wide boulevards and lots of trams. Sometimes
Mama and Papa would take us to an outdoor café and
we would be allowed to drink hot chocolate and choose
the most delicious cakes, and then we would watch
our parents dancing to the orchestra with the other
couples. They floated around the square to the waltz
and the foxtrot! In summer we would go to the beach at

Wannsee, make sandcastles and go swimming, or take
a picnic into the Tiergarten, and in winter we would go
ice-skating. At night people would come to our house
and make music and sing and play cards, and I used to
lie in bed and listen and think that I was the luckiest
little girl in the world.

Papa, your grandpapa. He was a banker and he
went to work every weekday at the family bank until
the Nazis took it from him. He isn't very tall and he's
round — he used to say that he could bounce back from
anything, because he was shaped like a ball. He has a
wonderful bushy moustache and his eyes are dark and
twinkly, as though something is always amusing him.
His favourite things in the house were his violins, and
he kept them in glass cases in the music room. They
were very old and precious and they made glorious
sounds. My brother told me that I must never pick
them up in case I dropped them, but I didn't want
to pick them up. He did let me touch one once, his
favourite one, because I drew him a picture of it. Then I
drew a picture of him playing it and put it in a wooden
frame for his birthday. Anyway, back to Papa. Most
of all I remember his lovely deep voice when he sings
prayers at Shabbat, and his laugh — he has a belly
laugh, rich and loud and he shakes all over when he
really laughs.

Mama, your grandmama. She is very beautiful and
very soft. She has soft hands and a soft kiss, and when
you kiss her cheek, her skin is soft. She is tall, with a
small waist (of which she is very proud!), a very straight
back and a long neck. I like to remember her as she
was when I was little — before the Nazis came — and
she seemed to glow. She had a green silk dress and it
shone in the light, and she wore pearls and diamonds.

When she walked, her clothes rustled. When they went out at night she would bring me back a chocolate, and when I woke up, and the chocolate was beside my bed, I knew that she was home, safe and sound. She took me shopping, and people would smile and give a little nod and say 'Guten Tag, Frau H.' I loved going to the big shops where everyone wanted to please her.

Lee, your uncle. He is my eldest brother and he lives in London now. After the war is over, I am going to find him and hug him very tight for a long time. He played the piano every day, and that was what he wanted to do, play piano in a nightclub, but Papa said no, so he decided to make lovely furniture instead. When he couldn't go to university (because they wouldn't allow Jews anymore), he worked for Papa in the bank. He has a tenor voice and I can hear it whenever I think about the prayers we used to sing together. He left home a year before the war started, and I gave him a poem and a drawing of him playing the piano to take with him. Was that only three and a half years ago? So much has happened since and I feel like a different person.

Cee, your uncle. He is my middle brother, and he is with Dee. Whenever I think of Cee I think of his violin — it's like they are joined together in my mind. He looks like Papa, quite short and stocky, with dark hair and brown eyes. He used to read me stories, and I used to sneak into his room and 'borrow' his books. He is an earnest young man, and he took his job of 'eldest boy at home' very seriously after Lee left. He is also amazingly brave. When the Nazis came and took our house, Cee put up a fight and gave the horrid Nazi a bloody nose! I don't know why he hit the officer, but in my heart I believe it had something to do with

*his precious violins. He was struck on the hand with
a truncheon and was trying not to scream when they
pushed him into the truck. The last thing he called to
us was to go to Meme because she would help us. Even
then he was thinking about us.*

*Dee. He is my twin brother. He adores exploring and
making maps and reading a compass, playing football
and Ping-Pong, and he loves cats. I could make him
giggle by tickling him during the Shabbat prayers. For
so many years he was just Dee and he annoyed me and
we fought, but it was just play-fighting. He always told
me what to do and I used to wish he wasn't there so I
could make up my own mind. I can't believe I thought
that. Now I haven't seen him for two and a half years
and it feels like half of me is missing. I would give
almost anything to see his silly, grinning face and hear
him tell me that everything will be fine because he will
always take care of me.*

*I like to believe that Lee is safe in London, but
the truth is we never heard whether he made it. Papa
tried to find out for a year, but all the authorities
could tell him was that Lee had made it to the border
with Switzerland. Then last year Mama went to join
him. She had been hiding with a Catholic family and
working as a tutor to their children. She had false
papers, too, and I thought she was as safe as we can be
in all this madness. But she decided she wanted to be
with Lee. I believe she made it, too, and one day I will
see them both. I didn't tell her I was pregnant, because
then she would have stayed here to look after me, and
who knows what will happen. With every passing
month our situation grows more precarious.*

*As for Papa, Cee and Dee, I know they were taken
to the work camp at Dachau on the train. So was my*

uncle. At the start, Meme tried to get them released, but it was too late: war had been declared and nothing her friends could do made any difference.

My knowledge of everything that has happened since tells me that they are dead, maybe, possibly, probably. We know about the atrocities the Nazis are committing 'in the East', and we hear very bad rumours about those camps. But my heart finds that too hard to accept. They are such good people and they have done nothing wrong. Maybe I will be one of the lucky ones and G-d will keep my family safe so that we can all be together again. In the meantime, I pray daily and I do what I do because of them and to honour them and to make sure that, if they are dead, they did not die in vain. I also pray that you will understand, and that, in years to come, my choices will make sense to you, and when we have won, it will all be for the best.

Your dearest Mama

CHAPTER TWO

Melbourne
July 2014

The night before Kobi Voight left for a three-month sabbatical in Berlin, his mother, now a widow but still living in the family home, came to his inner-city apartment to visit him. He was packing.

'Shouldn't you take a singlet, just in case?' she asked.

'It's July, August and September, Mother. I don't think I'll need a singlet, and if I do, I'll buy one. Did you know they have the largest department store in Europe in Berlin?'

She smiled at him. 'Actually, I do know that. Now, I didn't just come over here to say goodbye. I have something for you.'

He dropped a shirt into the open suitcase on his bed. 'Really? What sort of something?'

'Something for you to take with you.'

Kobi was surprised. He doubted very much that it was anything from her childhood, as she never spoke of it. She went to her handbag, which she had left on his dresser, and took out a black plastic bag.

'I found these in your grandmother's desk when I was going through her things after the funeral. I suppose I kept them because of the lovely drawings, and I thought you might like to take them with you.'

She handed him the bag. He opened it and drew out a bundle of letters, which were tied together by an old, stained pink ribbon.

'What are they?' he asked.

'Letters.'

'To Grandma Gunther?'

She shook her head. 'No. I don't think they have anything to do with her. I don't know where she got them from. Maybe she picked them up in some sort of market or curio shop, she was always doing that. They're written in Hebrew, although some of the words are German. I thought you might like to look at them because the most interesting thing is the beautiful illustrations. If the artist is German, it might make an interesting study.'

'Illustrations? What sort?'

'Mostly pencil, and some pen. Look at the paper. They were written a long time ago, maybe during the war; there are some maps and diagrams and pictures of people playing musical instruments.'

Kobi put them back in the plastic bag and tucked them into his suitcase, then he leaned over and kissed her on the cheek. 'Thank you, Mother. That's intriguing and a very nice gift. I shall spend some long summer evenings looking at them as I sip my beer.'

The gesture genuinely moved him. It was highly unusual for his mother to give him anything with a connection to her homeland; all his life it had been a subject riven with secrets.

Kobi Voight was quite different from his elder brother, Andrew, who was hardworking and earnest and saved his money in a kangaroo money-box. His sister, Lisle, was more relaxed about life; she loved making things and going to flea markets and singing in the shower.

His father's parents had immigrated to Australia as a young couple. Their front room had little beer steins on the shelves, and cuckoo clocks on the walls. Kobi used to move the hands of the clocks around to make the birds pop out and sing when no one was looking.

When he took the train north from Melbourne, with his older brother and sister, he knew that they would put away their 'Australianness' and become honorary Germans for the time they stayed with Greta and Karl Voight senior. Lisle loved the traditional costumes that her grandma had in the cupboard, and she wore hers with pride when they were taken to the local German society for schnitzel and *spätzle* and proper German beer and dancing.

But this was a small portion of their lives; something they kept hidden from their parents. Their father, Karl, wouldn't have minded, in fact he would have been secretly pleased. Their mother, Elizabeth, didn't like conversations about Germany and they were used to seeing her exasperation when her in-laws sent German memorabilia for their home. The children didn't understand her attitude but they were sensitive to her moods and the way she would stiffen whenever anyone mentioned the fact that she was born in Germany. They were certain she would have been furious and would have forbidden any more trips north. So the last thing the children did when they disembarked from the train home was to remind each other that most of the holiday was a secret.

Kobi had picked up coloured pencils when he was in kindergarten and drawn pictures of the flowers in his mother's garden. His teachers were so surprised by his talent and by his subject choice that they had telephoned his parents and asked them to come in for an interview.

'It's not that usual to have little boys drawing flowers, Mrs Voight,' the teacher said as she held the colourful piece of paper up in front of her. 'And look at the detail. The petals on the roses, the variations in the colours and the drops of water on the leaves. Most of the children are still drawing stick figures.' On the way home Karl asked his wife whether they should be concerned about Kobi's love of flowers.

'Not at all, dear. Maybe he'll be a florist. Or an artist. All the best ones are men,' she said happily.

Kobi liked guns and running fast in races and playing tag and hide-and-seek, but he also cast a critical eye over his sister and her friends as they played dress-up with Elizabeth's clothes. Their lack of organisation frustrated him.

'Can't you even try and match the colours?' he asked one day.

Lisle laughed at him. 'You sit on the bed and you watch.'

'I know,' he jumped up and grabbed his mother's hairbrush, 'you have a fashion parade and I'll do the talking.'

They thought this was a wonderful idea and spent the rest of the afternoon prancing around the room while Kobi stood on the bed, hairbrush to his lips.

'And now we have Kylie, in a lovely aqua polyester dress and matching sandals. The dangly earrings are her own.'

Kobi also had a sensitive side, and he cried easily when Elizabeth read him sad books or they saw a tear-jerker movie. One of her favourite memories was of a conversation she had had with him after a tantrum had resulted in him being sent to his room. He was lying on his bed looking at the coloured rainbow on his ceiling.

'Feeling better, little man?' she asked as she sat down.

'No.'

'What can I do to make things right?'

He looked at her, his cheeks tear-stained. 'You tore my feelings all up, like a piece of newspaper.'

'Oh dear! Well, we better glue them back together again then. Would some music do that? Or how about a jigsaw?'

When each of her three children turned five, Elizabeth enrolled them in classes with a local piano teacher. She had brought them up with classical music on in the background, a love she had inherited from her father, and she was proud of the fact that they could identify composers and singers from the recordings. She loved the old-style tenors — Giuseppe Di Stefano, Carlo Bergonzi, Nicolai Gedda and Richard Crooks — whereas Lisle and Kobi liked the newer ones — Luciano Pavarotti and Plácido Domingo.

Andrew lasted two years and told his mother he wouldn't go back; he couldn't see the point of the piano, and he'd rather have advanced maths coaching. Lisle took to it like a cat to a tree and wanted to add modern and folk music to her repertoire. Kobi mastered the basics very quickly and used it to express a latent flamboyance and a performance gene he didn't even know he had. His parents gave him a guitar for his thirteenth birthday. He had expressed an interest in learning the violin, but his father had squashed that idea by telling his mother to choose between a violin-playing son or a husband.

Kobi went to the same all-boys secondary school as his elder brother. It was academic and sporty and he felt like a fish out of water.

'So, Voight, how come you have a German name?' The older boys pushed him up against the lockers and glared at him.

'My dad was born here and so was I!' he'd remonstrate with them.

'But your mother is a Kraut, isn't she?'

Again and again the 'German factor' seemed to rear up and confront him. He tried to start conversations at home about his heritage but his mother shut them down, firmly and quickly. So he turned to books and tried to fill in the gaps in his knowledge through reading in the library at school.

To try to fit in with his peers, he pretended to develop a passion for cricket. He was good in the field, fast to the ball and a secure pair of hands, a fine middle-order batsman with a technique honed in the backyard with his dad. But all too often his concentration let him down, his eye was inevitably caught by something happening on the side-line and he was bowled. Throughout his secondary school years his greatest passion was art, and, when cricket started to interfere with time spent in the art studio at school, he gave an inward sigh of relief and abandoned cricket.

'Why do you come to school, Voight?' his form teacher asked in an exasperated tone as he surveyed yet more unfinished homework.

'To eat my lunch and to paint, sir,' Kobi replied with a perfectly straight face. The answer got him a few whacks with the cane, but the satisfaction of seeing the teacher trying not to laugh was worth the pain.

When he was fourteen his grandpa died of cancer, and six months later his grandma had a massive heart attack. The family had gone up to Sydney for both deaths, and his mother had borne the traditional German funerals with difficulty. The hardest part for Kobi was knowing that their 'German' visits to Sydney would now come to an end. At his grandma's funeral, Andrew had asked if he could speak. Kobi thought that was very brave. It was only the second funeral he had ever been to, and the Catholic church and all the finery were magnificent, but intimidating. Andrew unfolded his notes and stood for a moment to compose himself in the pulpit.

'My grandparents were German. They may have lived for many years in Australia, but they were always very German. From the time I was a small boy I used to come to Sydney on the train, with my younger sister and brother, and stay with them. We were taught basic German words for everyday objects and we ate lots of German food. My grandma watched me eat a whole jar of herring once. We went to the local German society clubrooms and danced and ate schnitzel.'

What was Andrew doing, Kobi wondered? He knew Andrew had loved their grandparents very much and it felt right for him to be speaking, honouring them. But when he paused to breathe and let his words sink in, Andrew looked straight at his mother. There was something else in his facial expression, a look that filled Kobi with admiration for his elder brother. It was defiance; he was daring their mother to react. Andrew started again.

'I remember the first time Grandpa gave me a sip from his beer stein and I liked it, so he poured me a little of my own. When we came home we kept all of these things to ourselves. We told our parents that our grandparents had respected their wishes and not shared their German culture with us. That was a lie. Our grandparents believed that we were, on balance, more German than Australian.'

Kobi looked at his mother who was sitting beside him. She was twisting a handkerchief between her fingers. Her face was white and pinched, and he could see by the spark in her blue eyes that she was absolutely furious.

In his last year at school Kobi took art history, which hadn't been available any earlier. His teacher was a young woman who wore long skirts and had her dark hair in plaits. She took him for art as well, and was astonished by his talent. Throughout the year he compiled a portfolio of paintings and etchings, and he was influenced by some of the books he read without his mother's knowledge. Books about life in Soviet East Berlin, escapes over the Berlin Wall, the treachery of the Stasi and the lack of freedom. He was appalled by some of what he learned and with no one to talk to, his emotion came out in his art.

'What's this?' his art teacher asked as she studied his latest painting. Black buildings and spotlights and barbed-wire mixed together with blood in an abstract portrayal of repression.

'East Germany,' he said. 'The wall and the oppressive State and the Stasi. People trying to escape.'

'Is your mother East German?'

He nodded. 'But my grandparents brought her here before the wall went up.'

'Did she tell you about this kind of stuff?'

'No, she doesn't talk about it, but I've read some books.'

She shook her head slowly. 'It's very good, Kobi. Very powerful, and your use of the brilliant white light to showcase the wire and guns, very strong.'

Art history students had two choices. They were given a list of names and could choose one painter for their major and another one to study on a minor level. Whether their two choices would appear in the exam paper was a matter of luck. After much thought, Kobi choose Raffaello Sanzio de Urbino, known as Raphael, over Leonardo da Vinci as his minor painter. There was never any question about who would be his major: Albrecht Dürer. When his art history teacher asked them to explain their choices to the rest of the class, Kobi's hand shot up.

'I chose Albrecht Dürer because he's the greatest artist of the early Renaissance to come from Germany. Think about his versatility. He painted in oil and watercolour but he also created some of the world's greatest engravings and woodcuts.'

The teacher nodded her approval and Kobi grinned with happiness. He spent the year in seventh heaven, poring over text books and prints, and trying to copy the Master's engravings in pencil. His diligence was well rewarded — the essay question about Dürer helped him to secure a scholarship. A lifelong passion was born.

He'd started some time ago to feel genuinely different from the other boys. All around him his friends were getting girlfriends and experimenting with sex. As time progressed he waited to feel that spark when he met a girl, someone he wanted to invite out for coffee and to a movie, but it never happened. He felt much happier in the company of his friends and some of their older brothers. If he felt anything at all, it was for the smouldering Italian boy who served him in his local deli. Did this mean he was gay? He had no real idea and the health lessons at school weren't geared to give him answers. He didn't feel able to confide in anyone so he stayed silent and kept his distance.

The years after graduation from school flew by. His older brother had qualified as an accountant and was working in the city for a finance company, and his sister was studying graphic design at art school, but she really wanted to be a potter. Kobi went to fine art school and lived on a loan from his parents. He flatted with a group of other young men, drank a bit and smoked some dope, but was happiest in the studio creating his portfolio.

He lost his virginity in a drunken encounter at a party and was horrified by the experience; it was mortifying and he was convinced she found it highly amusing. Then he had his first gay affair and lost his heart to an older man, who stayed around for a few weeks and then skipped town when he got bored. Devastated, Kobi decided that relationships were sad, messy and hard work, and he'd concentrate on his career instead. Magnificent art made his heart sing and had no power to hurt him.

After obtaining his PhD in early German Renaissance Art, he became a lecturer at the University of Melbourne by the age of thirty. By 2013, when he was forty-two years old, he was a strange mixture of creative and academic, both artist and lecturer. His art was dark and abstract. His followers knew which galleries agreed to show his paintings and he sold enough to keep the dealers happy. He'd had a couple of shows over the years but found the pressure to produce to a deadline almost intolerable. Some of the critics understood him, seeing the work as an illustration of his conflict over his heritage, but the general opinion was that as an artist, he made a good lecturer.

He was a mix of personality, too; quick-witted, articulate and friendly, but hiding a basic shyness. His friends would never have guessed that he found it hard to enter a room full of people and join a conversation. Physically, he took after his mother — tall, slender, with a long back, rangy limbs and elongated fingers. His short hair and goatee beard were a deep auburn colour, flecked with the first signs of grey. He was single, childless, and preferred his own company, but he was also a people-watcher, with well-developed gut instincts, and he viewed all human beings as potential subject matter.

After twelve years at the university, he had now qualified for paid study leave, and he had leapt at the chance to take his sabbatical and study the works of Albrecht Dürer, in Germany.

CHAPTER THREE

Berlin

July 2014

Kobi had carried the letters all the way to Berlin, and at the first opportunity had taken them to be translated into English where he felt there were people who could translate them into English. That was the first step towards understanding what they were and deciding what to do with them.

Over on the kitchen wall the red cuckoo popped out of the white wooden clock and heralded another hour. He could hear the faint hum of traffic and road works from the Auguststrasse four storeys below his windows. He was lying on a black leather sofa in the lounge of his Berlin apartment. He had been there fourteen days, and it still felt vaguely thrilling to refer to this set of rooms as his 'Berlin apartment'. Only one letter into the English translation and already he had questions for Ruby. Had she ever worshipped at the splendid New Synagogue, and, if so, how magnificent had that experience been?

That very morning he had strolled down the full length of the Auguststrasse to where it met the Oranienburger Strasse. He had passed squat, grey buildings in the obvious style of Soviet East Berlin, intermingled with newer apartment buildings, some of them built to resemble the grand houses of the pre-war era. At street level there were shops, cafés and restaurants.

The pavements were cobbled, and he still found it hard to stick to the right-hand side instead of the left. When he wandered into the cycle-way, the occasional cyclist came up behind him and rang their bell.

At the T-junction he turned left, and a few metres down the road he came to the New Synagogue. This glorious building had formed the hub of Jewish life in Berlin for so many years, before being expropriated by the Wehrmacht in 1940, and almost destroyed by Allied bombing in 1943. The modern day community kept it open to the public as a memorial to Jewish life in pre-war Berlin and to house the fragments that were left of its former grandeur.

Three policemen stood on guard outside the building. When he nodded to them there was no response, although their eyes were watchful, cautious. So he walked through the gap in the iron fence and up the path to the heavy front door where he had to go through a security check: an x-ray of his satchel and a walk through a metal detector.

'*Guten Morgen,*' he said to the guard, who inclined his head in response. He collected his belongings on the other side.

'*Danke,*' he said.

'*Bitte sehr,*' said the guard.

He went into the little shop, and the young man behind the counter recognised him and smiled broadly. 'Good morning, Dr Voight, have you come to see Frau Goldman?'

'Yes, thank you,' he said, feeling a small sense of pleasure at being greeted by name in a city that was still so foreign to him. The man picked up a phone.

'I'll let her know you're here. Why don't you have a look about? I'm sure she'll find you.' He gestured towards the entrance-way.

'I'd like that, thank you,' Kobi said.

The first room contained two long red Torah curtains in a glass case, the beautiful embroidery gently fading. The remains of the lamp of everlasting light sat in a glass box beside them. In the centre of the room was some rubble reconstructed to look like a pulpit, and a washbasin. There were information plaques on the wall in both German and English. Pieces of a cherished past, preserved and revered.

This place was consecrated on Rosh Hashanah in 1866 and was once the largest Jewish house of worship in Germany. Kobi had seen the immense gold dome from the street, and couldn't help thinking that it stood out like a beacon of difference on the skyline. Such striking ostentation would have been dangerous under the rule of the Nazis, a frightening situation for a community who were obviously proud of their culture and had built this place of worship to celebrate it. As he passed through the arch he touched the walls and wondered how many hundreds of people had done so before him.

The next room held pieces of original stained glass stuck onto the plain windows and sections of painted scenes fixed to the arches; they looked delicate and fragile. He walked to the bank of windows and looked out at the huge area where the auditorium had stood, with room for over three thousand seats.

'Good Lord, that's vast!' he said quietly to himself and shook his head at the thought of such wanton destruction, but it was the undeniable reality of war. As he turned away from the empty space his gaze was captured by a large black-and-white photograph. Row upon row of men sat, all looking in the same direction, their facial expressions reflecting their deep concentration. They wore hats and ties and coats, some with fur collars, their hands clasped and their knees crossed. Something about their faces fascinated him and he walked over to scrutinise them.

'Do you wonder what they are listening to?'

The female voice shattered his reverie, and he swung around to smile at Frau Goldman. She was a petite woman in a quality skirt and jacket, her blonde hair cut short and glasses magnifying her grey eyes.

'Yes,' he said. 'A rabbi, I suppose.'

'Probably. There must have been some great orators.'

'They're drinking in every word.'

'My favourite piece of information about this place is the fact that they used to drive their horses and carriages in through the Great Hall entrance.'

He shook his head. What a building it must have been!

'And that dome would have been visible for miles,' he added.

She held out his plastic package. 'It still is. Here is your translation, Dr Voight, and the original letters. I have to say it was a fascinating exercise.'

He took it from her. 'Thank you so much. Please, call me Kobi; Dr Voight is so formal and only my mother calls me Jakob.'

Frau Goldman nodded towards the photograph.

'How many of them survived the terror of the Third Reich, do you think? As I read those letters, I wondered whether any of them were helped by the author.'

'Really?'

Her words surprised him, and he hesitated before following her from the room. She was talking over her shoulder. 'Yes, she was a Resistance fighter in Berlin, during the early part of the war. She is careful what she says, but it's clear she was a very brave woman.'

He caught up with her at the exit.

'And the sketches?'

'They refer to people. She doesn't name any of them — that would have been dangerous if they had fallen into the wrong hands. She uses nicknames. But she clearly loved them. Her family.'

He nodded thoughtfully. 'So there are no clues? About who she was?'

'Unfortunately, no.'

'I look forward to reading this. Thank you once again.'

She gestured towards the package as he put it into his satchel. 'You're welcome. You know, Kobi, you should consider donating the originals to one of the museums here; they would be relevant to several of them. When you have read them, I suggest you visit the German Resistance Memorial Centre on the Stauffenbergstrasse.'

CHAPTER FOUR

Berlin
June 1942

My dearest darling baby,
It's only a day since my last letter, but I have found
myself aching to write to you again. It feels as though
when I'm writing I'm close to you, with you in a funny
sort of way. I have a blanket in which we wrapped you,
and I sleep with it under my pillow. Your darling papa
suggested I keep a pair of your booties, but you only
had two pairs and I knew you would need them. I want
to make sure you know, in every word I write, that my
love for you flows out of my heart and through my arm
and into the pen and onto the page. I do this so that you
WILL know who you are and where you come from
and the extraordinary circumstances of your birth. But
I also want you to know me, so I shall tell you more
about my life before the war.

My life before the Nazis came was full of laughter.
My twin and I used to play Ping-Pong and hide-and-
seek. He was very good at hiding, and I was not very
good at finding him. My elder brothers played tennis
and went into town with their friends. On Saturdays
we all dressed up in our best clothes and went to the
synagogue, mostly the local one down the road, but

on High Holy days Mama and Papa would take us to the great big one in town. That was always exciting, women in their beautiful dresses and men in suits and coats. I loved the enormous shiny gold dome.

We all had our favourite foods, and Cook used to spoil me with treats when no one was looking. I went to a private school with both Jewish and non-Jewish children, and we all played together and learned together. Sometimes my friends slept at my house and sometimes I slept at their houses, and they all knew I couldn't come out on a Friday night, and no one minded.

The changes started very slowly. In fact they were so slow I hardly noticed them. One day some girls in my class were mean to me, pulled my plaits and accused me of being a 'Jew'. I told them that was what I was, and what was wrong with that? A boy punched Dee and called him a 'dirty Jew', so Dee punched him back and made his nose bleed. Dee got into trouble.

Shopkeepers started to look sideways at some of our friends and refused to serve them. I heard their voices full of anger and indignation when they told my parents what had happened. Papa told us it was just people being ignorant and stupid and we should feel sorry for them and not be frightened. We still had our music evenings, and Dee and I still sat on the steps of the staircase and listened to the sweet notes and the singing.

At the beginning of 1933 I remember a night when Papa was very angry and that made me scared. Dee and I were still very young and only just beginning to take notice of the moods of the people around us. Mama told us it was just silly old politics, someone called Hindenburg was the President and he had appointed someone called Hitler to be our Chancellor and Papa thought that was a terrible mistake.

Almost immediately they started passing laws and making things illegal. On the first of April there was a campaign to boycott Jewish shops. It makes me laugh when I think how upset we were over such a slight thing. There were men in uniforms outside the shops, and they said very politely 'Jewish shop' to people about to go in. We went around as many shops as we could so we could answer, 'Thank you, we already know.' The men always looked surprised, but they didn't stop us. In fact one shopkeeper painted a slogan on his shop window that said 'I'm Jewish — Aryans enter my shop at their own risk.' That made Papa roar with laughter!

On the same day it became compulsory to give the German salute, you had to raise your right hand and say 'Heil Hitler!' At the time we thought it was fun and Dee and I marched around the house doing it; now it makes me shudder every time I see it. And if a Jew does it on the street and a soldier sees it, he will shoot the Jew dead.

During the month of April the laws kept coming, new ones every day. Jewish teachers were banned, then doctors had to register, Jews couldn't work in the Civil Service, and in May we had the book-burning.

The destruction of books made Papa furious. He wanted us to see it, to understand how wrong it was, so he took us to the Unter den Linden, just across the street from the university. There were thousands of people there, and we stood holding hands and watching as storm troopers in uniform and students from the university threw books into the road and set them on fire. I don't mean just a few books; Papa told us later

*that they had burned twenty-five thousand books
in several pyres. We stood in silence, but the crowd
around us were chanting things, ugly words about what
the authors had done and then their names. It wasn't
just Jewish authors; it was books by Communists and
Catholics and Americans! The one that upset Papa the
most was when they burned All Quiet on the Western
Front, the book about World War I written by Erich
Maria Remarque. He loved that book, and I remember
him muttering that no one was going to make him
burn his copy, nor his copies of Helen Keller, Ernest
Hemmingway, Jack London, Bertolt Brecht or Sigmund
Freud.*

*Not far from us was a podium draped with a Nazi
banner, and a man stood there and spoke to the crowd.
He told us that the era of extreme Jewish intellectualism
had come to an end and there was a revolution
happening that would open the way for the true essence
of being German. When he spoke about the trash and
filth of Jewish literati, Papa made us all leave and go
home. A few years later I learned that the man speaking
had been Joseph Goebbels, and so when still a young
child I had looked into the face of pure evil.*

*At school some of my Jewish friends had fathers who
were doctors, dentists and lawyers, and their clients
left them and went to Gentiles instead. I remember the
first Saturday we came out of the synagogue to find a
group of people standing on the sidewalk, who shouted
at us. Papa had warned us that it might happen and had
instructed us to walk quickly, and to chat to each other
while making sure we didn't look at the angry crowd.
From then on we had a 'welcoming committee' every
Saturday, and some of them followed us, throwing dirt
and yelling and spitting in our direction. Mama wanted*

*us to stay home, but it was an easy walk and Papa
refused to let the mob affect our behaviour. We ignored
them, or sometimes Dee and I laughed at them and
they turned bright red with rage.*

*When I look back now, Mama and Papa must
have been worried about the bank and about what
would happen, but they never talked about it when
Dee and I were in the room. It didn't affect us when
the government made it illegal for Jews to carry guns,
but it did when we weren't allowed radios anymore. I
missed sitting with Mama by the fire, listening to the
programmes on the radio.*

*When I was eleven Madame St Claire told Mama she
could no longer teach me to draw because her parents-
in-law forbade her to, but she did leave me some
picture books to copy and lots of paper and pencils. It
seemed so unfair, and I cried bitterly when she hugged
me. I promised her I would always draw pictures and I
have kept that promise.*

*Over the years our food changed, too. Mama could
no longer order from the huge department store on
the Wittenberg Platz. It was originally owned by a
Jewish family but they were forced to sell, and Georg
Karg, who was chosen by the Nazis to run the store,
wouldn't sell to Jews. So there was no easy way to get
things like smoked salmon, champagne and chocolate
truffles. We bought food from Jewish friends who knew
sympathetic farmers, and dinner became boiled beef,
potatoes and cabbage instead of veal cutlets and apple
pancakes. When I compare even those bland meals
with what we can find now, it feels like we feasted.
Nowadays we live on dark rye bread and potatoes.*

*By 1938 Dee and I had stopped going to school
and Mama taught us from books she borrowed from*

friends. For a little while we went to a Jewish grammar school that was still open on the Grosse Hamburger Strasse, but it was very overcrowded, with more than fifty pupils in our class. It was hard to get to and people stood outside to hurl abuse and dirt at us as we arrived and left. We weren't learning anything and I was always frightened, so Papa said it was better for me to stay at home. Dee refused to go if I didn't, so we both went to school in the kitchen!

It wasn't yet compulsory to carry our identification papers, but Papa told us to do so, as that way there would be no excuse to detain us illegally. We didn't go out much, just to the synagogue and sometimes to have tea with friends. Most shops wouldn't serve us anymore. I missed my Sunday trips to the art gallery with Papa, and he promised me that we would do it again soon.

From 5 October our identity papers had to be marked with a large 'J' on the cover and a yellow 'J' on the inside. Our left ears had to be visible in the photograph because the idiotic Nazi doctors said that Jewish people's left ears revealed their Semitic roots. And it was compulsory to take the middle name, 'Israel' for the men and 'Sara' for the women, so anyone checking them would know we were Jewish. If you didn't obey these rules they would put you in prison for a month. Papa used to joke about Mama and I being his two 'Zores', from our new middle name of Sara. In Hebrew it means trouble and strife!

Many of our friends had left Germany by this stage, and, at night when I was supposed to be asleep, I heard Mama and Papa talking about emigrating. Papa had a brother who had gone to live in New York, and he was a banker there. We would only have been allowed to take a suitcase each and a little money, and Mama couldn't bear the thought of leaving all her beautiful things.

Papa still believed that people would see sense and get rid of Hitler, whom he called 'that little Austrian paper-hanger'. And he liked to say that we were German and always would be: we spoke German, our culture was Germanic, and his family had been bankers in Germany for generations. By now it would have been too expensive for us all to leave anyway — my uncle would have had to put up six guarantees and lots of money to get us all exit visas. I didn't know it at the time, but not long ago I overheard a conversation that made me realise that towards the end of that year my parents could have put Dee and me on a train to England with other children, but I suppose Mama just couldn't do it. She must have believed we were safer with her.

Then one day some of our closest friends came back from Palestine after living there for a year. They told Mama about the dirt, the lack of water and the plagues of insects and how chaotic everything was, and she thanked G-d we were still in Germany.

I remember 9 November 1938 very clearly. It was nearly bedtime and Dee and I were playing with his train set. Sometimes he let me move the signals up and down and fill the wagons with the miniature wooden logs. I remember wanting to push the buttons, but he said he was older than me and that was his job. Funny how much that five-minute difference meant to him.

The phone rang downstairs, then Mama hurried into our room. She looked upset.

'We have to go for a walk. Now. I want you to put on your coats, gloves and warm boots. It's cold outside.'

Dee always wanted to know what was happening and why it was happening.

'Where are we going, Mama?' he asked.

'Out. Don't ask questions, just do as I tell you and hurry up.'

'What about Lee and Cee? Are they coming, too?'

She thrust our coats at us.

'Never mind about them. Lee is already out and Cee is coming. Now get ready!'

There was anger and fear in her voice, but Dee's curiosity got the better of him.

'But I want to know why. It's night-time and bedtime, we never go out —'

'If I have to tell you again I'll get Papa, and he'll be very angry! Finish getting dressed and come downstairs as quickly as you can.'

When we came downstairs Mama and Papa were even more distressed, and we realised that it was because Cee wasn't at home. He had left a note to say that he had gone to find Lee, and that made Papa more furious than I had ever seen him. I was afraid of what he would do to Cee when we came back from our walk.

We left the house and walked very fast to the end of our road. Mama made me hold her hand and Dee took my other hand, then Papa held Dee's hand. I could hear loud noises everywhere and the wind was freezing cold in my face. It seemed a very strange thing to be doing on a night in winter.

Then Papa seemed to cheer up and he told us we were going to visit the friend who sometimes came to play our piano. He was very old, he liked Papa's wine cellar and he wrote slow music. He lived about two miles away. I couldn't understand why we were walking, but at least I knew where we were going.

*We went around the corner and into the first street
with shops, and Papa made us stop and hide for a
moment. There were men in SS and storm trooper
uniforms running up and down the pavement and
across the road. They were using axes, hatchets,
bats and truncheons to smash the windows of Jewish
shops, and glass was flying everywhere. People
were being dragged out of shops and flung onto the
cobblestones. If they tried to get up, the officers hit
them with their weapons. Everyone was yelling and
shouting and I could hear a symphony of angry voices.*

*'Oh dear G-d, I think we should go home!' Mama
shouted over the din.*

*Papa shook his head. 'No, once we get there the
cellar is the safest place,' he yelled back.*

*Mama hugged me so tight that I could smell her
perfume.*

*'Mama, I want to go home.' I had a sob in my voice.
She stroked my hair.*

*'Shhh, little one, we will soon.' Her voice was gentle
and comforting.*

*'But why is it safer out here than at home?' Dee
demanded, looking up at Papa.*

*Before he could answer, a black truck rumbled to
a stop not far away from the doorway where we were
hiding and I saw men being pushed into the back of it.
Some of them were Orthodox Jews with hats, beards
and ear locks. They looked very scared.*

*'What are they doing? I need to go and ask where
they are being taken. This is not right,' Papa said.*

Mama grabbed his arm.

*'Don't you dare! You stay with us. We're all that
matters right now,' she yelled at him. I'd never heard
her yell like that.*

After a few moments Papa said it was time to move down the pavement towards the road where his friend lived. We could smell smoke and Dee complained that it was disgusting. It made our eyes water. Papa told Mama that they were burning our synagogue. That made Mama cry, and I squeezed her hand. Just as we reached an intersection, a tall man in a fire chief's uniform came running up to Papa.

'Why are you out tonight, Herr H?'

'A friend rang and told us to come and hide in his cellar,' Papa said.

The man shook his head and pointed back the way we had come. 'Please, go home, now. If they catch you, they'll arrest you, and take you and your son to a camp. Go home and lock your front door. Don't open it for anyone until morning.'

Papa smiled at him. 'No one will arrest us. I have friends, clients. The police chief and the mayor know me —'

The man seized Papa's shoulder and turned him around. 'Don't take the risk! Look around you! Do you think these people will stop and ask who your friends are? They hit and ask questions later. I am ordering you to take your family home and lock the door.'

'Our synagogue is burning,' Mama said. 'Can you save it?'

'I'm so sorry, Frau H, we're not allowed to put out that fire. We can stop it spreading, but we have orders to let the building burn.'

When I look back, I can't believe that Papa thought that these men would keep him, and us, safe. He was so trusting, so good, so honest and so naïve. Anyway, we ran, over piles of broken glass and past mounds of burning books and furniture. Dee had a shard of sharp glass in his hand, and he told me that he would protect me if a Nazi tried to put me in the truck. That made me very scared.

When we got home, Papa slammed the front door and locked and bolted it. Mama took us into the kitchen and gave us glasses of warm milk to drink. Lee and Cee were still out and I told her not to worry, that G-d would take care of them and bring them safely home. That made her cry again.

Instead of sleeping in our own beds, we got blankets and pillows and slept on the sofas in the drawing room. I had my head in Mama's lap and Dee had his head in Papa's lap. Papa told us a story that we loved, about Grandpapa and his magic violin, and I must have gone to sleep before they got to the end.

The next day my brothers finally came home, with some violins in a box. Cee had seen a huge pile of burning violins outside Amos's music shop, and his description of Amos's assistant being beaten has stayed with me for years; it broke his heart, and I had never seen him so distressed. My brothers told us an exciting tale about a Gentile lady who had saved them. Mama and Papa were so relieved to see them that they forgot to be mad. That morning was the first time I heard about Meme, the Gentile who would later save my life. Papa got Lee to write down her address so that he could send her a thank you gift of some money, the most valuable commodity he had.

That was also the day Lee left. One moment we were listening to their tales of the night, and the next Papa told Lee that a visa had come through for him and he could go to London to stay with friends. When everything settled down he would come back. Mama was trying not to cry, and I was wondering who would sing with me now.

When I went to see him, he was getting dressed. He had packed some clothes into a brown leather suitcase, and Cee was helping him to put on as many layers as he could. He had just closed the suitcase when I knocked on the open door.

'I wrote a poem about us. I want you to take it with you. I drew you a picture on the back,' I said. I held it out towards him and he opened his arms. I ran and hugged him. Although I couldn't stop what was coming, I wanted to.

'I don't want you to go; I'm scared,' I whispered into his jersey, and he stroked my hair.

'Shhh, don't worry, little bird, it won't be for long. I'm just going on a bit of an adventure and then I'll come back and we'll sing prayers again together, I promise.'

He told me that Cee would take care of me, and he made me promise that I would take care of Dee. He read my poem and looked at my drawing of him playing the piano. Then he told me that it was beautiful and he would treasure it forever.

We had beef and cabbage for tea, and I remember Dee telling us a story about a cat his friend had rescued. His parents had said he could keep it, because having a pet was a very good thing for a child when everything was so uncertain. Cee said that if we got a cat, our neighbours would eat it. When the car came, Papa put his best woollen coat on Lee and we all hugged him goodbye. Mama held my hand so I wouldn't cry, and we stood on the step and waved to him. That was the first time I realised that things might not get better as fast as Papa had said they would and that I should practise being brave.

Your dearest Mama

CHAPTER FIVE

Berlin
July 2014

Five mornings a week, Kobi Voight caught the U8 line of the underground train from Rosenthaler Platz station, changed to the U2 at Alexander Platz, and rode it to Potsdamer Platz. Then he walked along the cobblestoned pavements to his office in the Gemäldegalerie, the Old Masters Art Gallery in the Kulturforum development. He had fallen in love with the place on first sight. It was a complex of cultural buildings that all spread out from a central entrance space. For him it epitomised the clean, geometric splendour of post-unification architecture. Every day he walked through this huge space, with its black marble floors, square white columns and light streaming in from the skylights, and felt a sense of anticipation.

During his first week he had taken photos of the building, his office, all the Dürer paintings housed here, and some of the other great works, and emailed them to his colleagues and his sister. They had replied full of admiration and envy, so he had promised to buy bookmarks, fridge magnets, carry bags, books and other bits and pieces from the bookshop and mail them home.

He began each working day by visiting the Dürer paintings that hung in the gallery. His favourites were Jakob Muffel painted in 1526, with his fur collar and black hat, Frederick the Wise painted in 1496, with his piercing dark eyes that looked straight back at you, and, most of all, the portrait of Hieronymus Holzschuher, painted in 1526 and still in its original frame. The man had a strong face with a beautifully painted nose, a penetrating gaze and an exquisitely rendered beard and silver hair. One of the things Kobi admired most about Dürer's work was his ability to paint the details — hair and beards and fur and folds of clothing — so realistically.

This day his heart raced as he moved from painting to painting. He stood in front of the painting of the Virgin praying, full of such amazing shades of blue, orange and pink, and the beautiful oval face with its up-cast eyes.

His mind returned to the Dürer portrait described in Ruby's letters. 'Who is it?' he said, his voice barely above a whisper. 'When was it painted, and where does it come in the catalogue of work?'

For a moment he allowed himself to daydream. Imagine finding it — the last great lost work by an artist like Dürer! He could write a book about it and present it to the world; it could tour the major art galleries. Without question it would make his reputation in the halls of academia. What would it be worth? A recent Raphael had been confirmed as genuine and priced at twenty-five million dollars US, so a Dürer had to be around ten. But the financial value was secondary to the aesthetic and cultural importance of a great work of art. And what about the Botticelli? What fate had befallen that?

The questions continued to plague him for the rest of the morning, crashing across his concentration and distracting him from the large book he was reading. At midday he decided it was time to visit one of the museums Frau Goldman had suggested. Not the Resistance Museum; he would leave that until he had finished reading the letters. No, today he would go to the Topography of Terror — even the name was a nod to the black history of this city.

The museum stood on the long-demolished site of the Nazis' terror and persecution centre: the headquarters of the State secret police, the infamous Gestapo; the leadership of the security service, the SS; and, from 1939, the Reich Security Main Office. Just the thought of what had gone on behind locked doors here sent an icy shiver down Kobi's spine as he entered the site.

He wasn't prepared for the outdoor presentation, a timeline of Berlin from the Weimar Republic to the post-war decade. As he walked slowly down the row, Kobi saw photographic evidence of much of what Ruby had talked about: the 1 April boycott of Jewish shops, the burning of books, the Kristallnacht pogrom that she had lived through and described so vividly ... He stood before the pictures of piles of shattered glass, terrified men being herded into vans, and a synagogue on fire. Overhead, above the trench that housed the photo boards, rose the longest continuous part of the Berlin Wall left standing. It was plain, with heavy steel wire sticking out of the thick concrete, and the word *WHY?* painted in red. Suddenly Kobi felt like weeping

He remembered the Germany his paternal grandparents had idolised, the beer steins and costumes and brass bands and sausages; it felt artificial and ridiculous, a million miles from these horrific images. With a quick cough and a hurried look at the people around him, he pulled himself together and kept walking.

The later panels showed the rounding up of the Jews left in Berlin, their transport by truck to the assembly points and their march down the streets to the train stations. Members of the public turned their backs on the rows of elderly, middle-aged, young and children, suitcase in hand, who shuffled towards death.

He read the photograph labels, written in German and English, and felt tears welling up again. Between 1941 and 1945, fifty-five thousand Jews were deported to Eastern Europe from Berlin, although six thousand (known as 'U-boats') tried to survive by hiding. Was Ruby one of them? Had she hidden and survived? If so, was she still alive and could he find her? This last question shocked him, and he almost stumbled through the rest of the display. It told him about the bombing by the Allies, the surrender and the immediate post-war years, the division of the city and the terrible food shortages.

He sat down for a few moments on a low concrete wall and took a swig from his water bottle. These later years were when his mother had lived in Berlin, from 1947 to 1950, before his grandparents had taken her to Australia. She had never spoken about them, never shared stories from her childhood. Maybe now he understood why. She had insisted that her three children spoke only English and grew up as Australians, telling them that the past was a 'foreign country'. But today he felt overwhelmed by a desire to know, to understand, to experience her early years. Maybe if he took the translated letters home and she read them, and he talked to her about the places he had seen in Germany, maybe she would open up.

Slowly he got to his feet and followed the gentle incline of the ramp to the door of the museum proper. Anxiety bubbled up inside him, almost a reluctance to go further because of what he might find. Yet he needed to see what sort of city Ruby had lived in, what horror and terror had been the fabric of her daily life. What had made her give up her baby?

It was brilliantly done. There was a whole world of new information here about a subject Kobi had thought he understood. He saw photos of rallies, masses of people listening with hands outstretched as if to touch the Führer. This man, so universally vilified by history, had been seen as a saviour by his countrymen in the early days. A broad section of the 1933 German population had seen Hitler as a guarantor of internal security and order after years of hardship, 'a widespread sense of release and liberation from democracy'. If you were German and Aryan, what did the Nazi government promise you? Work, food, a rising income, a home, marriage loans, a child allowance and a financial reward for every child you had, and new opportunities for leisure and recreation. Was this the way his grandparents had lived? Had they attended these events, chanted and saluted and applauded Hitler?

Then there were processions through the streets, women, their heads shaven, accused of consorting with prisoners, and a man wearing a sign that said *I have defiled a Christian* walking behind a marching band. The faces of the people watching mixed amusement with disgust.

Now he could see images, as war crept nearer, of the increasing sanctions and rules against the Jews. And the German public, enjoying their new prosperity, finding it easy to turn a blind eye. In hindsight it seemed so obvious, so ominous and so inevitable. Why had her papa, as Ruby called him, not seen what was coming? Why had he not taken them all to New York to live with his brother before it was too late? Although the questions begged to be answered, Kobi knew it was futile to ask them. He sighed. These people were gone, probably exterminated in the camps, so what was the use of trying to understand their choices?

A whole section was dedicated to the Battle for Berlin; first, the Allied bombing that left the city in ruins, and then the two and half million soldiers of the Red Army taking on one million Germans. Hitler ordered that the city be defended to the last man. Kobi's mother would have been about three years old — where was she? What did she see, what did she suffer, and how much did she remember? He knew that his grandfather had served in the German Army and had been wounded — how, by whom, and where was he when Berlin fell? Was his mother's reluctance to talk linked to something her father had done or been — had he run away from a dark past?

Kobi walked on to the post-war section, with its photographs of people queuing for water at old pumps because the city's water system had been destroyed, burned-out buildings and rubble everywhere, and two men carving up a dead horse for food. All of a sudden it was too much — too many unanswered questions about his own family and the family he was reading about.

Outside, the sun was shining and people were busy going about their daily chores. He swallowed hard against the bitter taste of betrayal and guilt and struck out for Potsdamer Platz and the underground network that would take him home. He'd never felt as 'German' before, as guilty about the actions of a race of people of whom he considered himself to be a part. If this sensation was what his mother had tried to protect him from, it hadn't worked. She had betrayed her heritage, tried to expunge it. Even if he understood her motivation it was a double betrayal, of her past and of her present.

Two issues rolled around his weary brain. He couldn't believe how many of the men and women guilty of atrocities had escaped punishment after the war, or were sentenced to light jail terms and then melted back into German society. He suspected his general sense of outrage was a common response to this information.

The second issue was more complicated and more personal. What would he have done? Who would he have become? Now he knew that there were choices, degrees of response, and he couldn't decide what road his twenty-first-century personality and character would have taken. Would he have been part of the Resistance, creating anti-Nazi literature and hiding and feeding the persecuted? Would he have kept his head down and participated as much as was necessary to keep his family safe? Would he have collaborated and betrayed people he knew in order to gain extra food and promises of safety, or, worse, would he have been won over by the mass hysteria and rhetoric generated by the propaganda machine? Whatever the answers were, he needed to know what his family had done. By the Lutheran God his parents had raised him to believe in, he hoped that Ruby had made it safely through the war and been rewarded for her courage.

CHAPTER SIX

Berlin

June 1942

My dearest darling baby,
Harry asked me today why I seemed so much happier,
and I couldn't tell him it was because I was writing to
you. He might have told me that it was too dangerous
and I must destroy what I have written and not do
it anymore. I couldn't have coped with that, so I just
smiled and told him I felt we had reached a turning
point, the people were going to get sick of being at war
soon and demand that full and fair elections be held. He
gave me the smile that says 'Sweet girl, how wonderful
to have such optimism.' But I'm not a girl anymore,
I'm a woman. I may only be seventeen, but I have lost
my family and risked my life so many times and had a
gorgeous baby and am so in love with her father that
I want to stand on the roof and tell the world! When I
think back to the night when it all changed and how I
was so innocent and scared, I can't believe how much
I've grown up. Part of that is making decisions, decisions
so hard to make that your heart freezes and you are
afraid it will snap in two. In case you have forgotten
from the last letter, darling baby, I adore you and I'm
writing so you will know that you are the most gorgeous,

the smartest, most loved baby in the entire world. Now, on with the story …

It was a Friday in November 1939, just two months after war was declared. Everyone was nervous, and Dee and I used to discuss the fact that no one would tell us what we were supposed to be afraid of. We were teenagers now, and we lived in a society that despised us. On the streets we were spat on and shouted at. All around us the parents of our friends had lost their jobs. It was illegal for Jews to be lawyers, doctors, dentists, nurses, teachers, engineers, soldiers, shopkeepers, and to carry guns and to have radios and for Gentiles to rent us houses or commercial property … And yet the 'adults' in our lives kept telling us that everything would be fine and that nothing worse would happen. Did they really believe that we could go back to the way it was before the Nazis? So much hatred from so many quarters filled every moment of the life of every Jew in Berlin. When I look back I wonder why I didn't insist on honesty, insist that we pack up our essential belongings and move somewhere safe. Life was all that mattered in the end. Emigration was still legal; it was difficult and expensive and would mean leaving everything behind, but it was possible. And then one day it wasn't anymore.

It was nearly sunset and Mama had everything ready for Shabbat but Papa wasn't home. We waited in the music room so Cee could play the piano and we could all sing. Dee always reacted to stress by being a clown, and he made us all laugh with his new juggling trick. He wanted to juggle the Fabergé eggs and Mama told him that if he did, she would spank him. I told everyone about a story I had read in a book my friend Esther had given me about a Jewish family in Russia in the last century. Mama rang the bank to tell Papa to

*hurry up and come home, but no one answered, so she
rang my aunt and they discussed the fact that my uncle
wasn't home from the bank either. Men! I heard them
joking about how they never looked at their pocket
watches, but I could tell that Mama knew Papa would
never be late for Shabbat.*

*So Cee started to play again, as loudly and cheerfully
as he could. And then the knocking on the door started.
I sometimes think that life was ripped in half at that
moment. Family life before the knocking, and no family
life after the knocking. Dee and I sat with Mama on the
bay-window seat and she put her arms around us. The
noise from the street was muffled, but we could hear
what they were saying. I will always remember it; they
were yelling, 'Open up, Jews!'*

*Mama was shocked and told Cee to be careful, but
he had rushed out of the room and into the front hall
and to the door. Once again the voice bellowed from
the street. Mama and Dee and I followed him out
into the entrance hall. Someone was banging on our
big, heavy door with a fist.*

*We were all very afraid. I remember Cee looked at
Mama and told her that we had to open up and to be
strong because Papa would be home soon. He slipped
the chain and started to open the door, but it was
pushed from the outside and all these men in uniform
swarmed in. It was like a nightmare and I just wanted
to wake up. A big, fat man, in what I now know to be a
major's uniform, came up to Mama and thrust a piece
of paper at her. He shouted in her face and told her that
the house had been commandeered because Jews will
no longer live in houses like ours. He told her that we
had fifteen minutes to pack one suitcase each, clothes
and photographs only, no valuables.*

Cee ran back into the music room, but before Mama could call out to him some soldiers pushed us towards the stairs. She took our hands in hers and we went upstairs.

First we went to our own rooms and Mama brought us suitcases. She hugged me tight and told me to put clothes in the suitcase, woollen clothes, very warm clothes, and she needed me to be grown-up and brave. She put a coat on me and gave me my waterproof boots to put on, then she went to Dee. I felt numb with fear and I wanted to cry. Where was Papa? Why wasn't he home? He would sort out all these horrible men!

I took my singlets and underpants from my drawer and threw them into the open suitcase, then took two shirts and some heavy woollen jumpers from the wardrobe. What about skirts? And pyjamas? And my pencils and paper? All my precious things.

It seemed no time at all until Mama came back and helped me to close the suitcase and do up the leather straps. I looked around the room and bit my lip so I wouldn't cry. We had to be as brave as we possibly could, and anyway, it was all a mistake. Papa would sort it all out, we were special, and no one was going to throw us out of our home!

Dee was on the landing with his suitcase. He looked very pale and his eyes were wide, trying to take in all that was happening. Mama took too long and the soldiers came up behind us and pushed us onto the stairs. Dee cried out and they grabbed us by the shoulders and started dragging us down the stairs. That was too much, they were hurting me and I burst into tears. Dee was struggling and squirming against the tight grasp.

I could hear the rage in Mama's voice when she yelled at them to take their hands off us, but the soldiers ignored her.

Two men held the Botticelli portrait between them and the major was staring at it. As Mama reached the hall, he turned towards her. He told her that it was a sacred subject and for Jews to own such a work was sacrilegious, a profanity before G-d. He asked her why we hadn't registered our important possessions.

Mama was angry and she was taller than him. She faced him and, even though I was terrified, I thought she was wonderfully brave. She told him that Papa was an important man and owned a bank on the Pariser Platz so we were exempt from registration. He just laughed and said that wasn't the case anymore and that her son had seriously assaulted one of his officers. That was when we noticed that Cee was being held by the arms. Across from him stood an officer in a black leather coat, holding a bloodstained cloth to his nose. The major was speaking again, more like barking. He told the soldiers to take the two boys and turn Mama and me out into the snow.

What happened next seemed a strange combination of slow motion and lightning speed. The men caught both Mama and I off-guard and they literally picked us up and threw us out the front door and down the steps into the snow. It wasn't a soft landing, and I felt a sharp pain in my knee and the cold snow on my face. I looked up to see my brothers being marched with a guard on either side. Then the officer with the bloody nose yelled out for them to wait. He took a truncheon from his belt and hit the back of Cee's hand as hard as he could. Cee tried to swallow the scream, but it was obvious that the bones had shattered.

Dee tried to break away and run to Mama, but the guards caught him and held him tight. She put her arms around me and tried to bury my face in her coat but I forced my head around so I could see the boys being herded towards a large black truck. Cee called out to Mama just before they pushed him up and told her to take me to Meme. He was grabbed from inside and yanked into the truck. Mama screamed the names of both her sons as the truck rumbled off down the street.

We sat in the snow for a moment, and Mama stroked my damp hair with her glove. There was a guard standing on the step outside the closed door to our house and he glared at us as the major got into a car and the soldiers climbed into another truck.

Mama whispered to me, asking me if I remembered where Meme lived. I nodded and looked up at her. She wiped the tears from my face and asked me if I could take her there. I nodded again. Suddenly we heard the sound of the front door opening, closing and opening again. The guard had a suitcase in each hand and he threw them down onto the snow beside us. Then he took up his position on the top step and looked away. Mama scrambled to her feet and picked up both suitcases. She thanked the guard, but he ignored her. When I stood up my legs felt very wobbly for a moment and I thought I was going to sink back down, but Mama took my hand in hers and smiled at me. She told me to take my suitcase and come with her and we would pretend we were going for a nice evening walk in the snow and were off to visit a friend, and I could tell her more about the story in the book that Esther had given me. I remember I thought she was very brave.

It took a long time to find the right street. I don't know what the time was, but it was dark and snowing *and my suitcase was very heavy when we got to the entrance to Meme's house. Mama knocked on the door and we waited. Nothing happened, so she knocked again. I had gone with Cee and Papa to deliver gift boxes of food to Meme on at least three occasions during the past year. I liked her. She was plump and welcoming and she smelt of home baking when she hugged me. I thought that maybe she wouldn't hear us, but then the door opened.*

Meme was shocked to see us, we must have looked very cold and tired, and she wanted to know what we were doing out at such a late hour. I could tell by her eyes that she knew the answer. Mama told her that we had been thrown out of the house and the boys had been taken, and Cee had told her to come here. Mama's voice broke, and Meme moved swiftly to put her arms around her and then ushered us both inside.

We climbed the stairs into her house. The room was cheerful and full of light. Mama and I sank down onto her sofa and let her fuss. She brought us blankets and pillows and cups of coffee and sandwiches and cake. When I couldn't keep my eyes open anymore, Mama carried me through to the little bed in the spare room and tucked me in. As I fell into a deep sleep I could hear the two voices in earnest conversation and I knew the adults would fix everything.

Your loving Mama

CHAPTER SEVEN

Berlin

July 2014

Kobi was intrigued by the arrival of Meme. Who was this plump, warm, welcoming woman who had rescued Ruby and her mother? He found the use of nicknames frustrating; he understood Ruby's need for secrecy given her circumstances, but he ached to know them all by their names. Mary, Mildred, Martha, Maria? She had previously been referred to as the Gentile who saved Ruby's life.

She was obviously a hero, an example of the brave few who had risked everything to help those persecuted by the Nazi regime. The more he thought about her the more his confusion grew. He wanted to pick up the letters and read on, but something was stopping him. Something he didn't understand. Was he afraid that his grandfather had been involved in this wholesale genocide? Had he torn apart families like Ruby's? Was that what his mother had kept hidden? Or was the opposite true? Were his grandparents like Meme? These questions distracted him and as he rose to make himself a cup of coffee, he realised he wanted a reason to procrastinate. There were so many museums commemorating different aspects of the war in Berlin. And the one he felt like visiting now, on a Saturday afternoon, was the museum to the 'silent heroes'. The one that honoured people such as Meme.

The entrance-way was deep in Berlin's pre-war Jewish quarter, between two shops on the Rosenthaler Strasse and led, under an arch, into a courtyard surrounded by tenement buildings. The high walls were covered in graffiti and tagging, posters for out-of-date events and a huge painting of a young Anne Frank. Slowly, Kobi picked his way over broken tiles and tufts of grass to the back of the courtyard and the door to the Silent Heroes Memorial Centre.

Kobi wandered from story to story. These were just a fraction of the known Gentiles who had helped the Jews escape genocide during the war, but they were extremely impressive. After all the hatred and pain he'd seen these stories restored his faith in human nature. He felt a surge of relief at the courage, goodness and kindness on display and couldn't help hoping that this was where his family fitted in. This was how his grandparents would have reacted, how he would have reacted in the same situation. That belief certainly made his mood lift.

He became engrossed in the story of Ilse Lewin. She was young and vulnerable and yet she'd decided not to immigrate to London. She wanted to stay with her mother, Gretha. Kobi marvelled at her loyalty in the face of such danger, but then her fortunes took a turn for the worse. Her mother was arrested at the end of 1942.

Ilse took the logical steps to avoid deportation. She had hidden with friends and then, when that became too dangerous for them, she lived on the streets. Kobi tried to imagine what that must have been like, sleeping in abandoned buildings and surviving on scraps of food smuggled to her by Gentile friends.

She wanted to earn some money by sweeping the floor of a tailor's shop but the owner tried to sexually harass her so she ran away and stayed in hiding. Other Gentile friends forged papers for her, even using their own names, and then in the summer of 1944 they found her a safe place in the Prenzlauer

Berg district of Berlin, and she hid there until the end of the war.

'Isn't it amazing how many heroic Gentiles it took to save one Jewish woman?'

Kobi turned towards the voice. It belonged to a man about his age; the accent was English, polished, public school. 'I was just thinking that myself: she could have been betrayed at any point, and yet she wasn't.'

The man smiled at him and held out his hand. 'George Ross. Where is that accent from?'

Kobi shook the proffered hand. 'Dr Kobi Voight. I'm Australian.'

'But your parents were German.' It wasn't phrased as a question.

'My mother was born in Berlin, my father was Australian-born, but his parents came from Munich.'

'So what brings you to the Silent Heroes, if you don't mind me asking?'

Kobi hesitated. Better to be general. 'I'm on sabbatical in Berlin, at the Gemäldegalerie and I'm taking the opportunity to get around some of the museums.'

'What's your field?' George asked.

Kobi took a slight step backwards. 'Northern German Renaissance. I'm an art history lecturer and I'm writing a book. I'm here because the book is on the paintings of Albrecht Dürer.'

George inclined his head. 'Dürer? I have an engraving, a print, from the early eighteenth century. It's a naked woman, full-frontal, with one hand raised and the other behind her back. Bought it on the Left Bank in Paris in 1994.'

Kobi was genuinely impressed. 'How wonderful! Do you live here?' he asked.

'No, just a tourist. I live in London, for my sins. Well, I think I'm about done here, and it feels like time for a sit-down and a coffee. Care to join me? There must be a little cake shop around here somewhere — this city seems to be full of them.'

Kobi hesitated. Coffee with a man he didn't know, a stranger, even a good-looking one, wasn't his style. Something about it smacked of a pick-up.

George smiled. 'Just a coffee,' he said.

Kobi felt a faint blush rise from his throat to his cheeks. Had his hesitation been that obvious? He gave a bashful smile and a slight nod. 'Sounds like a plan.'

It didn't take long to find a café. They ordered hot chocolates and a huge slice of strawberry torte to share.

'I've fallen in love: I've never tasted better hot chocolate. I have one every day,' Kobi said as he sipped from the huge cup.

'Godiva hot chocolate from Harrods — nothing better. It's basically melted Belgian chocolate, ridiculously rich, but my God, the one with a hint of chilli is sublime.'

Kobi dug his cake fork into the sponge. Cream oozed out between the layers.

'This feels very decadent,' he said.

'Doesn't it just? I had a huge slice of *Sachertorte* the other night, and God knows what my personal trainer would say about that. Clearly he knew there'd be temptations, though: he suggested I weigh myself every day and then decide what I can eat.'

Kobi chuckled. George was good company and easy to talk to. 'So what brought you to Berlin?' he asked.

'A nostalgic trip — France, Germany, Austria and Poland. One set of grandparents came to London between the wars.'

'To escape the Nazis?'

'In the 1920s, to escape the Depression. But if they'd stayed, I doubt they would have survived Hitler.'

'From Germany?' Kobi asked.

'From Poland. My mother's family weren't so lucky; only her father survived and immigrated to England after the war. When did your mother leave Berlin?' George asked.

'In 1950, she was eight. Her parents wanted a new start, and democracy, and they lived in the eastern sector so emigration was a logical choice.'

'And you grew up on a beach.'

It wasn't a question. Kobi smiled to himself. 'Not really. I grew up in an Art Deco suburb of Melbourne, quirky but not posh. My father was proud of his German heritage, but my mother insisted we speak English and have barbeques and go camping. She wanted us to be Australian. She won. But I'm not fond of beaches.'

George gave a soft laugh of recognition. 'My parents were first-generation Londoners and they wanted to leave every part of Poland behind. We changed our surname, spoke English and supported Tottenham.'

'Touché.'

He raised his cup and George clinked his against it.

'So, of all the greats, why Dürer?' George asked.

Kobi smiled. 'Too many reasons to list them all — colour, detail, innovation, extraordinary talent.'

'Versatility. I still find it amazing that the man who painted the portraits and the hare, the owl, the piece of turf, also did those engravings and woodcuts,' George added.

Was it coincidence or was he being played, Kobi wondered.

'I sense a kindred spirit. What do you do, George?'

'I work in the City. Used to buy and sell futures, but that's a young man's game. Now I invest other people's money and make it grow.'

'What do you invest in?'

'Shares, start-up tech companies, property, sometimes even the finer things in life: wine and art.'

Kobi raised his eyebrows. 'I'm an artist, as yet largely undiscovered, but I live in hope. Maybe some of your wealthier clients would like to grab a bargain while it's still cheap.'

'Are you any good?' George asked.

'Oh, I'm brilliant. That's why I work as an art history lecturer. My subjects are too dark for most people.'

'Dark?'

'I've always had a fascination with repression and Socialism, the symbols of Nazism and Soviet East Germany. Not the sort of thing people want on their walls.'

Now it was George's turn to look interested. 'I have a client who collects skulls decorated with precious stones. Another who would pay anything for a Goya. Another bought a painting at auction. The sellers were the descendants of a Jewish family who'd had it confiscated by the Nazis during the war. He's more interested in its wartime history than he is in the piece of art.'

'Imagine being able to buy a masterpiece, owning a famous work of art,' Kobi was musing, almost to himself.

George nodded. 'Plenty can and want to, trouble is supply.'

Kobi smiled suddenly. 'Perhaps I should turn my hand to forgery, create some unknown masterpieces for you to sell.'

'A new Dali,' George suggested.

'Or a Munch or a Bosch.'

'Punch a large hole in it, and by the time the restorers have finished everyone will believe it is genuine.'

Kobi shook his head. 'You're a devious man, Mr Ross. A thoroughly bad influence.'

George winked at him. 'I hope so, Dr Voight.'

CHAPTER EIGHT

Berlin
June 1942

My dearest darling baby,
I dream about you most nights. I can feel your sweet
milky breath on my cheek and hear your little chortle,
feel your tiny hand wrap around my finger, clutching so
tight. Last night I thought I could feel you at my breast
suckling, but when I woke up and I looked down, you
weren't there. I bet your hair is getting darker and redder
every day, just like your grandmother's, and your eyes are
the bluest blue, like the tiny little forget-me-nots that grew
in our garden. Every time I look into your papa's eyes I
see yours, and sometimes it makes me shake inside with a
longing to see you, and sometimes it just makes me happy
that you have inherited his loveliest feature.

I believe that things are starting to swing our way.
America is in the war now, and eventually they will
come and free us. Maybe within the year we three will
all be back together in our house by the lake, and we
can go and visit our families, back in their houses.
These daydreams of mine lift my spirits, and sometimes
I think they keep me sane.

Last time I wrote I told you how we found our way
to Meme. Mama was desperate for us to go into hiding

together, but Meme said that was too dangerous. If we were together and got caught it would be the end for both of us, but if we were separated then at least one of us had a chance of surviving.

The first thing we did was try to get the boys out of Dachau. We learned that Papa and my uncle had also been taken there after the bank was seized, on the same day and very probably on the same train. Meme went to see the 'important people' she knew. She told us that it was too dangerous for Mama to come with her and demand her husband's release, and Mama had to realise that their Gentile friends couldn't help them anymore. But Meme knew people who worked in the Nazi hierarchy and they might be able to intervene. We didn't ask her how she knew them; it was obvious that she was much more than an elderly woman living alone in an apartment in the Mitte.

She found out that my aunt and our cousins had disappeared and had probably been taken into hiding. This cheered Mama up, as maybe they would be safe. No matter how hard Meme tried, the answer was always the same: it was too late. War had been declared and the opportunities to 'buy' prisoner releases had almost totally shut down. Papa was a banker and that was a particularly 'Jewish' occupation. The Führer wanted to make examples of Jews who had controlled money.

Mama was very distressed, and she and I cried together, but Meme consoled us and said that it would be over before too long. The Western European governments would never tolerate Hitler's power-mad land-grab if it went too far.

Sometimes I used to lie in my bed at night and pretend it was all a bad dream and tomorrow I would *wake up in my own bedroom and go to my old school. Often Dee visited me in my dreams and made me laugh and told me to be strong and brave. I drew him every day, and looking at those pieces of paper helped me not miss him so badly, for a moment. I used to remember the times we had argued and wish that I could go back and tell him that I wasn't really angry and that I loved him. Mama said it was fine, he knew that. She was sure he was being looked after by Cee and Papa and that he was thinking of me, too.*

Mama had been teaching us at home, and she was very well read, so Meme had no difficulty getting her a job. We had forged papers, and Mama was Petra Becker (not quite but close enough). Meme found a Catholic family with three daughters who lived in Wilmersdorf and wanted the girls taught at home, so Mamma became a governess. I remember the day she left, it was snowing and the sky was very dark grey, and we both tried not to cry. We hugged for a long time and then we hugged some more. I remember that hug; I could feel her heart beating through her coat. Meme said that she would make sure we both knew what the other was doing, and that we'd never lose touch and it was only temporary. I couldn't go and see her, as she was supposed to be unmarried and childless, but Meme told me that she had a lovely bedroom and they had bought her some new clothes and fed her very well. I was so happy to hear that.

I stayed on with Meme for another two weeks. My new name was Francesca Albrecht. I have black hair and very dark eyes and olive-coloured skin, so we made up a story that my mother was Italian and my father was German. He was fighting in the army in Poland, and my mother was ill so she had gone home to Milan to be nursed. I was a good Catholic girl and I was strong and could cook and clean, so I could work as a maid. Thank goodness I had enjoyed helping both Mama and Cook in the kitchen and had learned so much!

Meme had watched me drawing and copying pictures from magazines. I had made an exact replica of my papers to help me get my new name into my head. One night we were sitting in front of the heater and eating our soup when she asked me the most important question I had ever been asked. It was January 1940, and I'd just had my fifteenth birthday. She asked me whether I would rather be safe or useful. I didn't know what she meant by useful, and when I asked her she took a while to answer.

She told me that she could take me to a farm outside Berlin and I could work for a couple there who had a small boy. It would be a good life, better than in the city, with plenty to eat and I would be away from the soldiers and the Gestapo.

So then I asked what the useful option was. She said she had some friends who lived in Charlottenburg, in a lovely apartment. They were also a couple but they had no children, were younger than the couple on the farm, and they both had important jobs. He was in the air force, working at the Air Ministry, and she worked in movies! How wonderful that sounded. She hated cooking and cleaning, so I could do those things for her. They were very social and they entertained, had lots of parties, and went out into the countryside, to lakes and a castle. A castle! It sounded so exciting. Meme smiled at me and I could see that she was sad.

She said that unlike the couple on the farm, these two would know who I really was. And I would be part of what they did. Then she stopped, almost as if she didn't know what more to say, or she was frightened of saying the wrong thing, getting me involved in something. Suddenly I understood. I was where I was because of Hitler, and my mama, my papa and my brothers were all where they were because of Hitler.

I told her that I wanted to live with them, to help, to be useful. She got up and came across the room to me, and kissed me on top of my head and hugged me to her. She told me I was a very brave young woman and that my mama and papa would be so proud of me.

Two days later I wasn't living with Meme anymore. She took me by train to Charlottenburg, and we walked from the station to the big apartment building that was to be my new home. This couple have become the most important people in my life for the past two years. I shall call them Harry and Suzie. What can I safely tell you about them?

Harry is very tall and handsome. He comes from a Prussian military family and spent some time in England before the war. He speaks eight languages — German, French, English, Swedish, Norwegian, Danish, Dutch and Russian — and that ability is part of the job he does for the air force. He is so charismatic and full of energy, and when he speaks people listen, and they want to agree with him and do what he suggests. In 1933 the Nazis arrested him because he was writing things they didn't approve of, and Suzie told me that as part of his torture they beat him with rubber torches and carved a Nazi swastika into his thigh. He says that at that stage he decided to 'put my revenge on ice' and joined the Luftwaffe to train as a pilot. And he has a bottomless hatred for the Nazis and Hitler.

Suzie is like a ray of sunshine. She's pretty and blonde, and wears her hair in a very modern bob. She's an outrageous flirt and has a nervous laugh. She plays the accordion and we all sing. Sometimes when we feel brave she plays 'The Marseillaise' and 'It's a Long Way to Tipperary'. They had been married for three years when I met them, and they got married in a chapel in the castle that belonged to her grandfather. In fact, she is the daughter of a Prussian prince! Harry calls her his 'social butterfly', but that doesn't mean he thinks she's shallow: she is very bright and she is as committed to our cause as we all are.

In those early days I lived in a room downstairs and I worked in the apartment. I cooked meals and cleaned and got everything ready when they had dinner parties or more informal gatherings. Suzie told me that when summer came, and they would go sailing on the lakes, or bicycle out to the castle for picnics, I would go too. She would sit cross-legged on my bed and tell me about her childhood: she went to finishing school in Switzerland and she stayed in amazing hotels in Rome, and she used to ride her horse through the grounds of the castle. It all sounded so glamorous!

In my spare time I drew pictures, of my family and of things I copied from magazines, of people I saw in the street. I got to know the friends who came often to the apartment, and I shall tell you about some of them later. But I didn't stay for their discussions; I could tell when it was time to leave them alone. Meme had told me to do my job and wait for them to offer to include me.

Harry and Suzie knew my story, who I was and what had happened to my family. All their friends were supposed to believe I was Francesca Albrecht but some were a little suspicious. I heard one of them say to Harry once, 'She's very dark — are you sure she's not a Jew in hiding? Wouldn't matter if you were hiding a Jew, but it'd be nice to know.'

Then one evening Harry called me into the sitting room. He had a pile of my drawings on the coffee table in front of him. He asked me how I felt about the men who had thrown us out of our house and taken away my family. I didn't know what to say, but I did admit that I sometimes dreamed of revenge and thought about what Dee would have done to them with his knife. That made him laugh. He has a laugh like my papa's when something amused him. I still love his laugh.

Then he asked me how I felt about the laws the government had passed, all the stupid laws that had denied us our human rights. I still found it all confusing and unfair, and I told him that. I failed to see what we, as a race, had done that was so wrong. He corrected me gently: the Jews are not a race but a culture who believe in the Old Testament and worship the God of the Hebrews, and I must not listen to the idiotic nonsense that the Nazi doctors spout, because they only say it because it is what that thug wants to hear. It makes me smile when Harry talks about Hitler that way. Our fight is not his fight, and yet he feels so strongly about what has happened to us. I was sitting next to him on the sofa, and couldn't help noticing how very tall and thin he is.

He told me that he and his friends call themselves a circle because it grows all the time, every day. One friend introduces another friend, and other people have their own circles and members overlap. The thing they have in common is that they all feel the same way about Hitler and the Nazis. I knew that already, but I didn't say so. When he said that I'd probably heard them talking, because they are pretty loud — because he is pretty loud — we both laughed.

Then he told me how beautifully I drew and copied things, and that I could put these wonderful skills to good use. He asked me whether I would like to join them and start to take my revenge. At last, he asked! It had only been a few weeks but it seemed to me like I'd been waiting forever to be included in what they do.

He was asking me to help. He'd said I had wonderful skills. The most charismatic man I have ever met in my life, and he sat me down and talked to me and asked me to help. I looked up into his very bright blue eyes, and at that moment my life changed again.

In my next letter I will try and explain to you what we do and how important it is, why I do it, and why I have had to keep doing it after you were born. I have no choice, but it is the hardest thing I have ever done.

Your loving Mama

CHAPTER NINE

Berlin
July 2014

The young author of the letters had obviously given her baby away to keep it safe until the war was over, but the decision was tearing her apart. Kobi resisted the urge to rip through the letters and find out what happened. There was a deep-seated anxiety that kept him reading one at a time, often delaying the act of lying on the sofa and picking up the next one until late at night. Whatever the outcome, his heart ached for Ruby, and he very much feared for her fate.

The day they met, Kobi and George decided that the next day they would visit the Memorial to the Murdered Jews of Europe. Kobi knew that Ruby had become involved in the Resistance, and he suspected that her story would not end well. George was Jewish and had lost some of his Polish family in the Holocaust. He was clearly on a pilgrimage, and his determination fired Kobi up — he felt a need to pay his respects and learn more.

Unlike other museums, this one was hidden beneath the memorial itself. As they approached the site, the sheer scale took their breath away. Two thousand, seven hundred and eleven concrete blocks stood in elegant, sombre and silent reverence. They were all the same width and length, but their heights differed from almost ground level to over four metres high in the centre, and they were placed in tight rows. Kobi wandered down the slope towards the tallest blocks. The ground was uneven under his feet and he felt somewhat dwarfed and surrounded. The sunlight played on the stone and created patterns of shadows on the ground. The blocks felt warm and smooth to the touch; the surface was a gently sparkling grey.

As he touched the blocks he silently dedicated them to the people he was reading about, the tantalisingly vague nicknames that represented human lives shredded like cardboard. George was reading a pamphlet and looked up as Kobi returned to his side.

'It's a brilliant concept,' George said.

Kobi took his iPad from his satchel and started to film the scene. To their left a group of young students piled out of a bus and bustled into the memorial field. They were laughing and talking in French, their loud voices at a high pitch of excitement.

George jabbed Kobi in the ribs. 'Look,' he said, pointing at them.

Inevitably some of the students climbed onto the stone blocks and jumped from one to another.

'They won't get away with that here,' Kobi said, almost to himself. The incongruity of their actions in this sacred place irritated him. Within minutes a uniformed guard had marched up and remonstrated with the adults in the group. The students were quickly ushered towards the entrance to the underground museum.

'Let's go underground,' George said.

Kobi turned to him and smiled. 'Lead the way.'

They had to queue for the entrance, and at the bottom of the descending stone staircase passed through an x-ray security check and a metal detector. They handed over their passports and got an audio tour in English.

The displays flowed seamlessly from one room to the next, bringing together the stories of individuals who had suffered, died or survived the global catastrophe of the Holocaust. At the end of the timeline were six huge portraits hanging from the roof, all of differing ethnicities and nationalities, and each one representing a million people.

It was the Room of Dimensions that most affected Kobi. Backlit panels were set in the floor, each displaying a diary entry or a letter excerpt or a last note to a loved one. There were pictures of the original documents and translations into English. *What is my life worth even if I remain alive ... for what and for whom do I carry on this whole pursuit of life, enduring, holding out for what?* read one, written from the Warsaw ghetto.

It reminded him of Ruby, writing her thoughts and story down for her daughter, uncertain, yet firmly believing that they would be reunited.

In the next room Kobi read about the fates of fifteen different families. When he realised that the names in white had survived and the names in orange had died, an involuntary shudder ran through him. What colour would Ruby be? And her brothers, and their mama and papa? Would he ever know?

He was sitting on a concrete block in the Room of Names, listening to the voiceover and watching as a name and a place of birth and death appeared on a blank wall in front of him, when George sat down beside him.

'There's a sign over there that says the names of all of the victims of the Holocaust, not just the Jewish ones, would take six years, seven months and twenty-seven days to recite continuously just once,' Kobi said quietly.

George shook his head. 'Who figures these things out?' he asked.

Kobi smiled sadly at him. 'People like me who sit at desks and write a thesis on the facts and figures.'

'It's a good thing they do. Otherwise the world might forget.'

Kobi pointed at the wall. 'No chance. Not while this voice keeps reciting their names.'

Just up the road from the Memorial to the Murdered Jews of Europe, they found the Brandenburg Tor. Ruby had mentioned that their house was not far from this immense landmark and looking up at it, Kobi felt suddenly close to her. It had been repaired after the war and probably looked much the same to him as it had to her. The massive quadriga on the top gazed down on a square full of people enjoying the hot summer sun. A man was playing the violin and singing songs in broken English. In Ruby's day there would have been no stalls selling Russian military caps, fur hats and stacking dolls and no modern information centre. Kobi and George ventured inside and bought colourful pieces of the Berlin Wall mounted on plastic stands.

'I shall take this home to my mother and hope that it inspires her to tell me something about her first years, here, before the wall was built,' Kobi said.

'Take it gently: she's spent more than sixty years blocking it out.'

Kobi grimaced. 'That's true. But it is worth a try, she can only say no.' He pointed towards a bicycle with a two-person carriage built on the back. 'How about a spin round the Tiergarten in one of those?'

'I've ridden in something like that, in Thailand,' George said as he headed in the direction of the cyclist. Kobi joined him in time to hear him laughing.

'Are your thighs strong enough to take the two of us?' George asked the man.

'Of course sir, I can take two … sturdy Americans, so you are no trouble. Where would you like to go?'

George pointed over the road. 'Around the park would be nice.'

They agreed on a price of eight euros and seated themselves in the back. It was a snug fit and their legs were pressed against each other's.

George grinned at Kobi. 'Do you need a blanket over your knees?' he asked.

Kobi snorted with mock disgust. 'No. Do you need a zimmer frame?'

The man kept up a running commentary about the park and its origins. Both men found it hard to hear him so resorted to nodding and agreeing every so often.

'I do hope he's not talking about Berlin's dark past and we're busy smiling and approving of everything,' George whispered.

Kobi laughed. 'What's that?' He pointed at a square concrete cube on a slope a little way in front of them.

'Shall we ask?'

George leaned forward. 'What is that, over there?' he asked, touching the man's shoulder and pointing.

The cyclist came to a stop. 'That is the Memorial to the Homosexuals. The ones murdered by the Nazis.'

George climbed out. 'I'd like to see that.'

Kobi shook his head and followed him out. They were nearly back at the park entrance.

'Thank you very much,' he said to the man, who nodded cheerfully and set off back towards the Brandenburg Tor.

Kobi joined George at the Memorial. It was solid and dark and had only one opening, a small rectangle. George peered through the window, then moved away.

'Have a look in there,' he said.

Kobi hesitated and then leaned in. He could see a film projected onto a screen on the other side of the glass. As he watched, the two young men on the screen, who were facing each other, touched and then kissed. He pulled away.

'Symbolic,' he said gruffly, turned on his heel and walked to a bench a few feet away. George watched the film again and then joined him. For a moment neither man spoke. They observed two young men sauntering off the path and photographing each other beside the concrete block. The men smiled at Kobi and George and gave them a wave.

'They think we're a couple,' George said suddenly.

'Well, they're wrong.'

George turned towards him and said nothing. Kobi glanced at him, looked away and then reluctantly let his gaze settle back on the other man.

'Indeed. But they don't have to be,' George said.

Kobi was looking for something in George's expression. Some marker that would show him the man was sincere.

He shrugged. 'They do.'

'Why?' George sounded surprised.

Kobi tried not to sigh; this was not a conversation he wanted to have or had expected to have. 'I was gay ... once. A long time ago. It ended badly. I'm ... nothing now.'

George frowned. 'Nothing? That sounds very boring. I could change your mind.'

George was handsome and funny and could easily be a massive distraction. He was also a window into a scary world Kobi had walked away from years ago.

'No. But I am very flattered. And I'm also very hungry. How about sausage for lunch?'

At a sausage stand, Kobi bought them both currywurst: a cut-up sausage with chips, spicy sauce and some curry powder sprinkled on top. They crossed the road and walked into the Tiergarten, down a shell path and deep into the park before they sat down on a bench.

'Oh, I do love a bit of bratwurst!' Kobi said.

'Better than the spicy sausage, far too hot,' George answered as he picked out a large piece.

'Since being here I understand my grandpa, my dad's dad. He really loved sausage and used to complain about the white bread in Australia, "white fluff" he called it.'

'I remember comments like that. "No decent black pudding!"'

'And the sauerkraut was too sweet, the beer too watery, and you couldn't get decent dark bread!'

They both laughed at the memories of immigrant parents trying to adapt to foreign food.

'Have you thought any more about our plan to make millions selling forged recovered old masters?' George asked eventually.

Kobi smiled. 'I have enough trouble painting originals, let alone trying to create something that resembles someone else's work,' he said.

'Pity. I know we're only joking, but it is frustrating, dealing in growing demand and shrinking supply. Most of the Old Masters are in museums and art galleries now, and the pieces in private collections hardly ever come on the market. As it happens, the best source is Holocaust art.'

Kobi looked at him sharply. This was a more interesting subject to him than George could ever know. 'You mean art returned to descendants that comes on the market?'

George nodded. 'Klimt, Degas, Vermeer and even van Gogh —'

'A van Gogh?' Kobi was fascinated.

George nodded again. 'Perfect example. Did you know that Hitler declared him a degenerate artist? When they cleansed the German culture, some of van Gogh's pieces were burnt. Can you believe that? But the *Portrait of Dr Gachet* was sold.'

'What happened to it?' Kobi asked.

'Aha, that's where it gets really interesting. In 1990, a hundred years after it was painted, the heirs of Siegfried Kramarsky sold the painting for eighty-two and a half million dollars. A Klimt sold in 2006 for a hundred and thirty-five million. The art gallery it went to in New York is dedicated to displaying art stolen from Jewish families during the Holocaust.'

'A whole art gallery?'

'A whole gallery. Kobi, there are so many examples of returned paintings that would make a fortune at auction. A da Vinci, a Rembrandt, a Dürer —'

'A print?' Kobi interrupted sharply.

George shook his head. 'No, an oil painting. The Horowitz Dürer. It was returned to a German family in 2008. Nobody knows much about it. Most dealers would give their right arm to be asked to sell some of the art that has been reclaimed in the past few years. And I have clients who would pay a king's ransom for it.'

Later that day, Kobi knocked on the door of the office of Professor Mikel Kribbler, his boss. 'Can you spare me a moment, sir?'

The professor looked up from his computer and gestured towards the empty seat opposite his desk. 'Of course. What can I do for you?'

'I heard a phrase today, in conversation, and I wondered whether you might be able to shed some light on it for me.'

Kribbler nodded. 'I will certainly try.'

'What is the "Horowitz Dürer"? Is it a nickname for a painting? Something to do with provenance?'

There was a moment's pause.

'Yes and yes. It is a name for a painting and it has everything to do with provenance. But I'm not sure I know the whole story ... I do know someone who might be able to help, though. Let me make some enquiries and see what I can find.'

Kobi stood up. 'I'd appreciate that, thank you, sir.'

CHAPTER TEN

Berlin
June 1942

My dearest darling baby,
Someone remarked last night that the longer this war
goes on, the more of your milestones I am missing. I
won't see you crawl, maybe I won't see you start to
walk. I won't stay up with you at night as you cut
your first tooth, and I won't hear your first word. If
you say 'Mama' or 'Papa' it will be to someone else
and not to us. I did ask Meme if I could have some
photos of you as you grow, but she said that was too
dangerous — they might get your pretend mama and
papa into trouble if they were found. So I have to use
my imagination and lie here and conjure up your smile
and the softness of your skin and your smell. I'm very
good at doing that, but it will fade as time passes. What
will never fade, my darling, will be my love for you: it
is as deep as the ocean, which Dee used to say was the
deepest thing in the whole world, and as high as the
mountain called Everest. I miss you to my core. I may
not be beside you, but I am inside you, in your heart,
and you are inside mine.

But I want you to understand how important the
work is and how it has captivated me from the first

day I became involved. It is the most exciting thing
I have ever done. Now, instead of leaving the room,
I stay and listen and the people closest to Harry and
Suzie know who I really am. There are several people
who have gathered regularly at our home since early
1940. Shooey is a sculptor and he is so Aryan, blond
and ruggedly handsome, and he winks at me when
he thinks no one is looking. Elly is a doctor and she
is very helpful, the loveliest little woman underneath
her serious exterior. Her practice is in Wilmersdorf,
and I am so tempted to ask her whether she knows my
mama but I dare not. Mama is supposed to be unwed,
and if Elly is her doctor she would be shocked to know
that I am her daughter! Himpy is a dentist and he is
one of my favourites; he treats Jews who need his help
even though it is illegal, and he forges ration cards and
travel documents. We have worked extensively together,
and he is very good at making me laugh. He fixed my
toothache once and told me I have very good teeth.

His lovely fiancée, Minty, is called half-Jewish by the
Nazis. But her mother is Jewish, so she is Jewish — like
you, my darling. She was a law student, but she isn't
allowed to graduate and they aren't allowed to marry.
That seems so unfair; she is absolutely beautiful and
very bright. Gunty is a playwright and he is a very
close friend of Suzie's, they work together a lot on film
scripts.

But the closest of all are two married couples.
Hacky and Yankee are very serious and intellectual,
but passionate about resisting the government on a
practical level. He is German and she is American. To
start with I thought they were quite intimidating, he has
a very important job and she is a teacher, but now we
can chat and even laugh sometimes.

*And then there are the Kucks, Getty and Ron, who
have the sweetest little boy. They are my bosses' best
friends, and Suzie spends hours in conversation with
Getty.*

*These people won't mean anything to you and
I can't tell you too much about them, but they
mean everything to me. Suzie has a friend who is a
professional fortune-teller and a psychic, and she gets
military officers who want their fortunes told to tell
her about what they are planning, and then she hands
the information on! She tells their fortune in her front
room, and in her back room she has a printing press for
printing out illegal pamphlets.*

*When I joined Harry and Suzie in early 1940
the lack of wood to fight off the cold, and the food
rationing, had really begun to hit us all, and then they
passed a law limiting baths to Saturday and Sunday,
which took away a very easy way to get warm. We have
baths on days when we aren't supposed to, but we have
to be careful that the neighbours don't hear the water
running.*

*The Berlin in which we now live is a long way from
the city in which I grew up. The official buildings are
hung with Nazi flags, and swastikas are draped over
many residential buildings. The streets are full of open
trucks carrying soldiers, and every second car is a long
black government car with a driver. I was too young to
go to nightclubs before the war, but the older members
of our circle moan about the changes, the Nazis in
uniform at every table and bar, and the way the local
women drink with them, dance with them and sleep
with them.*

*And everywhere you turn are the men in leather
coats or black uniforms, always watching, always*

*waiting for a chance to pounce and arrest you for
some anti-government activity. They are the worst, the
Gestapo in their plain black coats, or their uniform
with the red arm-band and black-on-white swastika.
Two SS officers stopped me once, checked my papers
and circled around me, laughing and touching my
curls, telling me I was 'ripe for plucking', but they were
ordered back to their car. I was so terrified I wet myself.*

*Harry used to bring home real news, things we never
read about in the papers or heard about on the radios,
which are all controlled by the government. In April
1940 our army over-ran the European countries to the
north and west, Norway and Denmark, and then in
May, Belgium, the Netherlands and France. Everything
we hear from the 'official' sources is full of our
wonderful all-conquering Führer and how we are going
to rule the world. The Third Reich will last a thousand
years. But the people in the city around us don't seem
to be very interested in the war. They are too busy
trying to find enough food to eat and making sure they
stay out of the way of the Gestapo. Harry and Hacky
are exasperated — they had expected the public to be
horrified at all the warmongering and rise up against
the Nazis. But that hasn't happened. By the time you
read this, I pray that all of those countries are free again
and not still part of the Third Reich.*

*Hacky has managed to get a shortwave radio to
listen to foreign news broadcasts. He writes newsletters
about what he hears and we all read them eagerly.*

*In May 1940, several members of the circle went
with us on a bicycling trip to the castle that was owned
by Suzie's family. She brought along her accordion,
and we all sang songs and went swimming in the lake
and cooked lunch over an open fire. After lunch we got*

down to the real reason for the trip. Harry had brought foreign press reports and we read them and planned the next anti-Nazi flyer.

Our circle has a printing press hidden in a paint and carpet supply shop on the outskirts of Berlin. We get our information from all sorts of sources — Harry's press reports, Hacky's shortwave radio, the soldiers that Suzie talks to — and then we all help write and illustrate our leaflets. I draw cartoons and maps and sometimes banner headlines. Paper is hard to come by, and we can't buy in bulk without attracting attention, but Hacky has a contact at the US Embassy who supplies him.

When the leaflets are done we distribute them to all sorts of different people, and we try to circulate them around the city. It is a dangerous occupation; arrest means immediate deportation to a camp or trial for treason. I ride my bicycle through the streets at night, putting flyers in mailboxes, dumping them in telephone booths, and sometimes I go to the train station and put them in the backpacks of soldiers who are distracted saying goodbye to their sweethearts before leaving for the front. Once I have emptied my bag I cycle home as fast as I can, keeping to the shadows and avoiding the checkpoints. I imagine how much Dee would love doing this; it would have been one big exciting adventure for him.

One area in which I can use my skills is the work Himpy is doing to help the Jewish people who are trying to escape Germany or are in hiding. I forge papers and ration cards and draw maps to guide them to where contacts will meet them. Himpy says no one can do it as well as me! Sometimes I have delivered food and medicine by bicycle to people who are hiding

Jews, and given what news I could of the outside world.
They are always so pleased to see me and so grateful,
but all they really want to know is whether I think the
war will end soon.

Through Himpy I have met a remarkable man
called Tutti. He is a Gentile and he owns a company
that makes brushes and brooms, but it is more of a
workshop for blind and deaf workers. Many of them
are Jewish. Once, Himpy took me to Tutti's premises
on the Rosenthaler Strasse, and I saw all of these people
busy at their benches putting bristles onto brushes and
broom heads. He has three Jewish people working in his
administration department, which is strictly forbidden,
and when the Gestapo make one of their regular calls
a bell rings and those workers run and hide in a hole
under the staircase.

Two important things happened towards the end of
1940. The English air force started bombing Berlin, as
retaliation for a raid on London. We had to incorporate
new routines into our lives, as high-pitched, invasive
air-raid warnings would send us running to hide in
underground shelters, followed by the thudding sound
of bombs exploding. We would find piles of rubble in
the street when we emerged. The first time it happened
was terrifying, and I just wanted that horrible
screeching to stop, but it is amazing how quickly we got
used to grabbing our little packed cases and scurrying
down the street to the nearest shelter.

If I was out on one of my leaflet delivery circuits and
an air-raid siren went off, I would park my bicycle and
follow the crowd. Most frightening of all were the two
nights when there was no shelter close to me and I had
to hide in abandoned buildings and listen to the bombs
falling, praying they wouldn't hit me.

Secondly, a new person joined the circle, introduced to us by Hacky. I didn't meet him, but I heard about him. When Getty went to meet him at a train station and pick up a radio transmitter from him, he was so nervous he dropped the suitcase on the ground, and when she got it home the transmitter wouldn't work. His name is Rusky and he is a Red spy, although I suspect not a very good one.

Suddenly the Reds want some of the men in our circle to become agents as well as resisters to our own government. This has caused much discussion and argument and friction. As well as trying to disseminate true and authentic information about the war and the atrocities committed by the Third Reich, we are now faced with the prospect of supplying military information to our enemies, information that could help defeat our own country. Harry has a younger brother and a father in the navy, and many of the others have siblings fighting for Germany. Is it high treason? No, most definitely not: it is our patriotic duty and we are very proud to do it.

Your loving Mama

CHAPTER ELEVEN

Berlin
July 2014

That letter kept Kobi awake. They had gone from being Resistance fighters to spying for the Russians, and in doing so he supposed the danger had increased exponentially. And yet, if you were caught you were going to be killed for being a member of the Resistance, so why not be a spy, too?

Their bravery astounded him, especially Ruby's. He was beginning to understand why she had decided to put her baby into hiding. She was so young and yet she had cycled through the streets at night with illegal pamphlets and delivered food and medicine to Jews in hiding, forged documents and joined in treasonous discussions. How proud would her parents have been if they had known?

When he arrived at his office the next morning there was a note on his desk asking him to drop in and see Professor Kribbler when he had a moment. He wasted no time. The professor shut the door behind him and gestured to the seat.

'Have you discovered something?' Kobi asked, trying not to sound too hopeful.

Kribbler nodded. 'Indeed I have! Last night I emailed a friend in New York and asked whether he knew anything about the Horowitz Dürer. He is an assessor for Christie's and he knows everyone, and, more importantly, he knows the gossip. I don't have to tell you how much gossip goes on in the art world.'

Kobi looked up at him. Kribbler was an entertaining man, an academic with a sense of humour and a love of adventure. Kobi liked him.

'And?'

'And he came back to me with this.' With a flourish he pulled two pieces of paper from a folder and handed one over. 'This is, apparently, one of the few photographs of the actual Horowitz portrait, taken at authentication. They keep it out of the public eye.'

Kobi found himself staring down at a Dürer portrait. The background was dark and the foreground light focused on the handsome face of a young German nobleman of the early sixteenth century. He wore a white silk shirt and a heavy robe of red silk damask with a fur collar and cuffs. The fabric fell in exquisitely painted folds. The hair under his black hat was auburn, the curls touching his collar. His vivid hazel eyes stared straight out of the picture back at Kobi. The painting was longer and showed more of the man's body than in many of Dürer's portraits. The nobleman held a broken pomegranate in one hand; the fingers were long and slender. Kobi gazed at it for a long moment, fighting the urge to weep with joy.

'It's the Paul von Hoch,' he said finally.

'I thought so, too. Tell me, Kobi, what do you know about the von Hoch?'

'He was a nobleman, painted in 1520. It's listed in the catalogue compiled after Dürer's death, but it had always been in private hands, and there has been no trace of it for over a hundred years.'

This was the subject he had been searching for. Who were the Horowitzs? Would they let him write a book on their hidden masterpiece? Surely they knew what they had? If he could make this happen, it would genuinely add to both the collective knowledge of his favourite artist and his own reputation.

'Who are these people, sir? And where did they get it from?' Kobi asked.

'In 2008, a Russian billionaire, Valentino, returned a Dürer painting to two old brothers who had been through concentration camps. Germans, who live in Vermont. It had belonged to their family before the war — their father was a banker — and it was looted by the Nazis. Somehow the Russian had it. I don't think he was very pleased about them turning up to claim it. They have kept it low key.'

'They must have gone to great lengths to keep it quiet,' Kobi said.

'There was something to do with a violin, a rare one. He had that, too, and the grandson is a child prodigy —'

'Now *that* I remember reading about! I didn't realise there was a painting, much less a Dürer.'

Kribbler smiled. 'And this,' he said, watching Kobi closely, 'is a copy of the black-and-white photograph that was attached to the back of the painting. It was also taken at the time of authentication. This is the Horowitz family before the war. The only image of the entire family that has survived.'

Kobi tore his gaze away from the painting and took the second sheet from the outstretched hand.

A man, short and stocky with a bushy moustache and a huge smile; a woman, tall, elegant and wearing a gorgeously detailed dress; a young man beside her, his face similar to hers, smiling self-consciously at the camera; a teenaged boy, shorter and stocky, like his father, with a cautious expression, serious eyes and no smile; and standing in front of the four a boy and a girl. He was grinning, his head cocked slightly to one side and his hands on his hips; she was smaller, elfin, shy, with long black plaits and haunting eyes.

They were familiar, and yet they weren't. Something, and yet nothing. The eyes, the hands, the cleft in the chins of some of them ... Could it be —? Surely not. What were the odds? There was only one way to know for sure. He looked up at the professor, who was waiting patiently.

'Can I take these, sir? I need to do a little ... research, off-site.'

'Of course.'

Kobi packed his satchel and caught the U-Bahn back to the apartment. On the train, every few minutes he took the copy of the photograph out and studied it, then put it away again. His brain was spinning with questions and possibilities.

He sprinted down the street from the U station to the apartment. Once inside, he laid the two pieces of paper out on the dining table and then carefully unfolded the letters and sketches and placed them around the photograph. It was them.

'I don't bloody believe it,' he whispered to himself.

She had drawn her middle brother playing the violin, his face turned to his left. The eldest was seated, his hands on a piano keyboard. Her father was also playing the violin in one sketch, and smiling out at her in another, and her mother was such a good likeness that it almost made him cry. But the twin was extraordinary. She had caught the glint in his eye, the mischievous smile and the tousled hair. *It feels like half of me is missing.* That is what she had written about him.

The faces were mesmerising; he couldn't look away.

An hour later he caught the underground to the gallery and went back to Professor Kribbler's office.

'Was your research profitable?' Kribbler asked, watching him intently.

'Indeed. I'm not sure where to start.'

'You know them, don't you?' the professor asked.

'Sort of. I have a pile of letters; my mother gave them to me before I left home. It's a collection of love letters of sorts, written in Hebrew during World War II. I had them translated by a Frau Goldman at the New Synagogue here, and I'm reading them. One letter a night.'

Kribbler's curiosity was palpable. 'And?'

'And the author was an artist who drew sketches of her family. She didn't name them, she only used nicknames. But she drew them, for her baby daughter. I didn't think I would ever know who they were.'

'And they are the Horowitz family.'

'They are. Undoubtedly. It's written by the daughter, Ruby. Does your friend know their names?'

Kribbler shook his head. 'Only the two old men. Simon and Levi.'

Kobi looked up, a multitude of emotions in his facial expression. He couldn't stop them.

'So, Cee and Lee are Simon and Levi Horowitz — clever. Levi went to London before the war, and Simon was taken to Dachau with his father and brother.'

'What are you going to do with this information?' Kribbler asked.

'I'm ... I'm not sure, sir.'

'I don't need to spell it out. If there is any way you can persuade them to exhibit that painting here, it would be a tremendous coup for the gallery and a career-defining moment for you.'

Kobi nodded slowly.

'I know. First, I need to finish the letters. Then there are a couple of places I must visit, one in Berlin and one will mean a trip to Munich.'

'Dachau.' It wasn't a question.

'If I am to return the letters to Simon, I must understand what he went through.'

'And in Berlin?'

'I suspect I shall find out the fate of Ruby at the German Resistance Museum.'

In the afternoon, Kobi took a taxi out to the beautiful suburb of Grunewald in the west of the city. On the Erdener Strasse he found an ivy-covered villa, the home of the Galerie Bassenge, one of Berlin's oldest and most prestigious auction houses. He had telephoned to say he was coming, and was told that Dr Boris Meyer was available to see him.

'You said you wanted to ask about our Dürer Collection?' Dr Meyer asked as he gestured to the chair on the other side of the large desk.

'Yes. I assume most of what you sell are prints of engravings?'

Dr Meyer nodded. 'Either rare prints or in the fifteenth- to nineteenth-century print catalogues.'

'And the average price?' Kobi asked.

'A couple of thousand euro; occasionally one very old print will fetch ten thousand euro.'

'What's the world record for the artist?'

'Just last January, Christie's in New York sold a private collection of masterpieces, and the top lot was *The Rhinoceros*. I believe it fetched eight hundred and sixty-six thousand, five hundred dollars US, a world auction record for the artist. The total value of the collection was in excess of six million dollars US.'

'All prints?' Kobi asked.

'As opposed to?' Dr Meyer sounded a little bewildered.

'Paintings. Oils.'

'Dr Voight, I assumed you understood that no paintings have come on the market for a very long time. They are all in art galleries, museums and two are in private collections.'

'Are you counting the Horowitz Dürer among those two?'

Dr Meyer stiffened. 'What do you know about the Horowitz Dürer? Have you seen it?'

Kobi shook his head.

'Not yet, but I am hoping to.'

'Good luck. I know several experts who have tried. They keep it in a vault. They won't sell — and they have been offered ridiculous amounts of money. They won't allow any reproductions, even for display.'

'Did you know it is the Paul von Hoch?' Kobi asked.

The man stared at him, naked astonishment on his face. 'Are you sure?' he asked quietly.

Kobi nodded. 'Absolutely.'

'And how do you know that?'

'I've seen a picture of it, taken at the time of authentication.'

'I'd ... heard rumours that it was, but some experts claimed to have seen it and said it was nothing special, a drawing for a known portrait, a crayon study —'

Kobi stood up. 'It's not: it's the Paul von Hoch. Thank you for your time, you have been most helpful.'

He extended his hand and the man stood and accepted it. He could see that there were questions the doctor wanted to ask, but Kobi wasn't ready to share his secrets. It was a competitive world and discretion was essential.

'Anything I can do, Dr Voight, at any time.'

Kobi spent the next morning researching on the internet. Sergei Valentino had a substantial public profile as a businessman in oil and gas production, and as an arts benefactor. Kobi read about how his grandfather, General Vladimir Valentino, had served with Marshall Zhukov in World War II, and his father, Koyla Valentino, had been an influential member of the Soviet ruling party.

Zhukov had 'liberated' Berlin, taking it from the Germans in May 1945. Kobi could fill in the blanks about the violin and the painting. Sergei's grandfather had acquired them somehow in the chaos that was the last days of war in Berlin and hadn't handed them in to Russian authorities. Sergei's aunt, Yulena, was a professional violinist who had played the del Gesú in the Moscow Philharmonic and had died on English soil in 1965. One website claimed that she had been murdered by the KGB, who believed she was going to defect.

Daniel Horowitz, the young violin prodigy, had an impressive website and was described as Simon Horowitz's grandson. The family had owned the violin before the war, and had lost it when their house was looted in 1939 by the Nazis. Valentino allowed him to play the 1742 Guarneri del Gesú violin, which was named Yulena, in concert. It was all good background, but it didn't help him find out more detail about the painting.

Paul von Hoch was mentioned in relation to the 'lost' Dürer painting. He was a burgmaster of the City of Nuremberg, and was known as a local patrician. Most interestingly, he was one of the group of men who loaned gold to Charles V in order to secure his election as Holy Roman Emperor. In return, Charles gave the family noble rank and sovereign rights over their lands and the right to mint their own money. They were leading members of the Catholic nobility; Dürer, also, was a devout Catholic. The idea of the von Hoch family being Jewish was about as likely as the pope of the day converting to Judaism.

In frustration, Kobi turned to a leaflet he had been given at the Memorial for the Murdered Jews of Europe. Something had rung a bell … Yes, here it was: a small museum on the Rosenthaler Strasse called Otto Weidt's Workshop for the Blind. It was a brief description, a brush-and-broom workshop run by a Gentile, for blind and deaf workers, and how he had hidden Jews and organised the release of many others because his workforce was classified as 'important for the war effort'.

It was the man Ruby had described meeting: Otto was Tutti. He couldn't help but smile at her nicknames.

The workshop was five minutes' walk away, definitely worth a detour on his way to work. As it turned out, it was in the same courtyard as the Silent Heroes Memorial Centre. Kobi had seen the sign, but it hadn't meant anything to him so he had ignored it.

Now he took the stairs to the first floor two at a time. It was a long, narrow set of rooms.

He read Otto's story and studied the black-and-white photographs of the middle-aged man. He looked gentle and ineffectual, but obviously he was not. The descriptions of how he braved Gestapo anger were impressive. When his workers were rounded up and taken to a nearby deportation assembly point, Weidt marched in and declared that his products were classified as 'necessary' and he had to have his workers. They were all released to him. It appeared he wasn't above a bit of bribery of corrupt Gestapo officers to keep the wheels of his business turning.

Kobi looked at the little wooden benches and the vices, some with brushes still in them, and imagined Ruby standing on the same spot with Himpy, watching the people work. Suddenly he felt very close to her.

He read about the people who had helped Weidt, including a Jewish doctor who treated seriously ill Jews in hiding. His non-Jewish wife got them medicine from the chemist. Others obtained food and forged ration cards to make it easier to feed hidden Jews. Kobi assumed Ruby and Himpy were two of those.

Hedwig Porschutz, who worked in Weidt's factory, hid twin girls for part of the war until they could be sent to the United States, and then hid another worker and her niece. Porschutz was arrested in 1944, and Kobi dreaded to read what her fate had been, but she was just sentenced to eighteen months jail for trading on the black market. He felt a sense of awe. How brave were these people? What risks did they take to hide those to whom they were unrelated and whose only crime was being of another religion?

The final room was a windowless space that was approached through a hole in a wall, hidden by a cupboard. Chaim Horn, his wife, Machla, and their two children, Max and Ruth, were hidden here for all of 1942 and most of 1943. It was dark, square, and box-shaped; the four walls were the difference between life and death. He peered into the room for a full two minutes, and then he stepped out and read about the family. On 14 October 1943, they were betrayed and the workshop was raided. They were arrested and deported to Auschwitz where they all died.

Kobi felt his stomach turn over. Somewhere in this city there must be stories of people who had escaped and survived and gone on to lead happy lives, surely? Once again the atmosphere became oppressive. He took out his handkerchief and wiped his mouth, turned on his heel, and tried not to stumble on his way out. Groups of foreign children were being lectured to by teachers, and they eyed him suspiciously as he weaved between them. By the time he made it to the exterior door to the courtyard he felt his legs starting to wobble, and he just made it to an iron bench before they gave out completely. Work was out of the question today; it was back to the sofa and the letters.

CHAPTER TWELVE

Berlin
June 1942

My dearest darling baby,
Today I have been daydreaming about the young
woman you will become. Will you paint and draw?
Will you love music? Will you have long plaits? Will
you love school? What will you become when you grow
up? And of course, who will you fall in love with? How
many children will you have? My grandchildren! Will
they be girls or boys or both? I know you will live in
a free Germany, in a free world. I pray with all my
heart that you will be a good Jewish girl and a good
Jewish wife and mother. I imagine you making a cake
for my birthday, and bringing it to me, and all my
grandchildren wishing me 'Mazel tov' and kissing me on
my old, wrinkly cheek.

But for now we live in the present and so many
people are disappearing every day, so I know I should
finish these letters and take them to Meme. I have to
trust that she will give them to your pretend mama to
keep them safe.

I have been thinking about some of the things I have
done over the past year and wondering what I can tell
you, what you should know. The most important of

all was falling in love with your papa. It wasn't love at first sight; it was awe and wonder and then a gradual understanding. I remember the first time he kissed me: it was on the roof garden under the stars. He has such strong arms, and why wouldn't you want to be held by a pair of strong arms when darkness and danger threaten to engulf you at every moment? But, most of all, he makes me laugh. He was concerned because he is quite a bit older than me, but I convinced him that it doesn't matter. When we are alone and we pretend the war has vanished and we live by the lake together, there is no age difference.

Meme was the first person I told I was pregnant, and who the father was. She was angry with me. At first she wanted me to say that I had been raped by a German soldier. But I wouldn't consider that for a second: it was a lie, and I won't have something as beautiful and perfect as you based on a lie. But she persuaded me that if the others in our circle learned the truth they would be angry with him and would say he had taken advantage of me. That I was vulnerable because my family had been ripped from me and I was aching for some love to fill that gap.

So Meme and I invented a story about a young lawyer called 'Hans', which Meme would use if she ever had to explain who the father of my baby was. Hans was handsome and ardent and committed and he had swept me off my feet. Hans was a codename your papa used sometimes, but I didn't tell Meme that.

The truth is that your papa is all of those things, maybe apart from 'young' and apart from the 'lawyer' bit. He is as intense an anti-Nazi as I have ever met, and I love that about him. But he is also married. I explained to Meme that he and his wife have had an open relationship for years, and her long-term lover is part of our circle, too. She has other lovers besides that one, too. Your papa never objected to that, and he never intended to fall in love with me. The intensity of the world we live in and the nature of what we do — the danger, the fear, the joy at little victories — it was almost inevitable. When this hell is over and we're safe, we will be together and we will bring you back.

1941 began with Harry being transferred to Potsdam for his job. It made it even easier for him to access the information he was passing to the Reds via Rusky. He came home for two days a week, and we still had parties and dinners with friends. I know that all of the men involved with the Reds were very angry and frustrated, because they weren't taken seriously and their detailed information was discounted. They weren't members of the Communist Party, and the Reds were highly suspicious of their motives. There were raised voices and the banging of fists on tables, but nothing changed.

Sometimes when they had meetings in parks or nearby woods, Suzie and I, or Getty and I, would go for a walk some distance behind them and chat away, but we were really watching to make sure no one was following them.

Then in June of last year Hitler invaded the Soviet Union, and to start with it all went very well for Germany. The Reds were unprepared, in spite of all of the information that had been sent to them. I have never seen people as disappointed about how well their own country was doing in a war! Sometimes it felt very strange.

Around that time I joined with my dear friend Minty in her work, helping Jews escape. She and her mother are Catholics, but her mother was born Jewish, and that means Minty can't finish her law degree or marry her lovely fiancé, the dentist Himpy. She showed me some sermons that a Catholic bishop had given, publicly denouncing the government and especially their euthanasia policy. It was a very brave thing for him to do. No one was allowed to read the sermons, so we typed lots of copies, as did other German Catholics, and we distributed them. Soon they were all across the country and everyone was talking about it. Hitler made a speech and officially reversed the policy of euthanasia of the mentally ill. I'd like to think it hasn't continued, but the evidence suggests otherwise. Still, it was a victory of sorts.

Another of our circle, an artist called Cally, showed me what she was doing for the French forced labourers and prisoners of war. One day we went to the nearest train station and watched them being herded onto subway cars. At the last moment we jumped into the car, too. Cally had brought things for them, soap, cigarettes, sweets, gloves and bundles of our flyers and we stuffed them into pockets. Some of them had notes for her and some gave me notes, too. We promised to post them home to France. It was thrilling and I told her I would do it again. That night I filled a whole sketchbook with drawings of the faces of the soldiers and workers.

Not long after I told Meme that I was pregnant, she came to see me and asked me whether she should get word to Mama. I told her that I didn't think so, not until I knew for sure that I was going to be able to carry the baby.

Two weeks later she came back and told me that Mama had decided to join a group who were going to

Switzerland. She was living very happily with the family Meme had found for her, but she wanted to join Lee in London and this was her best chance. She had a proper exit visa in her false name, and the last group had got through the border with no trouble.

Meme said I had to make up my mind about telling her. If Mama knew I was pregnant she would probably decide not to go, but instead stay in Berlin and wait out the war to be near me. I asked whether Mama knew the kind of work I did. Meme said it was better that she didn't worry, so Mama thought I was safe on the farm outside the city. In that case I decided it was better not to tell her — it would mean shattering all her illusions and she might try to 'save' me, which could be disastrous for both of us. Meme agreed and promised to give her all my love and G-d speed for a safe journey. I must admit I did cry that night in my bed. I had often dreamed of seeing Mama again, and I so wanted to tell her about your papa and the gift Life had brought me. But it is a time for us all to be strong and make sacrifices. I like to think of her with Lee. I daydream about them drinking cups of tea and taking walks in the park.

So how did I tell your papa? I took him up to our favourite place, on the rooftop. I gave him his favourite scotch and then I told him. I was afraid he might be upset, but he wasn't — he was so happy! We did our little happiness dance that we used to do to cheer ourselves up, and he gave me a new nickname. I am 'Rabbit'.

I remember the day that Cally brought someone new to the house. She was young and absolutely beautiful, and Cally told us that she was an artist, a painter.

Her Jewish fiancé, Karl, was a student who had been imprisoned in Sachsenhausen concentration camp since the Kristallnacht in 1938. When I told her about my experience of that night, she wept bitterly and admitted that she was Jewish, too. She had kept in touch with Karl's mother and young sister, who lived close by. But that day, when she went to see them, she discovered that they had been deported to the camps. She was so upset that Cally had brought her to join us.

We listened to some music, Bach from memory, on the gramophone. When Harry got home I could see how shocked and scared she was of him in his German officer's uniform, but I told her not to be frightened. Harry listened to her story, gave her a big hug and reassured her. I knew then that she would join us and so it has proved to be the case. She is Katy and we all love her dearly; she delivers messages and has even hidden Jews in her studio.

Honestly, my darling baby, I don't know how many we have in our circle now, but it grows daily. Most of them work in the centre of Berlin, and some are teenagers and some are young, some are middle-aged and some are grandparents. They are Lutherans, Jews, Catholics and atheists. Within the group there are little sub-circles who meet on their own and hear the news that comes from the centre, Harry and Hacky.

Last October another Red spy came to see us. He called the house and Suzie answered the telephone. As soon as she hung up she said she had to go out and she wanted me to come with her. We walked to the railway station and met a man there. She told him about how the radio transmitter we had been sent didn't work. Our radio expert had got one message through in June and that was all. She stressed that our group had all

of this vital information and very little way of getting
it back to the Reds efficiently. Then she brought him
back to the apartment and I made tea for him. He
sat with Harry for more than four hours, and I saw
him feverishly writing what he was being told in his
notebook. Afterwards Harry was very happy and we
had a grand party that night!

By Christmas time I was eight months pregnant and I
didn't go out much. I did lots of drawing and copying at
home, and stayed warm beside the fire. You were active,
and I used to like to lie with my feet up and feel you
kicking me. Harry and Suzie and I joked that you were
going to be a gymnast and you had started practising
your moves already. It was hard to get me any extra
food, but I know that some of the meat and vegetables
that were supposed to go to the Jews in hiding was
saved for me. And when she could, Suzie would bring
me a piece of cake from her work!

She has changed jobs and now works for the Reich's
Kulturfilm central office. She tells me all about how she
gathers footage to make films for the Nazi propaganda
machine, about art and Germany and other peoples
and countries in Europe. It gives her just the cover she
needs to collect evidence of Nazi atrocities and file it
away. Some of the things she has shown me are truly
terrible. I admire the way she talks to the soldiers who
bring their photographs in and finds out why they have
done these things, whether they have children and what
their plans are for after the war. She records all of that
and their names and addresses, so that someday it can
be used for war crimes trials. It will be incontrovertible
evidence of what they did. They show her photographs
of their children, and then pull out a snapshot from 'the

*East' of them about to hurl a baby against a wall or
pulling their bayonet out of an elderly woman's body.
I know doing this upsets Suzie so much, but she keeps
going. It is her contribution.*

*I gave birth to you on 17 February 1942; it was a
Tuesday. The wind was howling around the building,
and there was a snowstorm outside. Suzie had fetched
our friend the doctor, Elly, and the dentist, Himpy.
Fortunately it wasn't a long or difficult labour, and you
were two weeks early and small. Going to a hospital
or getting further help was impossible, so if it hadn't
gone well there was very little they could have done. I
remember that I so wished my mama was there with
me, and I might have called out for her, but there was
no use getting upset about things we couldn't change.*

*Elly held you up by your feet and gave you a gentle
slap on the back and you started to cry. Then Suzie cut
the cord and wrapped you up straight away in blankets
warmed in front of the fire, and I nursed you. You
were hungry! Your papa came in to see you, and he
almost cried. I had never seen him so emotional about
anything before, and when he held you he promised you
that he would create a better world.*

*But life had to go on, and everyone had to go back
to work. Meme came to be with me for the early days.
You were a good baby from the beginning: you slept
well and drank well and we had lots of cuddles. I
remember when we gave you your first bath and you
seemed to like it straight away and kicked your little
legs. And you put your tiny hand up by your cheek
all the time, and Meme said you must have done that
in my womb. I hadn't realised it was possible to love
something as much as I loved you — your smell, your*

soft skin, the sound of you snuffling into my neck and the way you squeezed my finger in your hand. Most of all I remember I wasn't lonely anymore, and I used to want you to wake up so I could tell you about my family and count your fingers and toes.

Four months flew by and you were strong. You could hold your head up and smile and focus your bright blue eyes on me. I didn't do much work apart from housework, washing your clothes and making meals and cleaning the house.

Then two weeks ago, your papa took me aside and told me that Meme had found a place for us, you and me. We could go and live in a village out of the city. We would be out of harm's way and we could wait for him to join us after the war. I was shocked and wanted to know if I could see him in between now and then. He said it was too dangerous, but Meme could let him know how we were. I tried to imagine how life would be without him and I refused. He begged me, he ordered me, and still I said 'no'.

I told him that as soon as you were a little older I could go back to work, and what I do is the only thing I can do to honour my family. Not even my precious baby can stop me doing that. I have had to learn to live without the people I love, but I am not going to learn to live without him. He wanted to keep on discussing it, but you woke up and were crying for me, so I told him the subject was closed, we weren't going anywhere!

That night Meme came to visit, and she and Suzie and Harry sat me down. Meme told me that they thought I should give you to her. She would find a home for you until the war was over, a safe home. Having you here was endangering all of us. How would they explain you to the Gestapo if they came calling? And maybe the neighbours would report you and we would be accused of hiding someone illegal. And how was I going to feed you when the time came to wean you? You were four months and my milk was already being affected by the lack of food and so much stress. They couldn't keep finding me extra food so I could make milk.

At first I refused point-blank, and said I would take you and live on the streets and take my chances. Harry got angry with me and said I was condemning you to certain death. That I was being ridiculous and he would not allow it.

I had tried very hard not to cry but I still cry easily, especially over anything to do with you. I refused to talk to them and slammed the door on my way out. You were asleep, but I picked you up anyway and lay down on my bed, with you asleep on my chest. I sang you a lullaby that my mama used to sing to me.

After a while Meme came in. She told me that she knew it was the hardest thing I would ever do, but I would know that it was the right thing to do. The Gestapo could come bursting through the front door tomorrow and take us all away. They wouldn't want to bother with a baby; they would probably bash your head against the nearest wall. When she said that, I thought I was going to be sick.

She promised me that she would choose the people very carefully and that they would take good care of you. And that it would only be temporary. As soon as it was safe, your papa would take me out to them and we would pick you up. But what if you don't remember me? What if you cry for your pretend mama? She said babies adapt very quickly, and you would know that I was your real mama — you wouldn't forget my smell and the sound of my voice and my smile.

But they wouldn't know what you like. How would they find out that you need your back rubbed from the bottom to the top, and that if I blow raspberries on your tummy it makes you laugh, or how you curl your fingers up when you drink? She said that they would work those things out, and she would tell them what I had said.

She knew that I have lost EVERYBODY, just everyone in the world apart from your papa, and now it seemed like I was going to lose you. But I shouldn't look at it that way, I should believe that by doing this I was making certain that you would survive and be there for me when the war was over.

I have seen so much pain, so many people marched away and loaded into trucks. So many innocent people shot and left to die in the gutter. I have seen pictures of what our soldiers do to people 'out East', bodies lying in open graves, and men kneeling in a row before they are shot in the back of the head. I know that nothing is certain and we could all be killed. Most people would say that what we are doing is treason, and that we deserve to die for undermining the Third Reich and the Führer. So it is too dangerous for you to stay here. And I can't leave your papa and the work that we do. But I need you to know that it was the toughest decision of my life, the cruellest thing anyone has done to me and I grieve for you every day.

That night I held you very close to me and sang you all the songs I remembered from my childhood. I told you, once again, all about my family and who you came from. I cut a tiny lock of your hair and tied it with a piece of cotton, and I keep it with me always, tucked into my bra strap. I didn't sleep at all, but it was the best, and worst, night of my life so far.

The next day Meme came and told me about a couple who lived on a farm. She showed me a photograph of them, and they looked very nice, very blond, very German, very Aryan and very Lutheran. The woman was smiling. He had fought and been injured in the war, and now he was discharged and worked on his farm. They had one son and would dearly love to look after baby Ebee until the war was over. They supplied excess food and milk to help feed hidden Jews, and sometimes their barn was used to hide fugitives on the run. Harry told me that they were good people, people who believed what we believed, and people I could trust. I can't make up nicknames for them, I can barely think of them as people, but their initials are PG and SG.

So I kissed your face all over, gave you to Meme, and she took you away. I tried to stand at the upstairs window, but as the car pulled away I changed my mind and ran for the door. Harry caught me and held me as I sobbed and hit his chest with my fists. Then he hugged me very close to him until I stopped crying.

Suzie gave me a cup of coffee and Harry took me to the sofa to sit down. He told me that he was going to visit some mountains south of Frankfurt with a journalist who was another of our circle, to have a holiday. I knew there must be another purpose; they were going to meet someone and tell them, or find out, something important. But he thought I needed a rest and he wanted me to relax, so he asked me to come, too, and travel as his secretary. Suzie agreed to the plan, so I said I would go. I won't write about what the information was, or who we met; it is all part of the spy games we play. But Harry knew I needed to get back to work, and I can tell you that it was very important.

This has been my longest letter and it will be my last, my darling baby. The longer I keep these letters with me the less likely it is that I am going to be able to get them to Meme if something goes wrong. They could sit here, in the basement wall, for years and no one would ever know. If the end comes, it will come very quickly — that's the way the Gestapo work. I'm not afraid, I have experienced two great loves and I trust G-d to protect me.

So, tomorrow I am going to cover them with kisses and wrap them up in a ribbon and take them, on my bicycle, to Meme. I know she will agree to give them to SG, your pretend mama. I hope you never have to read them. I hope that before you are much older this horrible war will be over and the Nazis will be but a terrible memory. You and I will burn these letters and, with them, the tragedies of these past years. The Americans have entered the war and the foreign broadcasts say they will come and free us, and maybe the Reds as well. I can tell you there will be joy and relief in every corner of the land. And I will hold you and kiss you goodnight every night and never let you go again. With every passing day you grow closer to the age when you will understand who I am; if I could but hold you one more time, then, if I am to die, I will go to my death with a smile.

With all my love and lots of kisses,
From your loving Mama

CHAPTER THIRTEEN

Berlin
July 2014

Kobi had read the letters through twice. The second time he had written down in a notebook all of the nicknames, and the descriptions that went with them.

George had wanted to read the letters, but Kobi had decided that they weren't for anyone else at this stage. He could see that this hurt George but chose to ignore that. Something about this 'holiday friendship' had started to irritate him; he felt pressured to respond to the none-too-subtle hints in their conversations. George wanted to explore Berlin's gay nightlife and Kobi had never been a party-goer.

When George suggested that he delay his onward journey to Austria and they take the time to get to know each other better, Kobi had had to be honest with him.

'I enjoy your company, you're a fun guy, but it's not going to go anywhere.'

George had a way of looking at him, something between a sulk and a pout, that Kobi didn't find endearing.

'So, you don't find me attractive?' George demanded.

Kobi hesitated. 'I like you, as a friend.'

George grabbed his wallet and hotel room key from the café table and stood up. He reached out a slender finger and poked Kobi in the shoulder with some force. 'I'm disappointed in you. I thought you were up front, but you're just a boring old tease. You stick your head in books and life passes you by.'

Kobi rubbed his shoulder. 'Afraid so.'

George snorted with disgust and walked out the door. Kobi watched him go and smiled to himself. It was almost a flounce. Not what he'd expected from such an intelligent man who had seemed full of self-confidence. Perhaps it was a good thing that he hadn't added how reluctant he was to let a shallow romance distract him from the mystery at hand. Far from being buried in books, he felt centre-stage in an unfolding drama that spanned generations.

Kobi was engrossed in the last few pages. On one side of his list he wrote *Ebee*, *SG* and *PG*, and on the other side he wrote *Elizabeth Gunther*, *Sabine Gunther* and *Peter Gunther*. Elizabeth was his mother's name, and Peter and Sabine had been her parents. Sabine had had the letters in her possession. Yet Ruby had said that they had a son, and so far as he knew his mother was an only child. Both of his maternal grandparents had died before he was born, but he had seen pictures of them, and they were very blond and very German. Was it a monumental coincidence, or was he standing on the brink of a life-changing discovery?

That same day Kobi took the underground to Potsdamer Platz and walked along the edge of the Tiergarten to the German Resistance Centre.

His heart was heavy with anxiety over what he was about to find out. The centre was housed in the former offices of the Army High Command, the site of the attempted coup that followed an assassination attempt on Hitler in 1944. Before entering the building, Kobi went to the spot in the courtyard where the conspirators were hanged or shot. It was quiet, enclosed by buildings, in shadow on a brilliantly sunny day.

He tried to imagine this being the last scene you saw before you died. He trembled even though the day was warm.

The first floor housed a temporary exhibition all in German, and he cursed his mother for her refusal to teach him her mother tongue.

The next floor was divided into rooms; stark, efficient and chronological displays that traced the rise of National Socialism and the course of the war before leading into areas dedicated to specific Resistance groups.

Suddenly there they were. Boards of smiling faces and panels of information in German and English. They had been christened the 'Red Orchestra' by the Gestapo, because of the connection to Soviet Russia; loose groupings of large numbers of people who took part in Resistance activities until the ring was broken in late 1942. Only a couple of months after Ruby had finished writing her letters, her worst fears had been realised. Had she been frightened or resigned? Had she cried out for her baby?

A hundred and thirty people had been arrested. Of these, four committed suicide, five were murdered without trial, and seventy-nine were tried before the Reich Court Marshall and thirteen before the People's Court. The remaining twenty-nine were released through lack of evidence. The first eleven death sentences were carried out on 22 December 1942, and in all thirty men and nineteen women were murdered in Berlin's Plötzensee Prison, either by hanging or by guillotine. They were hanged with piano wire which took an agonising thirty minutes and resulted in near decapitation.

Kobi took the list from his jacket pocket and started to write. It felt like a giant jigsaw puzzle was rapidly falling into place.

'Harry' was Harro Schulze-Boysen, a first lieutenant in the Luftwaffe, or Oberleutant der Luftwaffe, born on 2 September 1909. He looked just the way Ruby had described him — very tall, aristocratic and handsome.

'Suzie' was his wife, Libertas Schulze-Boysen, a dramaturgic journalist, born on 30 November 1913. She was beautiful, with her blonde hair in a bob and a full, sexy mouth.

'Hacky' was Arvid Harnack, a highly ranked official who worked on economic policy in the Nazi Ministry of Economics. 'Yankee' was his American wife, Mildred Harnack. 'Ron' was Adam Kuckhoff, a journalist, and 'Getty' was his wife, Greta Kuckhoff. 'Shooey' was Kurt Schumacher, a sculptor, 'Elly' was Elfriede Paul, the doctor who had helped deliver the baby, 'Himpy' was Helmut Himpel, the dentist, and 'Minty' was Marie Terwiel, his Jewish fiancée. And so it went on, name after name. They were almost all killed, the most notable exception being Greta Kuckhoff, who had lived to bring up her son. Some of the nicknames made immediate sense, and some were obviously based on things other than their real names, things that had died with Ruby.

There was no mention of an 'R. Horowitz' or a 'Francesca Albrecht', but Kobi read that some of the more prominent members were Jewish and that they were sent to Auschwitz without trial, labelled as traitors to the State. So that was probably her fate. If she had survived, it would, undoubtedly, have been noted.

And then there was Liane Berkowitz, a Jewish, pregnant nineteen-year-old who had, like Ruby, delivered handbills and pamphlets around the city. She gave birth in jail to a baby girl and called her Irene, and when she came up before the court they pardoned her, but Hitler denied the motion, with a rage out of all proportion to the crime of which she was accused, and demanded that she be executed. She was guillotined on 5 August 1943 and her body taken to the University of Berlin where it was dissected and studied, a fate shared by most of the women in the circle. Her baby died in Nazi custody shortly after her birth; officially she was 'euthanased'. So would this have been the fate of baby Ebee if Ruby hadn't sent her away to the farm? Had she, indeed, saved the baby from a gruesome fate?

Kobi looked at their arrest mugshots, rows of three pictures, and the documentation about the trials and the appeals turned down by Hitler himself. Obviously the fact that there were traitors in high places in the administration had sent shockwaves through the Third Reich. What had given them away in the end was a complete blunder by their Soviet spymasters.

In October 1941 a soviet spy with the codename 'Kent', stationed in Brussels, had travelled to Berlin and met with the Schulze-Boysens. This was obviously the 'Red' Ruby had described meeting at the train station with Suzie/Libertas. He had been given a wealth of information about the state of the German war machine, which he had taken back with him to Brussels. For the next seven nights he had spent long sessions on his radio, on-air all night. This gave the German counter-intelligence officers ample opportunity to home in on his signal and record the coded messages. It was only a matter of time before they cracked the code, allowing them to decipher an earlier message sent to 'Kent' from Moscow, which contained the names, telephone numbers and addresses of the main members of the Schulze-Boysen circle.

Kobi couldn't help but wonder at the stupidity of people who made such basic mistakes and caused chaos and death. He imagined the hundreds of lives that could have been saved by the group had their work continued. And he could feel a growing determination to find out what had happened to baby Ebee. But if he was going to face Simon Horowitz and tell him about his incredibly brave little sister and the fact that he might have a niece, then he had to understand Simon's war, and to do that he had to visit Dachau.

As he turned away he found himself in front of a backlit panel, all in German. He couldn't read it, but he could see the name Harro Schulze-Boysen, and make out the words 'codename' and 'Hans'.

On his way home, Kobi caught a bus back to the underground stop. It was rush hour and the passengers around him were hanging onto straps and seat backs. Bodies. Tall ones, short ones, thin ones, fat ones, very fat ones, old ones mostly seated, and children listening to music through headphones, a baby in a pushchair, tourists, businessmen and women, schoolchildren. Someone right behind him and beside him and in front of him, all swaying to the movement of the bus as it crossed tram tracks and stopped at lights. Is this what it was like, he wondered? Not even close. These people had a small amount of precious space between them. On the cattle trucks they were packed so tightly that they were forced to stand. Even when you fainted you didn't drop to the floor. The bus reached the station and he joined the throng pouring out the double doors and down the steps to the platform. A mass of humanity on the move, this time of their own free will.

It was incongruous. In fact, it was the very essence of the word. It was a beautiful summer day, with a cloudless blue sky, the air full of birdsong and the vapour trails of planes. Tall trees, resplendent with green leaves, grew everywhere.

The day before, Kobi had caught a taxi from the airport to his hotel in Munich, driven by a young Iranian, a university graduate who had moved to Germany at the age of nine. His reaction to the news that Kobi was here to go to Dachau was to exclaim that he had been made to go there every year on a school field trip and he was heartily sick of the place. This surprised Kobi; it had not occurred to him that visiting a concentration camp could become routine, especially not for someone who had come to Germany from a place of persecution. He had decided that the country had come to terms with its past and wanted to tell the stories to the younger generation, although perhaps they didn't all want to hear.

In the morning, Kobi took the train from Munich to Dachau station and then boarded the 726 bus through the quaint Bavarian town with the unfortunate name, until he came to the KL Gleidsteimer stop. Almost all of the passengers on the bus piled out, and he wondered what the bus driver must think, a full bus every time he drove the route until this stop and then a full bus back from here to the train station, day after day.

Kobi made his way down to the first stop on the audio guide. He looked at the train tracks, still visible on the ground, and imagined Simon and Dee stumbling out into the daylight. Now he stood in the centre of the parade ground at Dachau concentration camp and drank it all in. He was surrounded by tour groups of all ages and all languages, some with guides and some with long-handled blue audio pieces like the one he carried. The square was a babel of voices, some happy, some laughing, some strained with emotion, and some openly crying. That just made the place, and the day, more incongruous.

Kobi stepped into the first of three reconstructed barracks with its three-tier, bare wooden bunks. In between the second and third barracks were the ablutions rooms. A long row of toilets ran down both sides of the room, brown, ceramic and with no seats. He tried to imagine how you kept your dignity when that most private of human functions had to be performed in such a public way. Did your fellow inmates look away and offer you what solitude they could? Next door were two huge round washing basins that looked like fountains, again very public.

More affecting were the row upon row of concrete foundations where all the other barracks had stood. The camp had opened in 1933 as a work camp, and the barracks had been built to house around two hundred prisoners; by 1944, they were each housing two thousand. That much overcrowding was almost more than he could contemplate. Now the rectangular holes were filled with clean white and grey stones, which shone in the sunlight. More incongruity.

He turned slowly and walked down the long road towards a bridge. To his left was the perimeter fence, the ditch, the wire (which had been electrified and which he assumed no longer was) and the watchtowers. The bridge was small and rose in a gentle hump over a fast-flowing stream. It was a pretty scene, full of flowers, trees and shell paths. There was that word yet again: incongruous.

The groups were still milling around outside a long, low-slung building, the sounds of laughter and half a dozen languages ringing through the summer air. As they climbed the steps to the first of a series of interconnecting rooms the talking ceased, almost as if someone had switched off the vocal power of everyone present.

They all shuffled through, from the disinfecting room with its fingernail scratches on the walls to the room where prisoners were told they were having a shower, on to the disrobing room and then the dark and foreboding gas chamber with its low roof and nozzles on the walls and ceiling, the room where they stacked the dead, and finally into the crematorium. The three brick ovens stood open, smaller than Kobi had expected. A sign on the wall told him that some prisoners were hanged in front of the ovens and then reduced to ash. He doubted very much that they were given the option of blindfolds. He could hear people sobbing in the room behind him. He stared at the ovens for a long moment, then walked out the door to the welcome sunshine. Whatever fate had befallen Papa and Dee, he knew that Simon had survived this terrible place.

His next stop was the religious memorials. These buildings were remarkably empty of tourists and that saddened him — surely they housed the only message of hope in the entire place?

The museum was vast. Three hours later he came to the last displays, liberation day and post-war. A colour film of the 45th Infantry Division of the US Army liberating the camp played on a continuous loop. Two German girls stood before it, and one raised a piece of paper to shield her eyes. Kobi felt a surge of anger and a desire to go over and pull the paper away. To his surprise her companion took her wrist and firmly lowered the paper. He couldn't understand what she said, but it was obvious she was having no hiding from the truth.

Once outside, he sat on a grassy hill and let the past few days wash over him. If his mother hadn't given him the letters he would have stayed in Berlin for three months and written a learned, and somewhat boring, treatise on his favourite Dürer paintings. Then he would have flown home to Melbourne and continued with his ivory-towered, and somewhat boring, life.

But now he was at the centre of a story of intrigue and murder and genocide, and had the ability to restore something that would be beyond price. In return he hoped to be allowed to write a book about a major piece of art, which had been lost to the world for seventy-five years. And, just maybe, he might be able to help this family find another member to add to their decimated ranks.

As far as his colleagues were concerned, he was cutting short his sabbatical and flying home from Munich for 'family reasons'. In reality, the next day he would board a jet bound for Washington DC and the unknown.

CHAPTER FOURTEEN

Washington DC
July 2014

When the young man emerged from the darkness of the wings, strode into the spotlight downstage-centre and bowed from the waist, Kobi found it hard to draw breath. A thousand questions and sensations threatened his composure, but Kobi's immediate thought was how like the pencil sketch of his grandfather the young man was. The modern version was twenty, tall, lean, with a mop of dark curls and a disarming smile.

The piece was Tchaikovsky's *Violin Concerto in D Major*. Kobi watched intently as Daniel tightened the screw on the end of the bow, nodded to the conductor and put the violin to his left shoulder. The lush sound of the opening orchestral bars floated through the air for fifty seconds, the strings asking the questions and the woodwind instruments answering them. The bow was poised above the strings, waiting. Then the orchestra fell silent and his right arm swooped down as the piercing, melancholic cry of the violin burst forth. He seemed to settle into a trance, swaying slightly, bending at the knees and then rising again, a dipping motion. His eyes closed and a frown of concentration crept over his brow.

Suddenly Kobi's mind was filled with the pencil sketch of the young man playing the violin in Ruby's letters. The expression on the face was so similar. Had Simon Horowitz felt like this when he played, had he got equally lost in the music, had he performed to crowds like this? And seventy-five years later, this genius, Daniel Horowitz, Simon's grandson, was standing here on the stage at the Kennedy Centre and giving a recital on his family's Guarneri del Gesú violin.

Entry to a post-concert party was included in the premium price he had paid for his ticket. The event was a fundraiser for a Jewish charity, and the crowd was a mixture of regular attendees and people more interested in giving to the cause. Regardless, they were all immaculately groomed, the women festooned with diamonds that glittered under the artificial light. He accepted a glass of champagne from a waiter and stood by a wall, watching, listening, and soaking up the scene before him.

In situations like this his artistic observational skills came to the fore. Take, for instance, tonight's conductor, Rafael Gomez, barrel-chested and broad-shouldered, a handsome, charismatic man in his late-fifties with silver streaks in his dark hair and a beaming smile. People congratulated him at every turn, and he shook hands, kissed women on each cheek and agreed enthusiastically with their comments on the young soloist. The programme notes had told Kobi that Gomez was the resident conductor with the Washington Opera and Symphony Orchestra, and Kobi's own research had confirmed that he was the main protagonist in the successful return of the del Gesú violin to the Horowitz family. Gomez seemed relaxed amongst this crowd, charming, self-confident and happy, but he exuded power from every pore.

The crowd parted to allow Daniel to enter. He was in an open-necked shirt and designer suit, and his shiny face and wet curls were indicative of a cooling shower. People broke into applause and Kobi joined them, gently patting his free hand against the champagne flute. What did it feel like, he wondered, to be that young and so talented and the object of so much admiration?

'Hello, there. Are you new to the Kennedy Centre?'

The proximity of the voice made him start, and he turned to see an attractive woman smiling at him.

'Er, yes. This is my first time.'

'Are you a visitor to DC as well? I'm sorry, I should introduce myself. I'm Magdalena Montoya.'

She was a mix of ethnicities, clearly Hispanic and First Nation among them, and the result was strikingly beautiful. He swapped his glass to his left hand and shook the one proffered to him.

'Dr Jakob Voight. Yes, I am a visitor. I live in Melbourne.'

'Goodness! What brings you to our lovely city?'

Kobi hesitated and then pointed towards the crowd of people, all turned towards someone in the centre. 'I came to hear him play, Daniel Horowitz. He impressed me.'

Magdalena touched his arm with her free hand. 'That's so wonderful! My husband was the conductor tonight and he is Dan's mentor. Please, allow me to introduce you to Dan.'

A wave of relief swept Kobi from head to toe — one problem solved. 'I would like that, thank you.'

He followed the woman across the room, careful to keep her in view as they zigzagged around small groups. As he passed a table, Kobi put his glass down so that both of his hands were free. Daniel saw Magdalena, excused himself and turned towards her.

'Mags!' He kissed her on each cheek. 'Did you enjoy it?' he asked.

Magdalena laughed. 'Of course not, you were awful and that violin certainly needs work.' It was obviously a longstanding joke and the look between them spoke volumes.

Kobi was as tall as Daniel and his gaze took in the young man's face, but his brain was strangely unable to grasp the situation.

'Dan, this is Dr Jakob Voight, one of your fans. He's come all the way from Melbourne to hear you play.'

The extended hand had long, slender fingers. Kobi had seen those fingers before, on a sketch of a young girl —

'Lovely to meet you, Dr Voight.'

'Please, call me Kobi. It is a pleasure to meet you. I thought the concert was ... exquisite.'

Daniel was clearly used to these conversations and gave a small nod of acknowledgement. 'Thanks so much. I try to give the credit to my violin; it's the true star.'

Kobi frowned. 'Without you, it is silent. Magnificent, but silent,' he said.

Magdalena nodded. 'What a beautiful way to put it. Dan is very bad at acknowledging his role in the music he makes. I will remember that answer.'

'I particularly enjoyed the Kreisler *Liebesleid* in the second half,' Kobi said.

Daniel smiled with obvious pleasure. 'That piece is special to Mr Sergei Valentino, my patron. It was a favourite of his late aunt, Yulena, after whom the violin is named. I like to include it when I can, for him.'

'And speak of the devil,' said Magdalena with amusement in her voice. Kobi turned to see Sergei Valentino striding towards Daniel, his arms outstretched. While Kobi had read about the man, the description hadn't done him justice. He was vast, a genuine man mountain. The Russian engulfed the young man and slammed him on the back with his massive hands.

'Dan, my boy!'

Daniel disentangled himself and allowed Sergei to kiss him on each cheek. Sergei's face was a pale, round moon and his mouth was red and moist. Something about him repulsed Kobi.

'We were just talking about you,' Daniel indicated towards Kobi. 'Dr Jacob Voight came from Melbourne, in Australia, to hear me play and he said he particularly enjoyed the *Liebesleid*, so I was explaining why I include it.'

Sergei turned his attention to Kobi and stretched out his hand. 'Good evening, Doctor. Is that a German name?'

His eyes were cold, and Kobi felt an involuntary shudder. He nodded. 'It is. My mother was born in Berlin and my father's parents came from Munich. I was born in Australia.'

'And what are you a doctor of? Music, perhaps?'

All three of them were looking at him. He needed to choose his words carefully. 'Art, actually. I'm an artist and I lecture at the University of Melbourne in art history.'

'Have you been to the National Gallery here in DC?' asked Daniel.

Kobi smiled at him. 'Not yet. I am very keen to see the *Portrait of a Clergyman*, the *Madonna and Child*, and *Lot and His Daughters*, all by Albrecht Dürer.'

Sergei's gaze had been wandering around the room, but at the sound of the painter's name they snapped back to Kobi. His smile vanished. 'You want to see the Dürers especially?'

The Russian's question felt like an interrogation. Kobi could hear a strange roaring noise in his ears and felt an overwhelming need to escape the confines of the room.

'Very much. My PhD thesis was on his influence on Northern German Renaissance art.' Kobi extended his hand towards Daniel. 'It was an honour to meet you, Mr Horowitz. I won't take up any more of your time. Good night.'

The young man's skin was warm and dry, and Kobi could feel the fingers inside his grasp. There was a sudden strong urge to squeeze, to send him a silent signal, and letting go was hard. What was it about this young man that shook him so deeply? What would their connection prove to be?

'Good night, and thanks so much for making the trip,' Daniel said, with another inclination of his head.

Kobi turned to Magdalena and Sergei. 'Thank you for the opportunity to meet this charming young man. Congratulations on your patronage, sir.'

Before they could answer he had walked away, through the crowd and out an open door onto the terrace. The cooling night air was a sweet relief. What had overcome him? he wondered. How had he planned to start the conversation? *Lovely to meet you and by the way, I have something that belongs to your family?* This was neither the time nor the place, but would there ever be another?

A burst of laughter from the room made him swing around and he saw the back of the conductor. Gomez was also in a group of admirers. His wife had described him as Daniel's mentor, and Kobi knew that he was a close friend of the family. Maybe ...

Rafael Gomez found his wife sitting on a sofa, in deep conversation with Jeremy Browne, the artistic director of the Washington Opera. Her musical knowledge was one of her strengths, and he never underestimated the role her intellect and charm could play. She stood up as he joined them.

'Hello, handsome. Pleased with the night?'

He kissed her on the lips. 'Very. I think we are in danger of taking that boy for granted, yet again, you know?' His voice was a deep, rich rumble and the accent was Spanish.

Browne smiled up at him. 'I don't think anyone could accuse you of taking Dan for granted,' he said.

Rafael gave him a small bow. 'I shall take that as a compliment, yes? Did you talk to Sergei? He was looking for you.'

Browne gave a small sigh. 'He had his guest list for me, for the Gala. I swear he could fill the opera house by himself.'

Rafael suppressed his smile and turned to Mags. 'Of course he could. Are you ready?'

She nodded and smiled warmly down at Browne.

'So nice to chat, Jeremy.'

'Jeremy has quite a plan for *The Magic Flute*,' she said as they made their way to the door.

'I know. Edwardian costumes, with over-sized tennis racquets and straw hats.'

She laughed. 'Well, I think the racquets are a very small part of the set design.'

'You would hope so. I don't remember seeing them in Mozart's score. Who is that?'

Mags had given a wave to a man standing alone in the corner of the room. His face was somehow familiar. The man squared his shoulders and approached them. Mags stopped and waited.

'Raffy, this is Dr Jakob Voight, and he came from Melbourne, just to hear Dan play.'

Rafael shook his hand. 'What a long way! I hope it was worth it.'

He could see emotional conflict in the eyes, but the man was trying to hide it and he couldn't identify the cause. Fear? Concern? Sadness?

'It was, indeed. Actually, Maestro, hearing him was not my only motive. Could I take up some of your time? Maybe tomorrow?'

Rafael hesitated; he was busy and his time was precious. Daniel's management handled fan enquiries. But there was a slight, long-buried hint of something behind the man's Australian accent, and Rafael suspected he came from a German-speaking household.

'May I ask why? I may not be the best person.'

Now it was Kobi's turn to hesitate. Rafael thought he detected a sharp intake of breath.

'I need your help. I believe I have something of value that belongs to the Horowitz family and they will want it back.'

Rafael tried not to display his surprise; this was something he had long anticipated. 'Why do you think that?' he asked.

There was that flash of emotion in the eyes again.

'I would like you to look at it first, before we discuss it any further. I can say it is in Hebrew, old and precious.'

It was, obviously, not something he was sharing lightly, and Rafael was aware that it was possible there were other Horowitz possessions to be found. He nodded thoughtfully.

'Of course. I have an office here. Please be there at eleven tomorrow morning.'

Kobi acknowledged his agreement with a brief incline of his head and a smile of obvious relief. 'Thank you very much, Maestro.'

'Is he the first person who has claimed to have something?' Mags asked as she massaged his shoulders. Rafael lay face-down on their enormous bed as she worked her magic on his tired rhomboids.

'As far as I know. I think they would have told me.'

'How plausible is it?'

'Perfectly plausible. I suppose he might have found something and it could have the name of "Horowitz" on it, you know? It might have come from the Berlin house or it could be completely coincidental. He has grown up in a household where someone spoke German, I think.'

'He said his mother was German and his father's parents came from Munich. He's an artist and an art lecturer, at the University in Melbourne.'

'Goodness! You did find out a lot.'

She smiled. 'Actually it was Sergei. He joined us. I think he inherited his grandpa's interrogation techniques. He made the good doctor feel quite uncomfortable.'

'Oh dear. I shall apologise for that tomorrow. I wonder if he knows about the Dürer —'

'I'm sure he does! He mentioned how much he wanted to see the three Dürers at the National Gallery ... Do you think he wants to sell whatever it is to them?' she asked.

He shrugged and she stopped the rhythmical strokes on his back.

'He didn't seem motivated by money; he was almost reluctant to share. We'll see tomorrow, yes?' he said.

'I wonder how they would react. Simon and Levi.' It wasn't a question, more of a spoken thought.

'Could be a huge thing in their life, or it could be something lovely but insignificant. People know their story and know that they have some priceless objects. That makes them vulnerable.'

Mags frowned. 'He seemed very sincere to me. Don't be too hard on him.'

He rolled onto his back and smiled up at her. 'Me? I will give him every chance.'

Kobi knew that sleep would be elusive so he didn't even try. He had a soak in the bath, then put on the hotel bathrobe, made himself a hot drink and sat in the comfortable chair to look at Ruby's sketches. He tried to put himself in Rafael's place, tried to view the letters as if for the first time. What did the conductor know of the family history?

Undoubtedly more than Kobi did, for he knew practically nothing. Not that long ago he hadn't even known who these people were. So why had he found it so hard to have a conversation with the young violinist? Why had he felt defensive when the Russian questioned him? Dürer was obviously a sore point, and it would be a lie not to admit he was dying to see the Horowitz Dürer; it was central to his plan. The hours ticked by and he traced the handwritten script with his finger, touched the blotches and stains, the sketches and the little rough maps. Finally, he drifted into a dream about paintings, Nazi soldiers and violins.

CHAPTER FIFTEEN

Washington DC
July 2014

Rafael sat at his desk, headphones on, watching his laptop. He was engrossed in Jeremy's choices for the 2016 production of Mozart's *The Magic Flute*, and his mind was searching for a charismatic Prince capable of making audiences believe he could rescue the daughter of the Queen of the Night. It took him some time to register that his PA, Jess, was standing in the doorway. He pulled the headphones off.

'Sorry. Have I missed the phone, again?'

Jess smiled. 'No. Your eleven o'clock, Dr Jakob Voight, is here.'

He nodded and shut the laptop. 'Ah, yes. Show him in, and can we have some coffee?'

'Of course.'

The man was nervous. After years of meeting people who were intimidated by him, Rafael knew the signs instantly. He came around the desk and shook the doctor's hand.

'How nice to see you again, Dr Voight. Please, take a seat. Would you like a coffee or a tea?'

The man seemed relieved and sank into the chair opposite the desk.

'Please, call me Kobi. Dr Voight is so formal and only my mother calls me Jakob. A coffee would be lovely, thank you.'

Rafael nodded to Jess, who closed the door as she left.

'And thank you for making the time to see me,' Kobi said.

Rafael smiled. 'Not at all. What can I do for you, Kobi? You have something to show me, yes?'

'Let me explain a little first. My mother was born in the countryside near Berlin during the war. Early 1942. In 1950 she left Germany and immigrated to Australia with her parents. From the age of eight she lived in Melbourne —'

The door opened and Jess came in, carrying a tray with two mugs, a sugar bowl and a milk jug. She set it down on the sideboard.

'Thank you, Jess. How would you like your coffee?' Rafael asked him.

'Just black, please.'

After Jess had left, Rafael stirred his coffee and looked at the man opposite him expectantly. Kobi seemed to be sizing something up. Eventually, he started again.

'I find it hard to explain what my mother and her parents faced in Australia. There was a climate of anger, fear and hostility. Many there saw them as the enemy. My grandfather was in the German Army and had been wounded in the war. He fought on the Western Front; he had nothing to do with the camps or the Gestapo.'

His face had contorted with the effort needed to express the emotion. Then he paused and relaxed.

'I'm so sorry, Maestro, this is a difficult subject for me and I'm still confused. There was much that my mother kept from my sister, my brother and me so we wouldn't worry. We spoke only English at home. My maternal grandfather had died by the time my mother married. My grandmother died before I was born, but I know she was very ... German.

'I am an artist, but I also lecture in art history, the Northern Renaissance artists, at Melbourne University. This year I was granted a three-month sabbatical to study at the

Gemäldegalerie in Berlin and travel around Germany. Before I left Melbourne my mother gave me a bundle of letters. I have no idea why she had them. She couldn't read them. They are written in Hebrew.'

Rafael nodded. The man had certainly captured his interest. 'Why do you come to me with these letters?' he asked.

'Mother found them amongst my grandmother's things after her death and kept them. They include pencil sketches and are beautiful works of art. She guessed that Grandmother had bought them at a street market after the war. I took them to the synagogue in Berlin and was told that they were written by a young woman during the war. A Jewish woman who worked in the Berlin Resistance. At my request they were translated so I could read them.'

He bent down and drew a square parcel of fabric from a bag at his feet, put it down on the desk and unwrapped the letters. They were obviously old — folded pieces of paper without envelopes. Rafael leaned forward, fascinated. Something, the slightest chance, a distant possibility, was stirring in his brain.

'May I see them?' he asked.

He extended his hand, but Kobi didn't pick the letters up.

'There are no surnames, Maestro. Some people have nicknames, others just descriptions. There are the sketches, but I didn't know who they were.'

Suddenly he bent down again, took a piece of paper from the bag and gave it to Rafael.

'Then, while I was reading the translation, a colleague told me about the Horowitz Dürer. He showed me a copy of the painting and of the photograph that was attached to the back of it.'

Rafael knew the black-and-white photograph well, and pointed to each figure in turn.

'Yes, yes, this is Benjamin Horowitz; his wife, Elizabeth; and their four children — Levi, Simon, David and Rachel.

Benjamin was a banker in pre-war Berlin. Levi and Simon survived the war, the rest did not. Rachel and David were twins. Simon is Daniel's grandfather.'

'Rachel,' Kobi said and smiled sadly. 'Ruby's real name *was* Rachel.'

Suddenly he thrust the letters across the table.

'These are the originals and I have the translations with me, too. For now, just look at the pictures.'

As Kobi spoke, Rafael took the top letter on the pile and opened it. He found himself looking at a pencil sketch of Benjamin Horowitz playing the violin.

'*Dios mio!*'

Kobi sat very still and returned his startled gaze. Rafael thumbed through the loose pages, then put them down and walked around to lean against the desk beside Kobi.

'So, you know now, who they are,' Rafael said softly. It wasn't a question, but Kobi pointed to the letters.

'Yes. I recognised the faces in the photograph from the sketches.'

In his heart Rafael could image what these letters would mean to two of his dearest friends, two very elderly men who knew that their German family were all long dead, and he found it hard to contain his excitement.

'Do you know who the author is?' he asked.

'She refers to herself as Ruby. It is Rachel Horowitz,' Kobi said.

Rafael nodded. 'They must have been written after the family were split up. I know she loved to draw, and she worked for the Resistance in Berlin.'

'She worked for a spy ring which was named the Red Orchestra by the Gestapo. It was broken and she died in Auschwitz in late 1942,' Kobi said.

Rafael returned to his seat. 'How do you know all this?' he asked.

'She refers to the people she lived and worked with by nickname. I went to the German Resistance Centre in Berlin and there they were — photos and information. Very brave men and women.'

Rafael wondered how all this made the other man feel. If his mother was born during the war that made her first-generation post-war German, even if she had grown up in Australia, and he knew many of them carried guilt. Yet he was relaying the information in a matter-of-fact, clinical way and seemed completely in control of his emotions.

'What I would like to do, Kobi, is take these to Simon and Levi. They live north of here, in Vermont. Levi is ninety-five and his health is failing. Simon is ninety-two and is still quite strong. It will be a shock for them, you know, but they will be overjoyed. When they have recovered I would like you to meet them, so they can thank you for this wonderful gift.'

Kobi seemed to hesitate. He was obviously affected by the situation. Rafael's experience told him that Kobi was surprised by this level of emotion. The question was, why? Perhaps he did want to be paid after all.

'There is more you wish to tell me, yes?' he asked.

'I came here from Germany, straight from Munich. I haven't been home and I haven't talked to my mother. She doesn't know that I have had the letters translated or that I have discovered who the people are in the sketches.'

Kobi took a sip of his coffee and Rafael waited. There was more; he could have posted, or couriered, the letters and then followed up with a phone call. This had become intensely personal.

'The old men will ask me how, why, I came to have them. I don't know the answer, for sure —'

'But they won't mind that! You've brought such happiness to them, which is all they will care about, believe me.'

Kobi shifted in his seat. There was a slight sheen of sweat

on his forehead. 'You see, the translation tells me why they were written. They are love letters, an explanation, written to Rachel's child. She had a daughter, called Ebee, after her moth —'

The words exploded in Rafael's brain. 'She had a *daughter*? I am sure that Simon and Levi don't know this!'

Kobi gave a slight nod. 'I suspected that would be the case. Rachel gave birth in early 1942 in Berlin. She had false papers and was living as a half-Italian Catholic and working with a couple she called Harry and Suzie. At the Resistance Centre I discovered that these people were Harro Schulze-Boysen, a first lieutenant in the Luftwaffe, and his wife, Libertas Schulze-Boysen. Rachel called the baby after her mother, and I now know for sure that that must have been Elizabeth.

'A woman she obviously loved and trusted, called Meme, took the child and gave it to Lutheran Germans to look after until the war was over. Rachel uses their initials — PG for the father and SG for the mother — and they lived on a farm. Rachel was desperate for her daughter to know that she hadn't been abandoned and to know about her Jewish family ... But I have been thinking about it and I don't think Elizabeth ever knew.'

Rafael leaned towards him. 'Why do you say that?' he asked.

'Maestro, my mother's name is Elizabeth, and she was born in 1942 on a farm. My late grandparents were called Peter Gunther and Sabine Gunther, and Sabine had the letters in her possession.'

His words swirled around the two men for a moment. The atmosphere was suddenly very charged.

'You think ...' Rafael's voice trailed off.

Kobi sat motionless.

'I think it could be a huge coincidence, but how likely is that, really? My grandparents were blond, fair-skinned and blue-eyed; my mother has colouring like mine, dark auburn hair as a child, with olive skin. Both my siblings have dark hair and dark eyes. The only thing that doesn't seem right is that Rachel said that they already had a son and my mother was an only child. But Rachel could have been mistaken in that. She never met them.'

Rafael shook his head, bewildered. 'And you have read a translation. In what, German or English?'

'English. I read German a little, but not very well. A scholar at the synagogue translated them for me. She speaks and reads perfect English and is used to translating Shoah documents. I am satisfied that it is a very safe translation.'

'And you were in Berlin when you read them.'

Again, it wasn't a question. 'I was in an apartment on the Auguststrasse. I read the letters and I visited the city at the same time. I walked where she walked, I felt her fear, and I discovered what happened to her.'

Rafael looked up at him. When he had first laid eyes on Kobi Voight he had been reminded of someone. Now he knew who: Levi Horowitz, and photographs he had seen of the mother, Elizabeth Horowitz. What a strange day this had turned into, and what a gift he had to take to his friends. He sighed and smiled at the concerned face opposite him.

'We need to go to Vermont,' he said.

CHAPTER SIXTEEN

Vermont
July 2014

It was a sight that always lifted Rafael's heart. As he got out of his car Simon and Levi Horowitz came down the path towards him, Simon with his arms outstretched. Behind them he could see the tall figure of Simon's son, David; Cindy, David's wife, looking as beautiful as ever; and their twenty-year-old son, Daniel. This family was as precious to him as his own.

'Maestro!'

Simon was shrinking by the year, bald and wrinkled, with brown eyes that glowed bright with determination. Rafael hugged the old man gently and kissed him on each cheek.

'Simon, my dear friend, how are you?'

Simon shrugged. 'You know what they say: I could complain, but who would listen?'

Levi was still tall, stick-thin and straight-backed, his shock of wavy hair completely white and his green eyes cautious and polite. 'Maestro, it is good to see you.'

They clasped hands. Rafael had learned that Levi was not the hugging type. The old men stood aside, and Rafael embraced Cindy, shook David's hand and enveloped Daniel in their customary bear hug.

'And who is this?' asked Simon, pointing to the man who stood beside the car, watching.

'Oh, forgive me, I forget my manners — I am so happy to see you all,' Rafael exclaimed. He went to Kobi and drew him towards the waiting group.

'This is Dr Jakob Voight. He is a new friend of mine from Australia.'

Daniel stepped forward and extended his hand. 'I met you after the concert; you had come from Melbourne to hear me play,' he said.

Kobi returned his smile and shook his hand. 'Indeed I had.'

Rafael caught Simon's glance from Kobi to his elder brother, then to his son and back to the stranger again.

'Come inside, we have tea waiting,' Cindy waved them towards the front door. Since Simon's wife, Ruth, had passed away, Cindy had assumed the role of woman of the house when visiting her husband's family.

'You said you have something to show us.' Simon looked up at Rafael with a questioning gaze.

'I do, my friend. All in good time.'

'It was Sergei's idea to install the security,' Simon said as he punched numbers into a keypad. The metal door hissed as it slid back into the wall.

'There are all sorts of things installed to make sure no one can steal him, alarms and pressure pads,' he added as he stepped back and extended his arm towards the room. 'After you, Dr Voight.'

It was the size of a double bedroom, carpeted, empty and with no windows, obviously temperature-controlled. Simon switched on a light and there he was, on the opposite wall.

'Oh, good Lord!'

Kobi moved swiftly across the room to stand in front of the painting. It was oil and tempura on panel. The photograph he had seen in Berlin had hardly done the original justice.

The brush strokes were exquisite, and the colours seemed to glow in the artificial light.

'He was Paul von Hoch, a Nuremberg nobleman, a friend of Dürer's. Painted in 1520,' Simon said.

Kobi turned towards him. 'Paul von Hoch was a burgmaster of the City of Nuremberg and part of a group who loaned money to Charles V for his election campaign to the position of Holy Roman Emperor. The pomegranate that he holds was a common symbol at the time. Did you know that it symbolised the Resurrection?' he asked.

Simon frowned. 'No, I didn't. He was a direct ancestor of my mother's, and so I always assumed he was Jewish.'

'No, he was Catholic nobility.'

Kobi turned his attention back to the painting.

'Are you sure?'

Something in Simon's voice made Kobi swing round. 'Absolutely. And Buddhists paint them to represent various degrees of enlightenment, in Chinese art they mean joy and in Japanese, triumph.'

'But the persimmon is also very important in Jewish life. Did you know it was extinct in Israel but now it is back, like the Jews? We eat them at Sukkot.'

Kobi smiled gently. 'I'm sure it is, but in this context, it is a Christian symbol. He was Catholic.' There was a tone of finality in his voice and the old man didn't reply. Kobi looked at the painting and shook his head slightly, his hand covering his mouth.

'He's absolutely stunning, painted by a genius at the height of his powers. Thank you so, so much for showing him to me.'

Simon turned towards a glass case that Kobi hadn't noticed in the corner of the room. 'You're most welcome. And this is our Amati violin, 1640. I keep it exactly as our father did.'

Reluctantly, Kobi followed him to the case. The violin, with its dark varnish, lay on a bed of white silk. 'It's beautiful. Where's the Guarneri?' he asked.

Simon smiled. 'If it is not travelling with Dan, it lives with Sergei Valentino. It will come to Dan when Sergei dies. That is our agreement.'

'But he gave you back the Dürer.'

Levi had joined them and he glanced sharply at Kobi. 'Of course he did! It was ours. His father stole it from the man who stole it from us. To keep it would have been wrong.'

Kobi turned to him. 'Forgive me, I didn't mean to sound surprised that he returned it. He obviously has a conscience. I have heard that art galleries have offered to display it for you.'

Both men nodded. They were looking at the portrait.

'And we thought about it,' Simon said, 'but for the moment we want to keep it near, and Sergei had this addition to the house built for us. When we die it shall belong to my son, David, and the decision will be his.'

Simon's voice was soft and non-confrontational, but Kobi could see that Levi was holding his tongue with difficulty.

Well, here goes nothing, he thought. *The worst they can do is kick me out.*

'There are so few Dürer portraits, compared to the woodcuts and engravings, and they are spread all around the world. What a great blessing it would be to the National Gallery,' Kobi said. He, too, stared at the portrait. It was one of the most beautiful things he had ever seen.

Simon shook his head. 'I shall try to explain it to you. When you lose something this precious for as long as we had lost this ... it is hard to give it up again.'

'I understand,' Kobi said, as he smiled at the old man, 'but I meant share, not give up. You could tour it for a short time, let the public enjoy such masterful painting.'

Simon shook his head again. 'But then they would know what it is and that it is here. The security experts say to us that keeping him safe once the public sees him would be almost impossible. Collectors would pay any price on the black market.'

Kobi revelled in his last moments in front of the portrait. It was too early to suggest a book, he could see that, but the seeds had been sown. Now it was time to play his trump card.

Simon shuffled the pages slowly, and occasionally he touched a drawing. Everyone in the room was looking at him. He spoke without raising his head.

'Your mother's name is Elizabeth?'

'Yes, sir.'

'Does she have another name?'

'Maria.'

Simon and Levi exchanged a sudden glance. Rafael could tell that Simon was daring to hope, while Levi was keeping himself safe.

'And you don't know why your mother has these.' There was a note of wonder in Simon's voice.

'No,' replied Kobi. 'They were in my grandmother's things —'

'Where was she born, your mother?'

'In the countryside near Berlin, during the war.'

Simon looked at Levi, and this time the two men held each other's gaze for several seconds.

'What year?' Levi asked without looking away from his brother.

'Early 1942.'

Finally, Levi turned away. 'No, impossible,' he mumbled under his breath.

Simon looked back at the pages and stroked one of the pencil sketches.

'Can you read them, Simon?' Rafael asked.

Simon smiled at him. 'Of course I can.'

Kobi was trying not to force their hand, but it was obvious he was desperate for some answers. He cleared his throat. 'I was in Berlin when I read them, the English translation. I visited many memorials and museums ... and when I was in Munich, I went to Dachau.'

Simon's voice was suddenly harsh. 'You *went* to Dachau?'

'Yes, sir.'

'Of your own accord. You *decided* to go there.'

'Yes, sir. Hundreds of people do.'

'It is a *tourist attraction*?'

There was an edge of horrified surprise in Simon's voice, and Kobi wondered if Simon's family had kept the fact that it was open to the public from him. He frowned.

'No, I wouldn't say that. It's a memorial and people go there so they can understand what happened.'

Simon shook his head. 'I can tell you what happened there, young man. My father and my brother are buried there, somewhere, without a grave.'

David shot a worried glance at Rafael, but the Spaniard raised his hand slightly. *Let this continue*, he thought. *They have to find each other, these two.*

'I wish I had known that at the time, Mr Horowitz. I would have said a prayer for them. The Jewish memorial is stunning,' Kobi said.

Simon smiled at him. 'Thank you. What was the camp like?'

Kobi hesitated. 'Hard to put into words. It would be easy to say heartbreaking, and it was, but also so much more than that. The museum is vast and full of genuine artefacts —'

'Like what?'

Again, Simon's voice had a hard edge. Kobi shrugged. 'Registration cards. A handcart. A knife, spoon and bowl —'

'Ha! The most precious thing you owned: without a bowl you didn't get fed.'

'I knew from the letters that you and your brother and father were there, and I thought about that, when I stood on the parade ground.'

Simon looked at him and seemed to be digesting his words. Rafael wondered if Simon would consider going back, closing old wounds.

'In parts it didn't seem real, like a recreated movie set, but in other parts you could tell that there had been great evil, but also great courage and human sacrifice,' Kobi continued.

'I survived five years there because of the courage of one man; a man who should have been my enemy had the courage to be my friend.'

'One day I would like to hear that story, sir.'

The two men smiled at each other, and Rafael could sense a bond forming. Suddenly the old man let out a huge sigh.

'Young man, these letters are, perhaps, pieces of a puzzle. And also, perhaps, at last all of the pieces are fitting together. You say your grandparents were called Sabine and Peter Gunther and that these letters refer to an "SG" and a "PG" who took in my sister's baby and raised her. I can add another piece to the story we are building. I, too, have a story about Peter Gunther.'

CHAPTER SEVENTEEN

Berlin
June 1947

'Where are they going to put all the rubble?'

Simon didn't answer his elder brother. He was staring down a wide street, full of potholes and littered with jagged lumps of concrete, twisted iron and bricks.

'There's enough here to build another city.'

The buildings on either side were bombed-out shells with chunks of blackened walls still standing. The night's rain had left puddles of muddy water in the holes. This was their city, their birthplace, in ruins.

'I remember that shop,' Simon said, pointing to a single wall to his left. 'Mama used to buy her furs there.'

The young men had been reunited in London six months after the end of the war, and had waited until now to come back to Berlin. They had no intention of staying — they were going to New York to live with their Uncle Avrum — but they knew that if they didn't come back here first, they never would.

Berlin was a hundred and sixty kilometres inside Soviet-controlled Eastern Germany. The United States, the United Kingdom and France controlled the western parts of the city, and the Soviet Union controlled the eastern part. The occupation zones were decided upon at the Potsdam Agreement in 1945, and were roughly located around where the armies were at that time. They were supposed to be temporary.

It had been quite a mission to get here, but the chaos of post-war Europe had aided them. Levi and Simon had crossed the Channel by ferry and caught a succession of military trains, which were still moving displaced persons around, until they reached Frankfurt. There was one rail link into Berlin, and that train ran only ten times a day, so getting seats was next to impossible. But there were three air corridors, from Hamburg, Frankfurt and Bückeburg, to Berlin. They had talked their way onto a plane into the American sector by promising to help unload the supplies at the other end, and, as soon as their job was done, they had slipped away.

Only the main streets had been completely cleared of rubble, and it took them some time to find the partially shattered Brandenburg Tor and work their way down the long square until they came to a point where they could leave the western section and enter eastern Berlin.

'Halt!'

It was a soldier, wearing the uniform of the Red Army. His German was basic.

'What are you doing?'

Levi saluted him. 'We are young German men and we want to see our house before we immigrate to Moscow. We want to work for the motherland.'

The soldier returned the salute and gestured down the street.

'Hurry up. Go!'

They scurried away and turned into a side street. Simon could feel his heart pounding and he grinned at Levi. 'You lied.'

Levi shrugged. 'God will forgive me. At least the soldier was dumb enough to believe me. Now come on, it can't be more than a couple of streets away.'

The once leafy street was deserted, but the houses were mostly still standing. Some had bomb damage and piles of bricks in their front gardens, and the trees were gone, leaving just blackened stumps beside the road.

'There it is!' Simon pointed to a house down the left-hand side of the street. 'Levi, there it is!'

Levi was standing beside him, gazing at the house. Then he wiped his face with his sleeve and jolted forward.

'Yes, I see it. What are you waiting for?'

Simon followed him, down the pavement, through the gate, up the steps and to the front door. Memories overcame both men and they stood stock still. Simon knew that Levi was remembering his mother waving him off from the step as the big black car supposedly carried him away to safety. He was remembering his mother and sister screaming and cowering in the snow as he and David were carried away to hell.

Suddenly Levi knocked on the door. The sound startled Simon. He could remember the insistent knocking and the calls of 'Open up, Jews!'

After a long moment the heavy door swung open and a young woman stood in the doorway.

'Yes? Can I help you?' she asked. She spoke German, but her accent was Russian.

'Do you live here?' Levi asked.

'Yes.' She frowned and looked a little scared. 'What do you want?' she asked.

Levi smiled reassuringly. 'Nothing bad. My name is Levi, and this is my younger brother, Simon. We lived in this house until 1939 and we would like to come in and see it, just for a moment.'

She hesitated. 'Wait here.'

She turned and ran back into the house. Simon looked at Levi.

'They're Russians,' he whispered.

'Not surprising, we are in the eastern sector. The Red Army chiefs like big houses and there won't be too many this big left standing,' Levi said.

A broad-shouldered man with a potbelly, a beard and a moustache, dressed in the trousers of a Red Army uniform and a white shirt, came to the door.

'Hello.' His German was more heavily accented than the girl's had been. 'What do you want?' he asked.

'We are German Jews and we have survived the war. My name is Levi Horowitz and this is my brother, Simon. He spent five years in Dachau. We used to live here and we have come back. From London.'

The man looked them up and down and frowned. 'What do you want with us?'

'Nothing, sir. We are going to America. Our uncle lives in New York. But before we go, we would like to see our house again.'

The Russian smiled slowly. 'Well, then, you had better come inside.'

The house was occupied by the Medvedev family from Moscow. They welcomed Simon and Levi and showed them where a bomb had damaged the sitting room and the music room, but the wallpaper was the same and the kitchen looked untouched. Both men ran upstairs to find their bedrooms, and Simon was delighted to see that his portraits were still hanging on his wall: Paganini playing his 1742 Guarneri violin, Il Cannone, and the other one of Antonio Vivaldi.

'Oh, how proud I was of those portraits,' he said.

'Do you want to take them?'

He turned towards Nicolai Medvedev and smiled. 'That is a wonderful gesture, sir, but they are too large for me to carry. I tire easily.'

The Russian nodded. 'It was very hard?'

Simon looked at him; the man's expression was sympathetic. 'Very. I try not to think about it, but here, surrounded by ...' Simon's voice trailed off.

The Russian put a hand on his shoulder. '*Da.* I was at the siege of Stalingrad, I know what deprivation is. Now, I believe my wife has a box of things that you might like, in the kitchen.'

Simon was joined by Levi on the landing and they followed the man downstairs again.

'He has a box of things,' Simon whispered, and Levi shot him a sharp glance.

'What sort of things?'

'Things we might like. Our things.'

The kitchen was still as large, warm and welcoming as ever. Memories of meals came flooding back, and both men could see their mama standing at the stove, their papa blessing them around the family table at Shabbat, and David pulling Rachel's plaits. They exchanged smiles as they sat at the table and drank a mug of bitter coffee.

Elena Medvedev was a plain woman with a broad smile that touched her eyes and softened the lines on her face. She took a shoebox from a cupboard and put it on the table. She spoke Russian and her husband translated for her.

'I put these away. In case anyone … came back.'

Levi lifted the lid and slid the box between them. The first thing he pulled out was a silver *mezuzah*. He opened it and showed Simon the small parchment scroll inside.

'It was on the front doorpost,' Simon said quietly. Levi kissed it and handed it to Simon, who also kissed it.

'Take it with you. Put it on your next house,' Nicolai said as Elena refilled their coffee mugs.

'Oh, we will,' Levi smiled at him. 'Thank you so much for keeping it.'

The next thing was a small wooden picture-frame holding a pencil drawing of a young Simon playing the violin.

'Rachel's drawing!' Simon took it and traced the outline with his finger. Then he looked up at Nicolai. 'My little sister drew this for me,' he said.

'She was a good artist. What happened to her?'

Levi shook his head. 'We don't know. We hope that we will see her again one day, and our mother. Our father and brother died in Dachau.'

Levi lifted a silver-backed tortoiseshell comb from the box. 'And here is Papa's comb,' he said.

Simon smiled at the memory, and suddenly stood up. 'Sir, could we possibly have a look in the attic? There might be a box there, and if there is, we would like to take that, too.'

Levi also rose to his feet. 'Yes, could we? We'll be very careful not to disturb anything else.'

The Russian shrugged. 'Of course you can. I didn't even know there was an attic. You know how to get up there?'

'Oh, we know!'

It was still there. A box of violins wrapped in sheet music. They carried it carefully down to the kitchen. The Medvedevs were stunned.

'What are they?' Nicolai asked.

'Seven violins. We rescued them from a shop. A luthier in town. On the night of the Kristallnacht.'

'The what?'

The young men looked at each other: so much pain and terror and destruction, and now people who lived in the city didn't even know it had happened.

'The first real pogrom, a year before the war started. We were caught up in it and Maria saved us from being arrested,' Simon explained.

Levi looked at his watch. 'And now we must go and try to find her. Thank you so much for your hospitality and for allowing us to take our things.'

'You're welcome anytime,' Nicolai said and laid his hand on Levi's shoulder. 'And I'm sorry the Nazi pigs took your house.'

CHAPTER EIGHTEEN

Berlin
June 1947

Levi carried the box of violins and Simon carried the shoebox. As they rounded a corner they came upon a line of people queuing at the first open shop they had seen. Some of them turned and, with curious expressions and dull, exhausted eyes, looked at the two men. Levi pulled Simon back around the corner and out of view.

'They're waiting for rations. If they think we have food they might attack us. Come, this way,' he pointed down another street.

'I know how to fight for food,' Simon said softly as he followed his brother.

An hour later and back in the western section, this time in the United Kingdom zone, they found the street. Levi counted the doors until he came to the one beside the alcove where they had sheltered all those years ago. He put down the box of violins and knocked.

'She may not be here anymore. We don't even know if she survived, so we'll only —'

He was interrupted by the sound of a chain being unlatched.

'Who is it?' asked a familiar voice from inside. The men grinned at each other.

'Simon and Levi,' they said simultaneously.

The door swung open.

'Oh, my God, it's my boys!'

She was older, thinner, greyer, more stooped and lined, but still unmistakeably Maria Weiss. Their saviour of the Kristallnacht. She hugged Simon very tightly for a long moment, and then Levi bent down to receive his kiss. There were tears on all of their cheeks. At last, someone from their past.

'Come up, come up. You must be exhausted and hungry and there is so much to know.'

She ushered them into the bare hallway, still lit by a naked bulb hanging from the ceiling. They followed her up the steep staircase and through the door. There were still two chairs and an overstuffed red sofa, but there was no ginger cat.

'Where is Wolfgang?' Simon asked.

She put her hands on either side of his cheeks and patted. 'Oh bless you, you remember him. He is gone. I would like to say he died of old age, but I very much suspect someone ate him.'

Levi laughed. 'Well, let's hope if that's the case he sustained some worthy soul for a day or so,' he said.

She gestured towards the seats. 'Before we talk, what can I give you? The rationing is so severe, I have a little bread and butter and some jam and enough coffee for us to enjoy a cup. I wish I could give you cake!'

'You are celebration enough,' Simon said as he sat down. 'And we hope you have news. Of family.'

She stopped on her slow journey to the kitchen and turned to face him. The grief was etched deep into her face, and her eyes filled again.

'Oh, darling boy, I wish it was better news. I fear we all have some tears to shed tonight.'

They told her what had happened to them. Levi gave his usual brief explanation about his eventful journey to London before the war, and Simon told her the basics about Dachau. He told her that his little brother, David, had become ill and was dead, although he never knew exactly how he died. And that Benjamin, his father, was shot by a German soldier when he was tripped up and dropped a box of shell casings. But mostly he told her about a guard called Kurt, and how he and his father had played the violins for the officers and received more food and some beer and were allowed to warm their fingers before the fire in the winter.

'I survived because of Kurt. He saved my life more than once. I don't know where he is or if he is still alive, but I hope he is: he is a good man. He saw me as his equal.'

She nodded thoughtfully. 'Thank God for such men. They restore our faith in mankind and go a little way to balancing all the evil.'

Levi shifted in his seat. 'And what about you, Maria? What kind of war did you have?'

Maria smiled at them, but they could both see the immense sadness in her eyes. 'As far as the local Nazis were concerned, I was a little old woman who kept to herself and lived quietly in her flat. I rode my bicycle, and sometimes I walked my neighbour's dog. Sometimes I had a parcel with me when I went out and didn't have it with me when I came back, but they never noticed. I was too old to be getting up to mischief.'

'You helped our people,' Levi said simply.

'Yours and many others, people who did not deserve to die or suffer. I did what the people in the Resistance needed me to do —'

Simon leaned forward. 'I told Mama and Rachel to come to you, when David and I were taken. Did they?'

She nodded. 'Yes, they did. They were exhausted, very cold and very scared of course —'

'But —'

Simon started to interrupt again but Levi leaned across and touched his arm. 'Sit back, Simon, let her speak. We have waited a long time for news, Maria.'

'I understand, and I will tell you what I know. I went to the local authorities and was told that you and David and Benjamin had been processed and were being held in Dachau. We tried to get you released, but it was too late; the people sympathetic to your father had been replaced. No one would listen. Your mama was very brave.'

Simon nodded. His heart was racing, and he felt such joy at the knowledge that his mama had tried.

Maria continued on. 'I went to your Aunt Sarah's house, but it was empty, looted. We knew that your Uncle Mordecai had been taken to Dachau with your father, straight from the bank —'

'He died,' Simon said. 'He got sick almost straight away and they took him. When they took you to the hospital, you never came back.'

She stared at him for a moment, and then she sighed. 'We are all so matter-of-fact about murder now. We have all seen so much of it,' she said softly.

'Do you know what happened to Aunt Sarah?' Levi asked.

'Yes. The family were hidden by the Grajerks, a Polish family. I think they were still safe well into 1940, and then someone betrayed them and they were all sent to Bergen-Belsen.'

The two men looked at each other: so the extended family were gone, too.

'What about Mama and Rachel?' Levi asked.

'I knew the right people and I got false papers for them, with new names and birth dates. They pretended to be Catholics and they lived, separately, with friends of mine. Your mama taught children as a governess and seemed quite content to live like that. Whenever I saw her she was well-fed and healthy.

I told her to be patient and she could survive, but she was missing you all terribly, and in 1941 she decided to try to get to Switzerland and on to London, to find you, Levi.'

Levi shook his head. 'I have never seen her. Could she be in London? Should I be looking?'

Hope lit up their expressions. Maria's face crumpled and her eyes filled with tears. 'I wish I could say "yes", but she never even got to Switzerland. I was told that they were stopped at the border and the Gestapo refused to believe their story. They had all the correct papers, all they had to do was stick to the story and eventually they would have been released, but they were interrogated separately, and one of them broke down and confessed that they were Jews running away. The Gestapo didn't hesitate; they shipped them all off to Auschwitz and I haven't heard anything about their fate.'

The men looked at each other again.

'Some survived,' Simon whispered. 'She might have —'

'No! We'd know by now.'

Levi's tone was brusque and Simon slumped back, his head down and his gaze to the floor.

'What about Rachel?' Levi asked.

Again the old woman sighed and clasped her hands together. 'My beautiful Rachel, oh how I miss her! She was so brave and I was so proud of her. She lived with two of the most glamorous spies in Berlin. Harro Schulze-Boysen was a lieutenant in the Luftwaffe Ministry, and his wife, Libertas, was the daughter of a Prussian prince. They ran a spy network and Rachel worked for them.'

'Doing what?' Levi asked, a note of incredulity in his voice.

'Cooking, cleaning and also drawing, copying, making false papers, maps, illustrating illegal pamphlets. She was madly in love with —'

'Rachel? In love?' Simon stared at her in astonishment.

'Oh yes!' Maria laughed. 'With Hans. He was a Resistance

fighter, too. Such a handsome man, funny and fiery, a lawyer, and how he loved her back!'

Levi shook his head slowly in bewilderment.

'She was a child —'

'She grew up very fast, Levi. She had no choice.'

'Was he Jewish?' he asked.

Maria's gaze was intense, almost daring him to disapprove. 'No, but they loved each other very much.'

'I'm almost too scared to ask what happened to them,' said Levi.

Simon was turning from Maria to Levi, following the conversation and trying to absorb how much his baby sister had changed. Maria beamed at them.

'They became parents.'

The words hung in the room. She had a glint of satisfaction in her eye, as if she had left the best till last.

'*Parents?*' Levi sounded disbelieving.

The shock was palpable.

'We ... are ... uncles?' Simon asked slowly.

'You have a niece. Called Elizabeth Maria. Rachel gave birth in early 1942, with Libs and two friends who were a doctor and a dentist. She kept the baby with her for a little while, but it was just too dangerous, so I found a home for Elizabeth with some friends who live on a farm. People who would take care of her until the war was over and Rachel and Hans could come and claim her back. Hans wanted Rachel to go with Elizabeth and live in safety on the farm, but she was a stubborn one, she was determined to keep fighting, to honour her family.'

Again there was silence.

'But she never came for her, did she?' Levi asked.

'No. In late 1942 the spy ring was broken and they were all arrested, over a hundred people. It was a very well-planned raid. One by one the main players disappeared. Libertas and

Rachel were taken into custody at the train station, as they were attempting to get to Switzerland. Harro was taken from his office at the Air Ministry in Potsdam. They were all sent to Plötzensee Prison. Some were executed very quickly, in December 1942; others took months to come to trial and most were executed in prison. Harro was hung and Libertas was guillotined. But they discovered, somehow, that some of them were Jews. I still don't know how. And they sent them to Auschwitz.'

Again Simon looked up and almost spoke, but Maria shook her head. 'No, my darling, you have to understand. By early 1943 the average life expectancy of a Jew in Auschwitz was four hours, and she had been branded a traitor. She is gone.'

'So,' Levi was looking out the window, not daring to catch the gaze of the other two, 'they are all gone, except us.'

Simon stood up. 'But we have a niece! How old is she now? About five?'

'I should think so. I haven't seen her since I went to tell the Gunthers that Rachel and Hans were dead. I wasn't made very welcome.'

'How will they react to us?' Levi asked.

'They don't have a choice,' Simon exclaimed. 'She's our niece and we are her real family!'

Levi ignored his outburst. 'Does she look like Rachel?' he asked.

Maria frowned. 'As far as I remember, she was more like her grandmother, and you, Levi. She has the auburn hair. And blue eyes, from her father. She was a very good baby, very placid.'

'Can we see her?'

'I can try. I'll have to get a car and permission for someone to drive us out of Berlin. But it is not impossible.'

Two days later, Simon, Levi and Maria were picked up by one of Maria's friends and driven out of the city.

It took them less than half an hour to find the farm. The land was flat and green, with stands of tall trees, and a river flowing through it. The car bumped over the gravel road and pulled up in front of a cottage. The windows were shuttered and the front door was locked. No one responded to Maria's knock.

There was no sign of a child, no bike or toys in the yard or tiny boots by the door and no washing on the line. A skinny dog loped over to say hello and give Simon's hand a lick. Just as they were discussing what sort of note to leave on the doorstep, a figure emerged from the treeline across the nearest paddock.

He was a man in his forties, well built, with short blond hair, blue eyes, pale skin and long limbs. He was wearing work boots, work trousers and a checked shirt, and was carrying a bucket in each hand. They stood by the car and waited until he crossed the paddock and came through the gate. He walked with a limp.

'Hello, Peter,' said Maria.

He nodded at her.

'Who are these people?' he asked. His German was clipped and brusque.

'Are Sabine and Elizabeth here?' she asked, avoiding his question.

He put the buckets down.

'Who are you?' He pointed at Levi.

Maria stopped Levi from speaking with a hand on his arm. She pointed to the driver. 'This is my friend, Stefan. He drove us from Berlin.'

And then she gestured towards the two young men, who were watching Peter closely. 'And these are Elizabeth's uncles. This is Simon and Levi Horowitz, Rachel's elder brothers. They survived the war and I have just told them about Elizabeth. They last saw Rachel in 1938 and 1939, respectively, and they find it hard to grasp that she had a baby.'

Peter returned their gaze. His eyes were very cold. 'Well, you're too late. She's gone. She died last January. Pneumonia.'

There was a long silence. Simon stared at the ground and Levi looked away at the trees.

'Is Sabine here?' Maria asked quietly.

He shook his head. 'No. She goes walking in the woods with our son. She's still coming to terms with the grief. It hit her very hard.'

'I'm sure it did. I would like to see her. Can we wait for her?' Maria asked.

Peter picked up the buckets and turned away. 'No. I don't want her to be upset by you. I want you to go now.'

'But —'

Maria cut Simon off. 'I really would like to see her —'

Peter swung around, his face contorted with anger.

'I said no! Now, get off my farm or I'll get out my shotgun and chase you off!'

'Have you got any photographs?' Levi asked, his voice calm and firm.

Peter shook his head more violently. 'One. I'll see if I can get a copy to Maria. Now, *go*!'

Stefan opened the car door. 'Come on, everyone, in you get.'

They were all still staring at Peter. He dropped the buckets and his fists balled. His face was very red, and he took a step towards them.

'Let's do as Stefan says.' Maria guided the two young men back to the car. 'Get in, boys.'

Simon and Levi reluctantly got into the car, slamming the rear passenger doors behind them.

'Tell Sabine I'm very sorry,' Maria said as she climbed into the front. He didn't react; he just stood very still and watched the car drive away.

'Why wouldn't he let you see her?' Simon asked.

Maria and Stefan exchanged glances.

'They're obviously very upset,' Maria said.

Levi was watching the countryside flash by. 'Do you think he's lying?' he asked suddenly.

Maria sighed. 'Maybe. I can do some research, see if I can find her death certificate. I have some friends who might be able to pay them a visit and make sure.'

'Don't hurt them!' Levi's concern was obvious.

She swung around and smiled at him. 'Oh no, of course not. Those days are long gone.'

CHAPTER NINETEEN

Vermont
July 2014

'So, did Maria confirm Elizabeth's death?'

It was Rafael who asked the question to which everyone wanted an answer. Simon looked at Levi, but the old man shook his head and turned away. However, Simon chose to reply, looking directly at Kobi.

'No, she didn't. She couldn't find any record of the little girl's death, and when her friends went back to the farm only a few days later it was deserted. The Gunthers had gone. Whether there were three or four of them, she couldn't tell us. There was nothing we could do, so we went back to London and from there to New York.'

Suddenly Levi swung around; his eyes were full of tears. 'What were we supposed to do? Berlin was chaos, and finding anyone was impossible. It broke our hearts, the thought that we might have left family behind.'

Rafael got to his feet and went to Levi. He laid his hand on the fragile shoulder. It was the most emotional he had ever seen the old man.

'We all understand that. Maybe there is a chance to make up for lost opportunities, yes?' he said.

Kobi gave them the original letters, and he and Rafael took their leave. The atmosphere had been stilted and uncertain, as if no one quite knew where to go from here. He had hugged the two old men and David and Daniel, but Cindy had turned away and, quite deliberately, snubbed him. Rafael promised that they would be in touch soon, and Simon thanked Kobi profusely for bringing Rachel's letters to them.

For several minutes Rafael let Kobi sit in silence, his face turned away, watching the scenery. Finally, the Spaniard coughed and wriggled a little in the driver's seat.

'So, my friend, what did you think of them?' he asked.

Kobi turned towards him. 'They're lovely people. I'm very glad I could give them a piece of their past.'

'Did they feel like they could be, you know, family?'

Kobi hesitated. 'I had a strong reaction to meeting Daniel the other night, he looks so like Rachel's sketch of Simon. If I'd had pictures of my brother and sister I could have shown them how like their father Andrew is, and Lisle has a cleft in her chin, which I see is a genetic thing.'

Rafael smiled. 'Simon and Daniel are very proud of that.'

Kobi waited for a moment. 'What do you suggest I do now?' he asked.

Rafael shrugged. 'It's not up to me to tell you. I think you need to talk to your mother. How old is she?'

'Seventy-one.'

'Is she in good health?'

'Remarkable. She's very fit and she walks every day. She leads a busy life.'

'So, she could fly over here?'

'She could, but I think it would be better if I flew home. I want to tell her the story in her own home, where she's comfortable. I'll let her read the translation and then see what conclusions she comes to. When she's ready, I'll bring her to Vermont.'

Rafael nodded. 'Sounds sensible. I wouldn't wait too long, yes? Those men are not getting any younger, and Levi is in poor health. It would be tragic if she never got to meet him.'

'I'll bear that in mind.'

'Before you leave, would you mind taking a DNA test? It would be just a mouth swab at a local lab in DC.'

Kobi stroked his beard and thought about the request. Rafael waited patiently.

'I think that's a very good idea. Will you suggest it to the Horowitz brothers?' Kobi asked.

'The whole family. Full testing. If we test you, we don't need to test your mother.'

Kobi smiled. 'Now that I have read the letters, I can see where my mother gets her nature from. She is very strong, very determined.'

'Very Horowitz,' Rafael returned his smile.

'And *very* Lutheran.'

Kobi's last few days in DC were busy. He went to a private genetic testing lab and had a buccal swab, a cotton swab of the inside of his mouth. He visited the National Gallery and spent a morning drooling over everything from Fra Filippo Lippi to Claude Monet and Vincent van Gogh. Then he went to the gallery shop and bought his mother a Monet *Water Lilies* scarf and himself a sketchbook with a picture of Dürer's *Dog Resting* on the cover.

When it was time to go, he had a last dinner with Rafael and Mags, and then boarded his plane for LA and home. During the long hours he read the English translation of the letters again, and planned what he was going to say to his mother, who thought he was still in Berlin.

CHAPTER TWENTY

Melbourne
August 2014

Elizabeth Voight considered herself Australian. She had lived in the country for sixty-four years, she had citizenship, she held an Australian passport, she could sing the anthem, and she supported the Baggy Greens, the national cricket team, in summer, and the Collingwood AFL team in winter. If her late husband hadn't been brought up to treasure his German heritage, all of her children would have had good Australian-sounding names; as it was, she named their eldest Andrew, he named their daughter Lisle, and then, after much debate, he named their youngest Jakob.

She lived in Yarraville, the once working-class suburb where her parents had set up home sixty-four years earlier. When Elizabeth married she moved only two streets away from her family home, and in recent years she and her local friends had observed the gentrification of their suburb — and the rising value of their properties — with some pleasure. Her older son, married with two daughters, and her daughter, married with three boys, were both an easy train or tram ride away. Only Jakob hadn't married, and lived in an inner-city apartment not far from his job at the university.

Every so often she went to St John's Southgate, a Lutheran church. Her faith was the only aspect of her early childhood she had carried with her; she was haunted by vivid memories of her father reading the Bible out loud and her mother encouraging her to pray beside her bed at night. There were other childhood reminiscences that could have risen up, but she kept them firmly suppressed and never spoke of such things.

On this cool but fine August day she had cancelled a coffee morning because, to her great surprise, Jakob had rung to say he was back early from Germany. She hadn't heard from him for a while and was beginning to wonder whether he had met someone, and then last night, there he was, on the phone from his apartment. He had lots of exciting things to tell her. Well, nothing new there. While she admired his creative spirit and enthusiasm for his work, his company was sometimes draining.

With a mother's intuition she had wondered whether he was homosexual and didn't know how to tell her; it didn't worry her, but she certainly wasn't going to raise the subject. Jakob was Jakob, and she was very pleased to hear that he had come home, though hopefully the experience hadn't made him hanker to hear about the 'German' past of his family. If so, that would have to be squashed immediately. The doorbell chimed and she got up and strode to the front door.

'Hello, Mother!' He gave her a kiss on each cheek.

'Hello, Jakob. How lovely to see you. Do come in.'

He had already gone past her and into the sitting room.

'I've made a pot of tea, or would you rather have coffee?'

He sat down in his usual chair. 'Tea would be lovely, thank you.'

She poured him a cup, aware of Kobi's eyes upon her. He definitely had something on his mind.

Suddenly he jumped up, put his hand into his jacket pocket and pulled out a square of material. 'I almost forgot, I bought you a scarf.'

It was silk, Monet's *Water Lilies*.

'It's lovely, dear. Thank you so much.'

He bent down and she kissed him on the cheek, then he returned to his seat.

'So, you're home early. How did it go?' she asked.

He gave a small sigh.

'It was wonderful. The art gallery was everything I'd hoped for, and I have found what I want to write about. The city was fascinating and I did quite a lot of sightseeing. Very clean, very efficient, but with a dark shadow over it. I don't know what it is — guilt, grief, sorrow — but it's definitely there.'

She stirred her tea, avoiding his gaze. 'Did you do all you needed to? Is that why you're home?' she asked.

'In some ways, but I'm home because of developments that I could never have dreamed of. Things I had to come and share with you.'

Finally, she looked up at him. His face was impassive and his eyes were guarded, not like the animated Jakob she knew.

'What sort of things, son?'

He hesitated. 'Those letters you gave me, the ones with the sketches and the writing in Hebrew?'

She nodded. 'I told you, I think your grandma bought them at a flea market. Did you identify the writer?'

'Much more than that. I had them translated into English, at the synagogue. And I read them and I found out who the people are.'

Her eyebrows arched with surprise. 'My, you have been busy. Did you return them?' she asked.

'Yes. I went to the US on my way home —'

'Goodness! What an extravagant thing to do. Did they appreciate you doing that?'

'Absolutely. I have so much to tell you. But before I do, I want you to read this.'

He bent down and pulled a plastic bag from his satchel. Inside was a bound pile of A4 sheets, the letters and sketches. He stood up again and brought it across to her.

'This is the translation, Mother. It's fascinating and heartbreaking at the same time. It is written by a young woman who lived in Berlin. She served with the Resistance and she died in Auschwitz; she was Jewish. The sketches are of her family, their name was Horowitz. Some of them survived, her two elder brothers, and they live in Vermont. I took the originals to them.'

She was flicking through the pages. 'I'm sure it's very interesting, dear. I'll put it on the pile, beside my bed.'

He shook his head. 'No, no. I need you to read them as soon as possible. Tonight. It should only take a day or two at the most. Then we need to talk again.'

He was anxious, which wasn't like him. She put the papers down on the table, picked up her cup and took a sip of tea.

'Why?' she asked.

'Because they are the reason I came home, what I found in there. But you need to read them first. Otherwise I'm telling you things that won't make sense. I promise you that is exactly as they were translated, word for word.'

'It's obviously important to you. Does it have something to do with Dürer?'

'Yes, very much. And a chance to write an important book. A vital book.'

She felt a slight surge of relief. It was about his work. And he wanted to share it with her. He wanted her approval. She smiled up at him.

'Of course I will, I'll start tonight.'

That night Kobi took a tram out to see his sister Lisle and her family at their home in St Kilda. Her husband, Mark, was a lawyer, and their three boys, Peter, Michael and Gary, were almost grown-up. The older two were at university, and Gary was in his last year at school. It was a relaxed household, bohemian and artistic. Lisle was a potter and made jewellery. The studio in the back garden was her haven. After dinner she and Kobi took their coffees and retreated to the peace and quiet amongst the pots.

'These are great!' he said, as he investigated her latest work.

She laughed. 'Thanks. I'm thinking about a stall at the art gallery market but it seems like a lot of effort. I'd rather give them away.'

He picked up a bright green glazed bowl. 'I'll have this if you're giving.'

'Oh, be my guest. It's a new glaze and I'm experimenting. Think I need to soften it down a bit. So, how was Berlin, really?'

He put the bowl down. 'As I said, fascinating, energising and a little scary.'

'Why scary?' she asked.

He sighed. 'I felt as if I kept running into my past. I wanted to ask Mother where she was when this happened, or did she see that, or where did she live?'

Lisle raised her eyebrows. 'Dangerous. I hope you haven't actually asked those questions.'

'Not yet, but I do intend to.'

'Kobi! You know what she'll say; she won't talk about when she was a little girl. I think it's like it happened to someone else and she believes she was born here.'

He shrugged. 'I don't think she's going to have a choice. The past is going to rush headlong into her present,' he checked his watch, 'around about now.'

She frowned at him. 'What do you mean? I wish you wouldn't be so cryptic.'

Kobi knew he wasn't really being fair; he was about to turn all of their worlds upside down. But at the moment it was still his secret.

'Kobi! Explain yourself,' she demanded.

'There's not a lot I can tell you at the moment. Mother gave me a bundle of letters before I left —'

'The ones in Hebrew with the pencil sketches?' she asked.

Kobi sat forward, surprised. 'You know about them?'

'She showed them to me and told me where she'd found them, hidden under papers in the bottom drawer of Grandma's desk. She told me she was going to give them to you.'

'Because of the sketches. And I took them to Berlin. I had the letters translated and I read the English version. This morning I gave that to Mother to read.'

'Why?' Lisle was clearly intrigued.

'Because … I want to talk to her about what's in them and I can't do that until she's read them. They may, and I stress *may*, have something to do with her childhood and why they came out here. And if they do, then she might, and again I stress *might*, be upset.'

Lisle digested what he had said. 'So you're giving me a heads-up in case she blows a gasket.'

He grinned. 'Something like that. I wish I could tell you more, but I owe it to her to talk to her about it first. Wish me luck.'

She grinned back at him. 'If you're going to bring up the "G" word and talk about immigration, then you'll need all the luck I'm capable of wishing.'

CHAPTER TWENTY-ONE

Melbourne
August 2014

Elizabeth's mother, Sabine Gunther, had died in 1970 when Elizabeth was twenty-eight and married with two children. She had been diagnosed with pancreatic cancer and spent her last days in a coma at the local hospital. Elizabeth was sitting beside her mother's bed when Sabine suddenly opened her eyes. Elizabeth got to her feet and bent over her.

'Hello, Mother,' she said softly. 'Do you want a sip of water?'

Sabine gave a little shake of her head, reached up and gripped her daughter's collar and pulled her closer. Then she said two words in a hoarse whisper, sank back onto the pillow and closed her eyes. A day later she was dead. Elizabeth had never heard the words before, or since, and hadn't mentioned them to another soul. Now, over forty years later, there were those words, staring out at her from a piece of paper.

She had read the document all the way through. The letters were, as Jakob had said, heartbreakingly sad. She was a mother and she couldn't imagine what it had been like to give birth and then give the child up because it was too dangerous to keep her. She had enormous respect for the courage of the young woman, and she hoped that her fate had included survival and reunion with her child.

Then she read the page that Jakob had attached. It explained who the nicknames belonged to and briefly outlined what he had found out at the German Resistance Centre, and then what Simon Horowitz had added during Jakob's visit to Vermont.

Rachel Horowitz had given her child to Sabine and Peter Gunther, who were obviously Elizabeth's parents. And there were those two words. She looked at the photo of the Horowitzs before the war. The family likeness was ridiculous: the father looked like her Andrew and some of them had Lisle's chin cleft, which no one had ever been able to explain.

She knew what Jakob was going to say to her, and demand of her, and why he was so anxious. And as she closed the document and let her glasses slip from her hand, she knew exactly how she was going to respond.

'You did what?' he asked, the shock evident on his face.

'I burned it,' she repeated firmly.

'*Why?*'

He was bewildered and she felt sorry for him, but her mind was made up.

'Because it's a load of nonsense. I've never read so much rubbish —'

'But, Mother!'

The force of his emotion drove him to his feet. 'Firstly, it is not nonsense, it's the *truth*. And, secondly, you have no right to destroy a document that doesn't belong to you!'

'Do you have another copy?' she asked calmly.

He nodded. 'I do, but that's not the point. You can't choose to ignore this, it's, it's just not … logical.'

She returned his angry glare with a cool, composed stare. 'I can choose to do anything I want. I loved my parents, they *were* my parents, and I am not interested in hearing any other story about my origins.'

'But you have flesh-and-blood relations —'

'Only if I accept what these letters say, and I don't. I was born on a farm outside Berlin and we came to Australia when I was eight. I have been Australian a lot longer than I was German. End of story.'

Kobi slumped back into his chair. He looked devastated, but she told herself that he would get over it.

'Go back to your work, Jakob, write your book and we'll say nothing more about this.'

For a long moment he said nothing, then he shook his head. 'You may not want to acknowledge them, but I have amazing great-uncles and a second cousin, and I'm extraordinarily proud of my biological grandmother. I'm also pretty sure I know who my biological grandfather was and he had family, too.'

She almost took the bait. This was one thing he hadn't put in the document, and she had to admit she wanted to know. But the mask slammed down again.

'Nonsense.'

He stood up. 'There's another thing. Believe it or not, they have a Dürer, an oil painting, an original. It belonged to the family before the war and it was returned to them in 2008. I saw it and it is possibly the best thing Dürer ever painted. Certainly the best thing I have ever seen. They keep it in a vault in Vermont and show it to no one. That's a travesty. I desperately want to write a book about it, tell the world. If you acknowledge them as family, that painting is part of your history, too. You have as much right to it as Simon's son, David, who is your first cousin.'

She stared at him open-mouthed. 'The Dürer she talks about in the first letter?' she asked.

He nodded. 'Imagine that, Mother. An original Dürer, the Paul von Hoch, and we're related to it. That's my best dream come true. If you deny your parentage, my access to the painting could be severely limited.'

She hesitated and her face betrayed the pain of her emotions. 'I can see that … Oh, Jakob, I wish I could help. But you ask too much. This is not me — I am not the baby in those letters!'

'Yes, you are. And giving you up broke her heart.'

'But she still did it, she still chose others. Sabine and Peter Gunter were my parents. They still are.'

He looked at her, then sighed. 'We're going to have to disagree. Don't think for a moment that I won't share this with Drew and Lisle —'

'Don't you dare!' It was her turn to get angry. Her blue eyes flashed as she reverted to the domineering mother who had always told him what to do.

This time he shook his head. 'You can't forbid me to tell them the truth about their background. They have a right to know and to make their own decisions.'

She shook her finger at him. 'You do and you'll not be welcome in my house!'

He raised his eyebrows with surprise. 'So be it, the price of choice.'

Kobi had imagined a variety of reactions — astonishment, upset, bewilderment, hurt — but this complete denial was beyond his comprehension. Even though the evidence was overwhelming she had retreated into the familiar world. There had to be a deeper reason. However, he knew her well enough to know that he wasn't going to get anything more at the moment.

Two days later he met his sister and brother for lunch in Chinatown. He didn't bring the translation; he would tell them the basics and then they could read it if they wanted to.

'So, what's this all about?' Andrew asked.

'All what?' Kobi replied.

'Mother rang me last night and told me not to believe a word you had to tell me. That's not like her.'

'She rang me, too,' Lisle added.

Kobi smiled. 'I wondered whether she'd do that. Remember, I gave you a heads-up about her blowing a gasket, Lisle?'

Lisle nodded. 'I do, and now I'm intrigued. What have you done to get her so mad?'

'Discovered some home truths, and she won't accept them.'

Andrew took a sip of his green tea. 'Start at the beginning and don't leave out anything,' he said. Kobi could see his curiosity.

'It all started with some letters …'

Half an hour later he sat back and watched them. Lisle was eating her meal and concentrating on her chopstick skills, her face blank. Andrew was frowning, and looked around the room until his eyes met Kobi's.

'And you think this Luftwaffe guy, this spy with the double-barrelled name, was the father of Rachel's baby?'

'I think it's very possible. She admits in one of the letters that she and Maria made up a cover story, and part of that was the name "Hans" for the baby's father because he was married. In the German Resistance Museum I read that Schulze-Boysen used the codename "Hans". Rachel says that her lover's wife also had a lover in the circle, and Libertas Schulze-Boysen had a longstanding affair with Günther Weisenborn. We'd have to get a DNA test from his surviving family and compare it to ours. They were a Prussian military family, aristocrats.'

'What were these Horowitzs like?' Lisle asked.

'Very nice, very gracious. Both old men have a fatalistic nature about them, as if nothing more could hurt them. Simon's son, David, is quiet but very smart, and his son, Daniel, is just a freak, a ridiculously talented violinist.'

She looked up at him, and he could see tears in her eyes. 'Great-uncles.'

'Yep.'

'We've never had any extended family. Just our grandparents and Mother and Father,' she said.

Andrew sighed. 'But Mother doesn't accept it,' he said.

'She's frightened.'

'I think she's terrified,' Lisle added, 'and I can understand why. This sweeps aside everything she has ever known. How on earth does she process that?'

Andrew seemed to make up his mind. 'She doesn't and I don't think we should make her. There are things in her past too sad to remember so she chooses to forget them. And that's her right. We can't force her to accept this new heritage.'

Kobi leaned forward. 'But these old men are in their nineties, they don't have years left while Mother comes to terms with the truth. If she doesn't go and see them now they'll be gone and they won't meet their niece. They've lost all the rest of their family. I don't think it's fair.'

Andrew looked from his brother to his sister and then shook his head. 'I understand what you're saying, but it is Mother's business not ours. She makes that decision. I'm afraid I'm with her: don't push it.'

Disappointment flooded through Kobi, and he felt a simultaneous desire to slap his brother's face. He was a supercilious, smug bastard and he always took the easy way.

'What about you, Lisle?' he asked.

She was torn, he could see that. While she was used to following her alpha-male elder brother, she wanted her sons to have more relations. On the other hand, Mother would not take kindly to her only daughter siding with her rebellious son.

'Personally, I'd love to meet them. I'd love to find out more about this incredible woman, who seems to have been my biological grandmother. I'd love for the boys to have contact with this new family ... But I don't want to cause Mother pain. She has her secrets and her reasons, and I respect that. If I did accept this and agree with you, I'd have to do it without her knowledge and that would make me deeply uncomfortable.'

He wasn't sure what she was saying. 'So, is that no, or is that yes?' he asked, looking at her intently.

She dropped her gaze to her plate. 'While Mother is alive, I think it has to be no.'

Again, the surge of disappointment. 'But she could live for ten years, maybe even twenty! So much lost opportunity.'

'Well then, you'll have to try and find a way to change her mind. In the meantime, let it rest,' Andrew said in a resolute tone. Clearly, he had given this all the time he was going to; his life was calling him back.

So be it. A solo path.

'I'm sorry you both feel that way. I'm going to concentrate on painting for a while. I'll make contact when I feel like socialising again.'

CHAPTER TWENTY-TWO

Vermont

August 2014

Simon had spent much of his old age using his brain, reading books, talking to his local rabbi and learning languages. He had put time into written and spoken Hebrew, extending the knowledge of his childhood. He had grown grateful for his papa's insistence that they become proficient in Hebrew at an early age. He remembered the elderly teacher who visited the house and taught them with genuine affection, but age had dimmed his skill and it had been a joy to discover the language again.

Consequently, he found his sister's letters an easy read, even with the idiomatic German words that crept in from time to time. So much in them reminded him of her — the way she had worn her heart on her sleeve, the way she was always drawing, the way she had cared for stray animals, and her determination to keep up with her energetic twin. Reading what she had written about David tore at the scars on his heart.

One rainy Sunday they all sat down around the large table and he read the letters aloud, first passages in Hebrew and then the whole translation in English. Everyone was transfixed, and silence reigned until the last 'From your loving Mama'.

'If only she had gone to live on a farm with Elizabeth,' David said quietly.

Simon shook his head. 'She was the only one of us who could do something from the inside, and she was too brave to take the safe route,' he said.

'What can we do to honour her?' Levi asked.

Simon looked at his brother, whose eyes were sad, his brow drawn into a frown. Levi was the only other person here who remembered Rachel, and they had shared a special bond, they had sung prayers together.

'Mama and Papa would have been so proud of what she did and the risks she took,' Levi added.

Simon smiled. 'And I love the way she says David would have been so jealous of her. Imagine how much he'd have loved to cycle through the streets at night and deliver illegal pamphlets!'

'Stopping to check his compass at every corner.' Levi laughed at a sudden memory. 'Remember when we went for a picnic in the Tiergarten and he insisted on drawing a map and we got so lost?' Simon was laughing as well. The old men had vanished into a world of recollection that was all their own. There was a moment of complete silence.

'What about a concert!'

It was Daniel. Simon could see the young man's excitement as the idea grew in his mind.

'I could get Yulena from Sergei and we could hold a fundraising concert. I know Raffy would help. And then we could use the funds, maybe to endow an art scholarship somewhere, in her name.'

'What a brilliant idea,' Cindy said, smiling affectionately at her son.

Simon nodded slowly. 'It is a brilliant idea. Should we wait for Kobi to return with Elizabeth?'

Now it was Cindy's turn to frown. 'Good Lord, no! They could take months to come back, they may never come back.'

Simon looked at her. 'Why do you say that?' he asked.

'We don't know how she'll react; maybe she won't want to be someone else's daughter. I know how hard I'd find that, and she's in her seventies —'

'She's our niece,' said Levi, quietly but firmly.

'Maybe.' Cindy's face was becoming defiant, an expression Simon knew so well — the don't-threaten-my-family expression. 'Let's wait until we get the results from the DNA tests before we welcome them with open arms.'

There was an uncomfortable silence.

'I think we owe Kobi,' said Daniel, purposefully not looking at his mother. 'He didn't have to bring those letters to us, he could have taken them home and put them in a drawer —'

'Are you kidding me? Do you think he's stupid? The Dürer, the possibility of recompense for the bank —'

'We never discussed that!' Simon cut across his daughter-in-law sharply.

'You didn't need to, he saw the painting. He's an art expert. If Elizabeth is Rachel's daughter, she has a claim to that. Am I the only one here who can see that he wants the Dürer?'

Simon looked at his son with a short incline of his head towards Cindy. Surely he could step in and stop her?

'Well let's leave all this for another day,' said David as he stood up. 'It's time we made a move for home.'

Daniel stood up. 'I should practise,' he said.

Cindy stood up. 'And I should shut up.'

Rafael was unaware of the beginnings of tension when he visited the Horowitz household later that week. He had decided to call on Simon and Levi in person, and then phone Kobi before he emailed the DNA result through to him. The welcome was as warm as ever. The housekeeper had been that morning and the home was spotless and orderly. Nearly seventy years after his ordeal had ended, Simon still couldn't stand the presence of dirt or the wasting of a scrap of food.

The two old men were sitting on the front porch listening to a CD of a Schubert concert.

'Maestro!'

Rafael hugged Simon and shook Levi's hand. There was a tremor in the formerly strong grip.

'Do sit down,' Simon said, as he paused the CD player.

'I am interrupting the *Rondo Brillant*.' Rafael smiled warmly at them as he sat down.

Simon returned the smile. 'It is one of our favourites, we listen to it often. Schubert can wait. What brings you back? Some results?'

Rafael nodded. 'I wanted to tell you in person, you know. The mitochondrial DNA confirms it. They do what they call a family reconstruction sequence and it is very stable. It is ninety-nine-point-ninety-nine per cent probable that you and Kobi Voight share a maternal ancestor. That would be your mother and his great-grandmother.'

Simon clasped his hands together. 'I knew it!' he exclaimed.

Levi was looking at him and smiling. Rafael hadn't seen such joy in the five years he had known them.

'I am so happy for both of you. It is not often you find new family,' he said.

'It is a gift from God,' Levi agreed. 'But the question remains: what are we going to do about it?'

Simon nodded. 'Yes! That's the issue now. When can we see her? There is so much I want to ask and share. Can we bring her here?'

Rafael hesitated. 'I'm going to call Kobi and talk to him, and then email the results through. He says his mother has read the English translation and she is thinking about it. I am sure this news will make a difference, yes?'

Simon looked from Rafael to Levi. 'Does she have an issue with the letters, Maestro?'

Levi answered before Rafael could collect his thoughts. 'You know, Simon, we have to be patient. It must be a huge shock for her. She thought she knew who she was and where she came from, and now she faces these revelations. I don't blame her at all if it takes her a little time.'

Simon frowned. 'Only a little time — let's be honest, we don't have years!'

Rafael smiled at them both. 'And Kobi understands that. For the moment, let us rejoice in the knowledge that you have a niece and David has a first cousin.'

As he drove back to Washington DC, the conversation played over in Rafael's mind. Levi understood that Elizabeth faced a life-changing revelation; Simon couldn't imagine why anyone would not want to be part of their family. Simon took his Jewishness for granted; he didn't think about what it would mean to a practising Lutheran to discover that she was Jewish, especially a German one. During the Third Reich it would have been enough to get her killed, and Elizabeth, possibly, had long-buried memories of living under that regime. How difficult would it be for Kobi to persuade her to make the trip? Maybe he needed some on-the-ground help?

The other thought that engaged his mind was the secret he had left in the envelope. He had asked for the results to be separated so he could email the mitochondrial tests to Kobi and leave the Male Specific Y-chromosome test out. At this point in time he was the only person who knew the result of David Horowitz's test. Simon's wife, Ruth, was dead and had, presumably, taken her secret to the grave. Simon adored David and Daniel and there was no need to wound where it would have no purpose. And perhaps even Levi was not aware that he was, in fact, David's biological father.

CHAPTER TWENTY-THREE

Melbourne
August 2014

Kobi hadn't visited or heard from his mother since their fiery exchange over Rachel's letters. He wasn't due back at the university until the end of September, so he had locked himself away in his apartment and painted. The works were dark, lots of tangled barbed-wire and swastikas and pale, gaunt faces. Plus one very plaintive painting of a young woman with Rachel's face holding out her hands to the viewer, tied together by a pink ribbon.

It was a rainy late-winter's day when the phone rang and he put down his brush and picked it up.

'Hello?'

There was a second of silence.

'Kobi? Is that you?'

He recognised the deep, gravelly Spanish accent immediately.

'Maestro Gomez! How are you?'

'Very well, and you?'

'I'm painting. I'm spending my spare time giving vent to the emotions from my trip to Germany.'

'That sounds very cathartic,' Rafael said.

'I think so. Do you have news?' Kobi asked. He could feel his heart beating a touch faster. There was a pause — was that a good thing or a bad thing?

'Yes, I do. I'm going to email the result to you, but I wanted to call and let you know. The DNA tests prove that you are related, yes? It is ninety-nine-point-ninety-nine per cent probable that you and the Horowitz brothers share a common maternal ancestor, and that would be their mother and your great-grandmother, Elizabeth.'

Kobi felt a warm rush of relief. He'd known it, he'd been absolutely certain of it, but now it was truth.

'Are you going to tell your mother?' Rafael asked when Kobi didn't say anything.

'I will show her the result when it comes through. I don't think it will make any difference. She already knows it to be true, but she won't accept it.'

'And your siblings?'

'They don't want to cause her pain, and I understand that. She's a very strong woman and they are not used to upsetting her. I'm afraid that's my role in her life!'

Rafael chuckled. 'I can relate to that, you know. I wondered whether it would make any difference if I came to see her. I could bring some family photos and I am neutral, no threat.'

Kobi felt hope rise and tried not to let it consume him. 'Would you do that? Come all this way?' he asked.

'Of course I would. I can visit a couple of venues and have some discussions about potential concert tours, and that makes it a business trip, yes?'

At last Kobi could see a possibility of some resolution. Rafael really was a remarkable man, and his commitment to the Horowitz family was obviously deep.

'I would be tremendously grateful if you could see your way clear to doing that,' Kobi said.

'Excellent! I'll be back in touch when I have it finalised.'

Later that week Kobi took the Sandringham line from Flinders Street and alighted at Elsternwick Station. He walked for a couple of minutes down a suburban street and found the Jewish Holocaust Centre. He was driven by a need to see how his hometown honoured the dead, remembered the tragedy that had befallen so many. The security wasn't as strict as in Berlin, and the welcome was warm. At the front desk he was asked if he would like to talk to one of the camp survivors who volunteered at the centre. Kobi agreed that that would be excellent, but he wanted to have a look around first.

The first thing he was confronted with was a display of bronze busts of members of one family who had perished, created by survivors in remembrance of loved ones.

Next was a photograph of five young women, naked, running down into a hole with their arms covering their breasts. It was obvious that they were going to be shot and their vain attempt to retain their modesty moved him deeply. The brunette reminded him of Rachel and he felt tears well in his eyes.

Most of the information mirrored what he had read and seen in Berlin — identity cards with the middle names of 'Israel' or 'Sara' and yellow cloth Stars of David for sewing onto clothing. But now he looked at the pictures and relics, the examples of clothing from the concentration camps and the video footage through new eyes. Now, he imagined Simon being herded out of the cattle truck and into a processing line. Now, he saw Rachel in the descriptions of the Resistance and the camp uprisings and the bravery of those executed. He wanted to ask someone to add Rachel's name to the lists and to honour her sacrifice that had led to generations of Melbournians.

One phrase made him stop in his tracks: *From her Resistance comes my existence.* That was it. From the courage of two people, Rachel Horowitz and Harro Schulze-Boysen, came a person, and from her another three people, and from them another five people, and more would come — generations that existed because Rachel had given birth and had given up her child. Somehow he had to find a way to make his mother understand this. He wondered whether she would come with him, see it for herself. Or would the connection to her childhood be too much to bear?

'Excuse me, sir?'

He spun around. 'Yes?'

It was one of the women from the entrance desk. 'If you would like to speak to Hana, she is free now.'

He gathered himself together. 'Thank you. That would be a real privilege.'

The woman gave him a warm smile. 'Thank you for seeing it that way.'

She led him to a bench in the corner of a display area. Hana was a small woman with jet-black hair. She was probably in her nineties, and she leaned on a carved walking stick, her back bent over. When she straightened up and held out her hand, he could see that her dark eyes were like Simon's, sparkling and fierce.

'Hello,' she said. Her accent was Eastern European, Polish at a guess.

'Hana, this is Dr Jakob Voight, he works at the university. Dr Voight, this is Hana Krakowski.'

He shook the firm, dry hand. Every finger sported a gold ring, some more than one.

'Lovely to meet you. May I call you Hana? Please call me Kobi.'

The old woman eyed him as they sat down. 'Are you German, Kobi?' she asked.

He shook his head. 'I was born here. So was my father. My mother was born in Berlin, but she came here in 1950. She was the daughter of a Resistance fighter, a Jewish woman who was murdered in Auschwitz.'

Her face softened and she patted his hand. 'Welcome, my boy. You are one of us.'

That simple sentence caused him to catch his breath and he almost choked. 'Why, thank you. I am very keen to hear your story.'

'I was a girl when war broke out, thirteen. We lived in a Polish village, but my mother came from Warsaw and her grandfather had been a very well-known rabbi. When the soldiers came, my family were all shot — my mama, my papa, my sister and my two brothers. But for some reason they took me and sent me to the Warsaw Ghetto. I lived there until 1941, and then I was sent to Markstadt labour camp, which was a satellite camp of Gross-Rosen concentration camp. I stayed there until 1944, when I was transferred to Peterswaldau, which was a camp for women.'

'My great-uncle survived Dachau,' Kobi said. It was the first time he had said that out loud.

She smiled. 'That was quite a feat.'

Kobi felt a new emotion: pride. 'He played the violin for the guards. And he worked in munitions.'

'So did I, but I did what I could to sabotage the war effort. I tried to put as little gunpowder as I could in the bullets.'

They both laughed.

'Did you get caught?' Kobi asked.

'Eventually, and every day for three months they threatened to send me to a killing camp, but it was too late by then. Auschwitz had closed.'

'What are your strongest memories of life in the camp?' he asked.

'Roll call, at five in the morning, in the freezing cold, and something that resembled potato soup with a small portion of bread. In Markstadt we had more food, a loaf of bread the size of your head that fed five people for a week, and a small pat of butter, a little jam, black coffee, and in winter two types of potato soup, with actual potatoes.'

'And the people?'

'Oh yes. Other women. We formed great friendships, but there was always the fear that someone would be shipped off to another camp.'

'What happened to you after the war?'

'I was sent to a displaced persons camp where I met my husband, who had also survived the camps. We got married and we went, eventually, to live in Israel. It was very hard. We had small children and life was tough, not enough supplies, food, water, nappies. But we did not complain — we were free!'

'When did you come to Australia?'

'My husband died in 2002, and one of my children had come here. So I came on holiday in 2003, and then I decided to come back and live. Eventually, my three boys all moved here, and all my grandchildren and great-grandchildren. I have seventeen descendants, four generations, because I survived.'

Kobi shook his head in awe. Suddenly, she looked very tired.

'Thank you for sharing,' he said.

She put her hand on his knee. 'Come with me, I have something to show you.'

He followed her as she walked slowly out of the exhibition, past the front desk and along the corridor to the volunteers' lunch room. She didn't say a word, she just dipped into a handbag and took out a small sepia photo, creased but laminated and stiff. She handed it to him.

'This is my family. I hid the photo throughout the war, behind a stone, in both camps. I kept it with me. It is the only record I have.'

He stared at the smiling faces, a man and a woman and two boys and two girls. The image was grainy and had faded before it was laminated, but it had been cradled and caressed with love for so many years, and it resonated with memories. Again, Kobi felt the lump in his throat.

'Thank you, Hana. I feel honoured to see it.'

'You are a good boy. You remember your ancestors. They died or they survived and their story lives on in you. Make sure they are never forgotten.'

CHAPTER TWENTY-FOUR

Melbourne
September 2014

'My son tells me you have flown over sixteen thousand kilometres to see me. I am flattered.'

Rafael sat opposite Elizabeth Voight. She was dressed in a copper-coloured blouse and a black skirt, with flat black court shoes and a long string of pearls. Her hair was dyed a sandy, reddish-blonde, covering the grey with honey-coloured highlights, and her eyes were blue. There was much about her that reminded him of Simon's mother, and nothing that reminded him of Rachel. He smiled.

'It is my pleasure. I have never been to Australia, you know, and it is very beautiful. And it has been also useful. I have talked to promoters about my orchestra and also about some of the soloists who play with it, including Daniel Horowitz, about potential tours. Concert tours.'

She nodded. 'Good. I'm glad. Then it hasn't been a complete waste of time.'

He shook his head. 'Nothing I do is ever a complete waste of time.'

They were fencing. Rafael had instructed Kobi to sit and watch and keep quiet, no matter what his mother said.

'So, Maestro Gomez, let's get down to business. Have you read these letters?'

'Not for myself. Not all the way through. I spent some time looking at the English version Kobi had in DC, and I have talked to Simon Horowitz about the original version. He has become something of a Hebrew scholar in his old age, and he read the originals to his family.'

'And you have come here to persuade me to embrace them as my new family.'

Again he shook his head. 'No, no, that is entirely your choice, yes? I have come to tell you my experience of them.'

As he spoke he got up, took an envelope of photographs from his inside jacket pocket and handed them to her before returning to his seat.

'I first met them when I was head judge of an international competition, in New Zealand, in 2008. It was a violin competition, you know, and the winner was Daniel Horowitz. That is his photo: he is twenty now, but he was fourteen when he won. He is a remarkable young man.'

'I've heard about him,' she said.

'And I met his parents, David and Cindy, at the same time. They came to a symposium I hold every year at the Kennedy Centre, but by that time Dan had decided not to play the violin anymore.'

She looked up from the photos. 'Why ever not?'

'He wanted to play baseball and his mother would not let him, and he felt, you know, different. He was going to a special music institute, and when he came home he was bullied. I am sure you know how much teenage boys want to fit in with their peers.'

She smiled, and for the first time he could see warmth in her expression. 'Not just boys, Maestro, and I know this more than you could possibly imagine.'

He nodded. 'I moved from Spain to the USA to study music, and I found it very hard. Not speaking English.'

He understood her pain. She seemed grateful for that. 'Please go on,' she said.

'To cut a long story short, I learned about the family and I met Daniel's paternal grandparents. I learned about their history at the hands of the Nazis and how they had lost a 1742 Guarneri del Gesú violin. One of the best violins ever made, yes? We managed to get it back, and Daniel now plays it in concert halls around the world.'

He sat back and took a sip of his coffee.

'You staged a sting.'

He raised his eyebrows and gave her an amused smile. 'Some might say that. We actually staged a concert, but we left the current owner of the violin with very little choice.'

'And is this what you're doing to me?' she asked.

'No, not at all! Your choice is perfectly clear. The DNA tests prove that Kobi shares a maternal ancestor with the Horowitz family. The letters indicate that it is Elizabeth Horowitz, who is Simon's mother and your grandmother. If we could test Sabine and Peter Gunther I am in no doubt that it would prove you are not genetically related to them at all.'

She sat up very straight and looked at him, one eyebrow arched. 'There are bonds that are deeper than being blood relatives.'

'I understand that. Answer me one question, yes? When years ago you first looked at the letters, before you knew who the people were, did you not look at the sketch of the woman and see a likeness to yourself? A likeness between Levi and Kobi? Between Benjamin Horowitz and your other son?'

For a long moment she didn't answer. 'It might have crossed my mind. But I believed my mother had bought it as a memento and that it had nothing to do with me. You don't see what you're not looking for.'

'Why would she keep something written in Hebrew?' he asked.

'She wanted them for the lovely pencil sketches.'

He acknowledged her victory on that point. 'Now you have read the letters, what do you think of Rachel?' he asked.

Again she hesitated. 'She was a very brave young woman and I was sad to hear of her fate.'

'She was your mother,' he said quietly.

Elizabeth looked straight into his eyes, defiant. 'Sabine Gunther was my mother. She cared for me, fed me and read to me and taught me to love Jesus.'

'If Rachel had survived the war she would have gladly done all those things.'

Now it was Elizabeth's turn to give him an amused smile. 'I doubt very much that she would have taught me to love Jesus.'

He couldn't help but smile back. '*Touché.*'

She took a sip of her tea. 'What are you trying to persuade me to do, Maestro?' she asked.

'Come to Vermont and meet them. If you do not come soon at least one of your uncles will be dead. Levi Horowitz is ninety-five and he is infirm. He is a wonderful man, a little aloof until you get to know him, but as sharp as a tack, yes? He adores music and art and has an encyclopaedic memory for fabrics and the history of costumes. I only need to look around your gorgeous house, you know, to see how much you would enjoy meeting each other.'

'Thank you. I'm sure I would like him very much.'

'And Simon is ninety-two and stronger, but he spent five years in Dachau and some of those experiences have caused him, you know, health problems. He watched his younger brother, Rachel's twin, get sicker and sicker until he was taken away, and his beloved father was shot in front of him. He never saw his mama again, and he is thrilled to have a record of them, handwritten by his baby sister. Family is everything to this man. He just wants to see you and hug you and welcome you and tell you about your mother.'

There was a long silence. Kobi was on the edge of his chair, obviously desperate to contribute. Rafael glanced at him.

'You know, Mrs Voight, it is not just yourself you are robbing of family. It is your sons and your daughter and their children. Generations that could offer each other support and love long after you have gone.'

They stared at each other across the room. He knew he was reaching her.

'I … I do see that.' Her voice was shaky.

'You have time, not much time because these men are very old, but some time, to repair your family. If you do this, then it is another blow to Hitler and the abomination that was the Nazis. Your family gets to win.'

Suddenly her hands went to her face and she burst into tears. Kobi moved swiftly to her side and put his arms around her. 'There, there, Mother. It's okay. I'm here for you, and so are Lisle and Drew. We love you so much.'

She buried her head in his shoulder and sobbed, large racking moans that shook her whole body. Kobi stroked her arm and looked over at Rafael, who gave him a small nod. He was doing the right thing. It was an avalanche, the release of years of pain, and he must let her cry until she was spent. Finally, she drew back and sat up. Kobi took his handkerchief from his pocket and gave it to her. She dried her eyes and blew her nose.

'Thank you, dear,' she said, patting his shoulder. 'I've made you all wet,' she added.

He leaned over and kissed her on the cheek. 'My jacket and I don't mind. Does that feel better?'

She nodded. 'I do apologise, that certainly was not my intention, Maestro.'

Rafael smiled at her. 'It wasn't my intention to upset you. It is a very emotional subject.'

She gave a little half-sob, half-sigh. 'It is, and I need to give you my response.' She finished her tea.

'I want you both to take a moment and think about what you are asking me to accept. I am not a young woman either, and suddenly I find out that I am illegitimate and that the couple I have always thought of as my parents took me to the other side of the world. That only happens in television shows!

'And not only that, my mother was Jewish — does that mean that I am Jewish? You don't know what that means to me. My teenage years were not as happy as you might assume. We were in a country that had just been at war with my homeland. Many of my schoolmates had lost relations in that war. They hated me. They bullied me. They called me a name I didn't understand until someone translated it for me. They called me "Jew murderer".'

CHAPTER TWENTY-FIVE

A farm outside Berlin
Late June 1942

'It's a girl.'

Peter Gunther stared at the baby in his wife's arms and tried not to show his disappointment. He was a farmer and he had wanted another son.

Sabine frowned at him. 'She's a baby and she's beautiful and she needs a safe home,' she said sternly. Then she turned to the woman who was watching them from the corner of the room. 'Of course we'll take her, Maria, and we'll love her like she was our own.'

Maria Weiss smiled with obvious relief. 'Thank you, Sabine. Her mother will be very grateful. Her clothes and her toy are in this bag, she doesn't have many nappies —'

Sabine gestured to Peter to take the small bag from Maria. 'That's as maybe. We'll provide for her.'

'How old is she?' Peter asked. 'Exactly?'

Maria hesitated. 'Now let me see, she was born on 17 February, and it is now 27 June, so she is four months, ten days. Her name is Elizabeth, Elizabeth Maria.'

Sabine looked down at the auburn-haired little girl who smiled happily and clutched at her necklace.

'When this madness is over, her mother and father will

want her back and they will want to raise her in her mother's religion,' Maria said firmly.

'Her father isn't Jewish?' Peter asked.

'No. He's Aryan, she gets her blue eyes from him. They both love her very much.'

Sabine gave her a tight smile. 'Of course.'

Elizabeth missed her mother — her face, her sound, her smell, her touch and the taste of the milk she was used to. She missed her father's face, too, but not as acutely. She cried with confusion and despair for several days, and nothing her foster parents did comforted her.

Then the survival instinct kicked in and she adapted. She slept through the night and was happy to be cuddled by this new, strange-sounding and -smelling woman, and to be cooed at by this strange-looking man and this young boy. They fed her, changed her, smiled at her, laughed with her and seemed to be at her beck and call.

Her brother, Mathias, was four, and he showed her his toys and carried her outside to see the cows and the dog and the birds on the riverbank. When he pulled funny faces at her, she laughed and clapped her hands. It was still hot and sunny, and Sabine put her out on the grass of the back lawn. She was a strong baby, long-limbed and well-covered. Within two months she was raising herself up on her elbows and swaying forwards and backwards.

'Peter!'

He latched the gate and looked up as his wife came running down the path. 'What's wrong?'

She shook her head. 'Nothing's wrong. Come and see!'

She was already heading back to the house. He followed her, around the corner and onto the lawn. The shrapnel in his legs caused him to limp, always more obvious when he tried to hurry. Sabine sank to her knees about six feet away from the baby, who was lying on her stomach on a rug.

'Come on, baby, come to Mama.'

She stretched out her hands and clapped. Elizabeth rose up on her hands and knees and crawled over the grass to her. Sabine turned to her watching husband.

'She's crawling!'

He joined her as she collected the laughing baby in her arms.

'Six months and she is crawling,' she repeated proudly.

Peter patted Elizabeth on the head. 'Good girl, she's strong. She'll be helping Mathias and I feed the cows by next winter.'

Sabine laughed and kissed the baby. A familiar sense of unease rose in Peter's stomach. He couldn't keep reminding her, keep suggesting she not get too attached. She was right to get angry when he harped on about it.

Mathias had been born after seven years of trying, and had been only eighteen months old when his father had joined the Führer's army. Peter was a good soldier and had fought bravely on the Western Front through Denmark and Norway and then south to Belgium and the Netherlands and into France. In late 1941 a tank shell exploded close beside him and ripped his legs apart. A skilful surgeon saved the limbs, but he was not fit for combat and, because his farm produced much-needed food, and Sabine was struggling on her own, he was discharged and allowed to return to civilian life.

There were rumours that some farmers supplied excess milk to an organisation in Berlin, who saw that it went to starving children, possibly orphans and children in hiding. Peter had been suspicious of such people. 'They may be trying to defeat the work of the Gestapo.'

'They're feeding children! Little ones who don't have political opinions and they're hungry. Surely it's not wrong to help with that.'

Sabine was stubborn, and Peter knew that helping these 'little ones' could fill the gap created by her yearning for further children of her own, so he agreed to see if he could find a contact.

The Gunthers made their own butter and cheese and baked their own bread, grew their own vegetables and slaughtered a beast when they needed meat. Their house was always a place of plenty and word spread.

One day Peter hobbled in from the farm to find a plump, middle-aged woman and a younger man in his kitchen, talking to Sabine.

'This is my husband, Peter ... Dear, this is Maria Weiss and Dieter Schonberg. They work with the people who have been taking our extra milk.'

He shook their hands and took a seat at the table. 'What can we do for you?' he asked.

They glanced at Sabine and she cleared her throat. 'They have come to ask whether they can use the barn, the old one at the bottom of the back paddock.'

He hesitated. All three of them were watching him. 'Why?'

'It is better if you don't know why, Mr Gunther,' Maria Weiss answered the question.

'So what you want to do is illegal.' It was a statement.

'We save lives, Mr Gunther. We believe in freedom and equality for all, and we don't believe that any of our fellow Germans are subhuman.' Schonberg's words were treason, against the express commands of the Führer, and as such were punishable by death.

Peter had feared this moment for some time. He was a patriotic German and he was proud to have served, but the direction in which the Nazi Party was taking his beloved Germany had begun to sicken him. To express these opinions out loud was madness, though.

'What have these things to do with my barn?' His voice was quiet, measured and calm. He could see that Sabine was frightened; she was pale and her eyes darted from one guest to the other.

'We wish to use your barn. If you don't go near it, you will see nothing. If you leave some food in it from time to time, that would be very much appreciated. But all we require is that you don't report, or shoot, anyone who uses it.'

Peter nodded slowly. 'And if the Gestapo raid us and find people hiding there, do you think they will believe that we knew nothing?' he asked.

Maria Weiss smiled at him. 'I am a Gentile and I live in Berlin. I have papers and I travel quite freely around my city. I'm in my sixties now, a widow and I live alone. What would the Gestapo want with me?'

'Nothing, I would imagine.'

'Precisely. But when I die and I come before my God, I will be able to say that I did everything I could to prevent the mass slaughter of my countrymen. I did not stand by.'

She held his gaze and Peter could see that she had conquered her fear of consequences. It was time to be counted.

'Very well, you may use the barn.'

By the time Elizabeth joined the Gunthers, their participation in the Resistance was well-established. They knew that if there was a flag on the fence-line by the old barn, it was time to take bread, cold meat, cheese and milk and leave it by the door. Sometimes Peter added a big flagon of beer, which he knew would be appreciated. Sabine left a pile of blankets hidden under hay in the corner of the barn in winter.

Just after Christmas 1942, when Elizabeth was ten months old and standing up against chairs and knees, Maria made another visit. The snow was heavy and it was bitterly cold outside. A fire roared in the grate and the room was beautifully warm.

'My, what a bonny baby she's grown into!' Maria said.

Elizabeth was playing with a gold bell on a red ribbon. She stretched out her hand to give it to the strange woman.

'Thank you, darling!'

'She's standing up and balancing, she'll be walking soon,' Peter said as he handed Maria a cup of coffee.

'I can see she's strong and obviously happy. Thank you —'

'What do you want?' Sabine asked as she scooped Elizabeth up in her arms and sat down on the sofa.

'I have news. Sad news, but I thought I should come and tell you. I'm afraid Elizabeth's parents have both died, serving their beliefs. So they won't be coming to take her back.'

Sabine closed her eyes and kissed Elizabeth gently on the top of her head. The baby looked up at her and giggled.

'Poor wee mite,' Peter said as he looked from Maria to Sabine. Maria nodded.

'She's an orphan and now we have to discuss what to do with her.'

'No, she's not! She's our daughter and she will stay with us,' Sabine's voice was firm and calm.

Maria looked at Peter. 'Is that the way you both feel?' she asked.

Peter was looking at Sabine. 'Of course it is, isn't it, Peter?' Sabine asked.

He nodded. 'Of course. We have more than enough to feed her, and she'll help on the farm when she grows up. You can leave her here, Maria.'

Sabine stood up. 'And I need to give her a bath and put her to bed, so you'll have to excuse me,' she said as she left the room.

Maria smiled at Peter. 'It's a good thing you're doing — without you, her chances of survival are slim to nothing.'

He shook his head. 'I don't know what the outcome of this war will be. But she'll grow up a Gunther and no one will ever know she was the child of spies.'

CHAPTER TWENTY-SIX

A *farm* outside Berlin

March 1945

Elizabeth's earliest memories were of happy times, riding around the paddock on the back of the house cow led by Mathias, baking bread with her mother, feeding out hay with her father and her brother, and summer picnics down by the river.

One day her father and some of his friends dug a huge hole in the backyard and lined it with concrete blocks and a corrugated-iron door. Her mother told her that if the planes came overhead during the night she might have to wake up and come with them to stay in the hole until the planes went away. Although they heard dull thuds in the distance on quiet nights, the planes never flew over their farm.

There was the odd moment when life became charged with dangerous excitement. When the trucks of soldiers came rumbling up the drive, her father told his children to do what they had practised: run like the wind down to the old barn and stand in the doorway and yell 'Soldiers are here!' at the tops of their voices. Then run even faster up through the trees to the back of the house and come through the laundry and into the kitchen.

Before her mother could object to her going, four-year-old Elizabeth was running, her hair streaming behind her. The grass tickled her legs as she followed Mathias across the paddocks, jumped over the stile and down the gully to the barn. It looked empty, but they both yelled anyway, as loud as they could, and as she turned to run back she could hear the bales of hay rustling with movement.

Just before he got to the house, Mathias stopped and caught his breath, so Elizabeth stopped as well. Through the trees they could see soldiers roaming around the courtyard, going into the implement shed and poking pitchforks into a pile of straw mixed with dirt.

'What are they looking for?' Elizabeth whispered as she tugged at his sleeve.

'Jews. People in hiding.' Mathias grinned at her. 'Well, they won't find them now.'

When his breathing was even, Mathias climbed up onto the laundry windowsill, pushed open the window and extended his hand down to his sister. She wriggled past him and he followed her inside. He could hear voices in the house, so he picked up the empty clothes' basket. Elizabeth shadowed him, skipping through the back door, down the passage and into the warm kitchen, where two soldiers in uniform stood with her parents.

'All done, Mama,' Mathias said in his best singsong voice.

One of the officers turned and looked at Elizabeth. 'Hello, little one,' he said.

'Hello.'

'What's your name?'

'Elizabeth.'

'You're very grown-up. Do you know who the Führer is?'

She nodded solemnly.

Mathias pulled himself up tall and saluted.

'My daddy fought for the Führer,' he said proudly.

'Bright boy. Who does the girl get the red in her hair from?'

Sabine went to Elizabeth and picked her up. 'My mother: I was a strawberry blonde when I was young, too. She's darker than I was, but I think she'll be a blonde when she grows up.'

He smiled at them. 'Lovely blue eyes.'

The two soldiers saluted their parents, who saluted back, and then they left. A few minutes later the trucks drove away.

Sabine was sitting at the table with Elizabeth on her knee when Peter came back into the room.

'Don't you ever do that again!' she snapped at him.

Peter scooped up Mathias and hugged him. 'Well done, son.' He turned to his wife. 'The children were the only ones who could get there in time and warn them.'

'And what about them? What if there had been soldiers in the barn and they'd caught my babies?'

The anger in her voice was obvious. He shook his head with frustration.

'If they'd caught anyone hiding in the barn they would have arrested us. The children are fast, Sabine. They knew what to do and they might just have saved us all. Leave it at that.'

Sabine held Elizabeth tight and kissed her on the top of the head. 'Very good girl, you did very well,' she said soothingly.

Elizabeth didn't really understand what the end of the war meant. Lots of people came to see her parents and they had a party, with singing and drinking and platters of food. She and Mathias hid under the table and stole food from plates when their parents weren't looking. Happy people kissed her, and some of them threw her up in the air and caught her again.

In the weeks that followed, new people came to the farm and filled boxes with produce and meat and steel pails of milk. The official ministry men didn't come anymore to collect the milk, but there was a never-ending stream of people from the city wanting to buy and barter for the black market. Her mother collected fruit in the neighbourhood and made jam in the summer and baked cakes and traditional biscuits, stews and vegetable dishes in the winter, and steaming hot puddings —

everything was snapped up by the people who came in the anonymous black cars.

By the time Elizabeth turned five in February 1947, her mother had taught her to write her name, to recite the alphabet and to count to twenty. Her father was trying to find a school that she and Mathias could attend, but many of the local ones had been closed. There was talk of children gathering at the home of someone who had been a teacher, but people were still frightened of congregating in anything that could be misconstrued as an anti-government protest.

One warm June day, when Elizabeth had been to the nearest town with her mother and brother, they arrived home to find her father pacing the sitting-room floor.

'Peter! What's wrong?' her mother asked as soon as she saw him.

'They came. Maria. And she brought two men. Her —'

Her mother turned and pushed Elizabeth towards the door. 'Go upstairs and get changed, darling. You can take your plaits out if you like. You go, too, Mathias. I'll be up in a minute.'

Elizabeth knew that tone of voice and she left the room, but she paused on the first step.

'Who came with her?' her mother asked.

'Two young men, both called Horowitz. Rachel's brothers. They have survived the war. She has told them about Elizabeth.'

Mathias was beckoning to her from the landing. The conversation was confusing and she didn't want to get into trouble, so she went up the stairs.

A few minutes later her parents both came into her room, and her mother started brushing the long hair she had just finished unbraiding.

Her father sat down on the edge of her bed. 'We're going to go on a little holiday, sweet pie, all four of us — so what do you think of that?'

She turned around and looked at him. 'Where?' she asked.

He looked excited. She had never left the farm for more than a day trip to the nearest town, and this sounded like fun.

'Berlin.'

That place she sometimes heard her parents talking about in hushed tones. Mathias said the planes had dropped bombs on it, and most of the buildings were just piles of concrete.

'Is that the city?' she asked, joy and anxiety mixing up in a bubbling feeling in her tummy.

'Yes, darling, the city.'

Her mother turned her around and hugged her tight. 'You and Mathias and I are going to pack clothes and toys —'

'Right now?' she asked.

Her mother nodded and kissed her cheek. 'Right now. Your father has some people to go and see, and then he'll come back and pack his clothes, and before you know it we'll be on our way to our holiday!'

It all happened so quickly. In a matter of hours they had packed the car with all the things they needed and left the farm. She hadn't even had time to say goodbye to the cows, or the dogs, or the cat that lived in the barn, but her father had promised they would still be here when they came home. It was late when they got to the apartment building in Pankow; Elizabeth was sound asleep and didn't see the rubble-strewn streets and the bombed-out buildings until the morning.

CHAPTER TWENTY-SEVEN

Berlin

August 1947

Elizabeth was horrified when she looked out the window on her first day in Berlin. The city was still gripped by post-war trauma. The streets were taking years to clear and the skeletons of buildings stood as stark reminders of the Allied bombing.

When she went out with her mother, she held her hand very tight. She and Mathias couldn't help but stare at people pushing handcarts loaded with possessions from one part of town to another, gangs of orphaned children roaming the streets looking for people to rob, trucks full of soldiers rumbling past, and lines of women and children passing buckets of rubble down to a vehicle waiting to take it to the outskirts of the city.

The water lines were still broken, and women gathered at old-fashioned hand-pumps on street corners to wash clothes and draw buckets of water for cooking and cleaning.

They were in the eastern part of the city. Everywhere she looked she saw banners of a man in a cap, with a bristly black moustache, a man her father called 'Stalin', and flags showing a hammer and a sickle.

The apartment was cold and dank and smelt musty, but at least it had all its walls and a stairwell that went all the way to the ground. At night, when Mathias had gone to sleep across the room, she lay in bed with her much-loved stuffed bunny rabbit and cried quietly for the farm and the animals and the sunshine and the fresh meat and milk. Her mother would come in and cuddle her and dry her tears and tell her not to worry, things would get better soon.

About a month after they moved, her mother's words came true. Her father came home full of joy: he had a job as a bricklayer and they were moving. He had found them a much better apartment in the Prenzlauer Berg, still in the eastern sector but closer to the centre of the city. There was much hugging and promises of a better life.

'And what is even better, princess, is the fact that there is a kindergarten around the corner and a school for Mathias! You can both learn and play with other children.'

This caused Sabine to burst into tears, which she assured Elizabeth was because she was so happy.

By the end of the week they were installed in their new home on the third floor of a nine-storey apartment building. It had curtains and carpets and nice furniture. She had a much more comfortable bed in a room of her own, with a view of a park from her window. And it had a bath with running warm water, so she didn't have to wash in cold water from a bucket anymore. There were many more shops close by, and her mother didn't have to queue for two hours to buy a loaf of bread, some butter and a little bacon. To celebrate their first night in their new home, Sabine cooked onion soup, followed by Mathias's favourite main course, goulash with potato dumplings, and Elizabeth's favourite dessert, tinned pear hedgehogs. She helped her mother put the almonds into the pieces of pear to make them look like hedgehogs, and stirred the chocolate sauce. They hadn't had cocoa since the flight from the farm, and she was so excited to try it that she burned her tongue.

Two days later there was a knock on the door. The head teacher of the local kindergarten had come to invite Elizabeth to join. She was five, so would only attend until her sixth birthday, when she would start school down the road where Mathias went.

'So she hasn't been to a kindergarten before?' the woman asked.

Sabine shook her head. 'No. We lived in the country. But I have taught her to write her name and count to twenty and we've read lots of books.'

The woman was stout, with glasses and her hair pulled back in a severe bun. She frowned at Sabine. 'What sort of books?' she asked suspiciously.

'Books I had saved from my own childhood. Fairy tales and adventures. Books her brother read when he was little, and he reads very well now.'

The woman looked over at Elizabeth, who was playing with a new doll and trying not to look scared. 'I can see she's been indulged, and that's all well and good when they're babies. But she has to start to learn the ways of the motherland. The process of her education will produce a well-rounded Socialist who is efficient, loyal and ready to defend their homeland. And she is behind the others of her age, so we will help her to catch up.'

Sabine hesitated.

'Mrs Gunther, the State demands that you allow us to educate your children. Please have her at the front door at seven-thirty tomorrow morning. Do you know where we are?'

'Yes. We have seen the children playing through the fence.'

The woman nodded. 'Excellent. And with Elizabeth and Mathias taken care of, you can find yourself a job. The State encourages both parents in a family to work. I know the workroom over on the Spandauer Strasse is looking for machinists. Can you sew?'

'Err … yes. I make the children's clothes.'

The woman stood up. 'Good. I'll tell them to expect you to call on them. We will see you tomorrow.'

With this abrupt exchange, Elizabeth's life changed again. The next day Sabine braided her hair and helped her into her very best dress, white socks and black shoes and took her to kindergarten.

It was big and loud and busy. The woman who had come to see them took her from Sabine at the door. She had no time for a goodbye hug or a word of encouragement. She was teamed up with a girl called Petra, who was the same age but who had been attending kindergarten since she was three. Petra showed her where to put her bag and where the toilet was and where to sit. She was a smiley girl, and when Elizabeth felt lost she squeezed her hand and whispered 'Stick with me' in her ear. Elizabeth decided she liked Petra very much and announced to her parents that night that she had a friend.

For a thirty-minute period twice a day they had a structured lesson, and Elizabeth found it fascinating. It changed every day, on rotation. Sometimes they talked about approved literature, or did maths and counted up to twenty, or talked about scientific things, like weather or the sky or stars or rocks, or made music and sang or did craftwork or played a team sport. All of these things she loved, and she caught up very quickly to the other children.

But sometimes they had an introduction to Socialist life, and that meant visiting factories or learning about traffic or reading from approved history books and repeating phrases from Socialist pioneers, and this she didn't like so much.

She watched Mathias doing his homework at the table. Whereas she had playtime and a few lessons, he did lessons and a little playtime. However, Elizabeth decided she was going to enjoy school, too.

Sabine went to the workroom and was asked to sew a demonstration piece, then was hired on the spot. She worked, as Peter did, a forty-three-and-three-quarter-hour week, excluding breaks, and had to queue for groceries on the way home. All four of them were so exhausted by the end of the day that they simply ate their dinner and went to bed. Sunday was their only day off, from work, school and kindergarten, and they treasured it.

The western sector was just a stroll or a tram-stop away; in some places you only needed to cross the street. So Sunday was the day they went to the American or French or British sectors by tram and had a fancy lunch, looked in the shop windows, and played in beautiful playgrounds. Sunday was the day of laughter and sunshine in summer and snow to play in in winter, swings and slides and luscious cake and Coca-Cola or hot chocolate. While they were enjoying themselves, they had no idea that they were part of half a million people who crossed from the east to the west and back again every day.

After Christmas 1948, just before her seventh birthday, Elizabeth brought home a notice from kindergarten inviting all of the families to watch a youth rally march through the streets to the Brandenburg Tor. She and Mathias were desperate to go, so their parents agreed. They got there early and found a good vantage point. Her father lifted both children up onto a statue on a street corner so they could see both ways. It was the most exciting thing Elizabeth had ever seen.

'Look, Lizzie, a marching band!' Mathias screeched with excitement as he pointed up the crowded street.

Next were rows of drummers, all in perfect time. Then came the girls in their blue shirts and black skirts followed by the boys in their blue shirts and black trousers. They looked so smart and so joyful that they made her heart jump. These were the FGY, Free German Youth. They were Party members, seen as the future by the party élite. She and Mathias looked at each other and nodded, she knew they were both thinking the same thing. *One day, I'll join them. I'll be a Socialist Party member and I'll march with the FGY!*

CHAPTER TWENTY-EIGHT

Berlin

February 1950

By the time she turned eight, Elizabeth had only vague memories of the farm. She was a true city girl. She adored school and worked diligently at her lessons six days a week. Sabine supplemented her school home education classes with Sunday cooking sessions, and was teaching her what her job as a machinist entailed.

They still went to the western sector every second Sunday, but Elizabeth and Mathias had become critical of what they saw there. They lectured their parents about the motherland and the Great Father Stalin, and some of their comments about the decaying West caused Sabine and Peter to glance at each other in consternation. There was nothing they could do about it; the school influence was all-consuming and children were encouraged to inform on parents who disagreed with the Party line. Elizabeth was counting down the months until she could join Mathias in the Pioneers, children in uniform who went door-to-door to collect paper, glass and rags for recycling.

The one thing her parents insisted upon was adherence to their Lutheran faith. Peter read the Bible aloud in the evenings, they said grace before meals and prayers before bed, and the whole family attended services at the old church down the road. Bombed by the Allies, it was still partly covered with a tarpaulin and was very cold in winter, but the altar was untouched and there were enough pews for the worshippers.

Elizabeth had never seen her father as angry as when Mathias told him that Karl Marx said religion was the opium of the masses and that his teachers said that the abolition of religion would lead the way from the illusion of happiness to real happiness. So she never commented on the services, she sang the hymns and listened to the sermons, but her parents suspected that when she was old enough to make up her own mind she would decide to stay away.

Peter used to tell them about what the Tiergarten was like before the war, a huge park full of trees. But much of it had been deforested due to the extreme need for fuel, and it wasn't nearly as pretty now.

Likewise he told them about the zoo his parents used to take him to every year on his birthday, but most of the animals had died in the bombing and the buildings had been at least partially demolished. When she looked around her at the devastation, Elizabeth hated the Allies for dropping all those bombs, although she understood that much of what Herr Hitler had done was evil. They didn't refer to him as the Führer at school, just Herr Hitler, the devil at the heart of the Nazi menace. It felt to her as if this city was waiting to be reborn, to rise from acres of debris and burned-out husks of buildings.

Their first encounter with tragedy started like any other Sunday. The four of them caught the train to the border, walked across the street and then caught a western-sector tram. One moment they were all holding hands and waiting to cross the road, and the next Mathias was pointing to a flagpole down the street where two soldiers were raising an American flag.

'I hate that flag! It shouldn't be allowed here,' he said.

Peter let go of his hand and reached into his pocket. 'Why would you say that? If it hadn't been for the Americans the Nazis would have won the war —'

'The Soviet Army won The Great Patriotic War! You know that, Father,' Mathias exclaimed, his twelve-year-old face full of exasperation.

Peter lit a cigarette and Sabine looked across Elizabeth to Mathias. She was cross. 'Now, dear, don't —'

He wasn't interested in hearing what his mother had to say. Without warning he broke away from them and ran down the pavement towards the soldiers.

'Mathias! Come back here, now!' Sabine's voice was a mixture of anger and fear. 'Don't just stand there, Peter — go after him.'

Peter looked at her with a helpless expression. 'I can't run,' he said.

Mathias reached the corner and ran blindly across the road towards the flagpole. An open American truck, with soldiers sitting in the back, came around the corner and ploughed straight into the young boy, sending his body hurtling up the bonnet, into the windscreen and then arcing into the air like a rag doll.

Sabine let out a terrible scream. '*No!*'

The impact and the sudden braking of the truck sent the soldiers in all directions on top of each other. The driver leapt out and ran towards Mathias, who lay in a crumpled heap on the road.

All three of them started to run. Peter, the slowest, was left behind almost immediately. By the time they reached the intersection, the driver was holding Mathias's broken frame in his arms. He looked up at Sabine as she threw herself onto the ground beside him.

'I'm so sorry, Ma'am. I didn't see him. He just ran out in front —'

Sabine grabbed at Mathias. 'No! Wake up, my beautiful boy. You're all right, Mama's here.'

She stroked his blond hair, matted with blood and bone. Blood was flowing from the head wound onto her dress and pooling on the street. The sound of a siren split the air. People were gathering around the couple by the time Peter reached them. He pushed his way through. Elizabeth stood by the truck. She had felt numb while she was running, but now the tears burst from her. She wasn't to know it at the time, but she would see her brother's body cartwheeling through the sky whenever she closed her eyes for years to come.

Their grief was intense. An investigation by the American Army ruled that the driver was not to blame; he could not have stopped in time. It was Mathias's fault: he had run across the road without a thought for traffic. Peter blamed himself for letting go of the boy's hand and arguing with him. Sabine turned her grief into an illogical hatred of all things American. She refused to buy anything from their stores or set foot in the American sector ever again. Elizabeth threw herself into her schoolwork and a renewed dedication to her Socialist beliefs. The West had taken her brother and the heartbreak she saw in her parents fuelled her resentment. They shut themselves into the apartment, leaving it only for work and school. Mathias's room was left exactly as it had been that morning when they had set off for their day in the west. Winter gave way to spring and then summer.

One Saturday night in June, Peter made a suggestion at the dinner table. 'I read in the newspaper that the department store on the Wittenbergplatz has just reopened two floors.'

'Where is it?' Sabine asked.

'In the British sector. They plan to rebuild it completely. I wondered whether it might be a nice idea to go and have a look, tomorrow.'

There was a silence.

Elizabeth looked at her mother. 'Could we, Mother?' she asked.

Sabine smiled at her. 'We haven't been out for a long time. Maybe a little trip might do us good. We could have lunch in a café.'

Peter reached across the table and squeezed his wife's hand. 'Perhaps a new dress, one for each of my girls, might be in order.'

It felt quite strange to be out and about again. Elizabeth loved the sun on her face. Even though there was a hole in their hearts and she held both her parents' hands instead of her mother's and Mathias's, it still felt like a family.

Just as they were crossing the square from the U-Bahn station, heading towards the massive grey building, her father stopped in his tracks. She nearly fell over with the sudden pull on her hand.

'What is it, Father?' she asked, looking up at him. He was very pale. In one fluid movement he swept her up in his arms and turned back towards the station.

'Over there,' he muttered to Sabine.

Her gaze followed his outstretched finger. 'Oh, good God! Hurry!'

Elizabeth could hear the panic in her voice. What had they seen? Peter couldn't carry her for very long and when he put her down both parents grabbed a hand each.

'This way, darling: quickly, back on the train,' he said.

'But why?' She knew her frustration was obvious.

'We'll go back into town and buy some ice-cream and some sweets,' her mother said as they pulled her down the steps and onto the platform.

No one said anything during the train ride, but her parents exchanged regular glances and also scanned the compartment. What were they so afraid of?

After an ice-cream, a packet of sweets and another train ride, they reached the apartment. The atmosphere was still tense. Elizabeth could see that her mother was trying to hide her distress.

'Elizabeth, I'd like you to go and read in your room for a little while. Will you do that for me?' her father asked as he gave her a kiss on the cheek.

She hugged him. 'Of course. Can I help cook dinner, Mother?'

Her mother smiled at her. 'Paprika schnitzel?' Sabine asked.

Elizabeth clasped her hands together. 'Oh, yes please!'

Once she had left the room, Peter closed the door and hugged his wife.

'It was her, wasn't it?' Sabine asked in a small voice.

'Yes, it was.'

'And she would have recognised us, and Elizabeth,' she added.

He nodded. 'She was a bright woman, Maria Weiss, and even though she is older and maybe her eyesight isn't what it was, she would have realised the truth with a glance.'

Sabine pulled away. 'I can't lose her, Peter. I'll go insane if I lose her, too ... What do we do now?'

He went to the window, raised the curtain and looked out at the street below.

'What is it?' she asked.

He came back to her. 'I've been thinking about our life here. That school she goes to, the nonsense in her head. She's turning into a little Socialist. I don't like it.'

His voice was low and his tone was cautious. Sabine just nodded, so he continued.

'I think we have three choices. We move to one of the western sectors and take our chances at getting new jobs —'

'You have heard what they say on the radio: there are no jobs in the west. And the people come here to shop!' she couldn't help but interject.

He could see that his words scared her. 'Yes, I know, but how much of that is true? How much is propaganda?'

She raised a finger to her lips. 'Shhh. Quietly, darling.'

'Or we move further away, into West Germany. Munich or Bonn or Frankfurt?'

She shook her head. 'And do what? We have to provide for her.'

'I'm a qualified bricklayer now. There has to be work in most cities. Just look at the bomb damage. And you're a machinist. People need clothes.'

'That's only two choices,' she said quietly, and the look on her face told him that she dreaded the third option.

'Or … we get right away and start again. I read an article the other day about Australia. They want German immigrants, strong people who can work and want to get ahead. It's warm and the sun shines and there's lots of food and no Socialist government.'

She sat down. '*Australia?*'

'It's worth thinking about, Sabine. No one would ever find us there and it would be a completely new beginning, no bomb-damaged buildings or bad memories.'

He stood and watched her, waiting for the arguments and the fear. She picked up Elizabeth's stuffed rabbit, which had been lying on the floor at her feet, and stroked it. Finally, she looked up at him.

'We were at war with them. Why would they welcome us?' she asked.

'We helped, remember? We gave extra milk and we hid people in our barn. We did what we could to resist the Nazi regime, and neither of us are happy under Socialist rule. I think that would count for a lot. They are intelligent people; they won't brand all Germans as Nazis.'

'You fought in the German Army,' she said in a matter-of-fact tone.

'I did what I was commanded to do. I won't be the only person applying who fought in the war.'

'We'd have to leave our son behind.' Her voice was flat, as if speaking of the subject hurt her.

'He's not here, you know that. He's with God in Heaven. For us, he is in our hearts and he will go wherever we go.'

She nodded.

'That's true, and it is the best way to keep Elizabeth safe. How do we do it?'

He took a deep breath. 'We pack up, just suitcases again. We take the train to Delmenhorst and we apply there. If we are accepted, we get on another train to Bremerhaven and we board a ship.'

'There's nowhere to apply in Berlin?' she asked.

'No. And if anyone hears what we want to do, they could arrest and interrogate me. Elizabeth would be a pariah at school, and we could both lose our jobs and be registered as asocial. I could be sent down the mines.'

She shuddered. 'It's a hell of a risk, Peter. What if they don't want us?'

'Then we try somewhere else. Canada, Britain, New Zealand. They are all looking for European migrants who will learn English and work hard.'

'We don't speak English!'

'They give you lessons on the boat, and when you get there they put you into a nice hotel place and they teach you what you need to know while you get a job. If we went now, it would be nearly summer by the time we got there.'

'You read all this?'

He nodded. 'They quoted people who had gone and they said it was wonderful, the best thing they ever did. If we stay here, we will look over our shoulders for the rest of our lives. We'll see that bloody old woman in every shop window. If she finds us, she'll tell those men and they'll come for Elizabeth —'

'No! I couldn't bear that!'

He pulled her to her feet and embraced her. 'Neither could I. You and she mean the world to me. She's our daughter, our princess. So we need to make her safe.'

He brushed the tears from her cheeks and she smiled weakly at him.

'I would kill to keep my baby safe.'

Elizabeth listened to her parents without interruption. Someone wanted to report her father to the authorities, to accuse him of treason. They might believe that person and take him away and interrogate him and torture him and throw him in jail. He hadn't done anything wrong, but that didn't matter. She had seen it happen to the families of children she went to school with, so she knew that they were telling her the truth.

Then they got out the atlas and showed her Australia and told her about the sun, the beaches and the plentiful food. But most of all they told her that her father would be safe and they could build a house and find better jobs and she could go to a school. If they had room, they would even get her a pony to ride. Secretly she wondered why they thought they could bribe her with a horse when all she cared about was her father's safety, but she didn't bother asking them that, she just agreed to the plan.

Peter and Sabine had withdrawn all their savings from the bank over several days. The next Sunday they packed a suitcase each and made a picnic lunch, caught the U-Bahn to the main train station and bought three train tickets for Delmenhorst. No one asked them why or tried to stop them.

The building that housed the Australian Immigration Department offices was called 'Canberra' after Australia's capital city. The process, which began the day after they arrived, was remarkably straightforward. Peter filled out an application form and they all had their photos taken. Then they had separate interviews, Peter by himself, and Sabine with Elizabeth. The officials asked both adults questions about their educational qualifications, their language capabilities, their employment history, their political history and war service record, and their proposed employment in Australia. Their processing sheet would show that the interviewer wrote 'altogether a nice-sounding family'.

Then they had comprehensive medical checks, tests on their hearts, blood pressure, sight, hearing, lungs, teeth, and so on. The medical examiner paid close attention to Peter's leg wounds, but agreed that they had healed and didn't stop him laying bricks or working with his hands.

Whenever they saw wild-eyed, terrified people yelling and arguing with the officials, Elizabeth's parents soothed her, removing her as quickly as they could. Her father explained that some of the applicants had been in concentration camps, and the interviews and medical checks were too much for them to stand. They were petrified that they were going to be interred again. Likewise, some of them reacted to being given a number; one frightened Elizabeth by starting to scream about being tattooed again.

Finally, the Gunthers were each given an identification number and accepted as immigrants. The departure hall at Delmenhorst was so huge that Elizabeth was scared that she would lose her parents in the crowd.

Peter, Sabine and Elizabeth had a four-bunk cabin on the MS *Nelly* which sailed out of Bremerhaven. For many years Elizabeth could close her eyes and see that little cabin, the striped sheets and the blue-checked blanket, a wooden dresser, a white china basin with gold taps, wall-mounted lights and a narrow shelf for ornaments.

They could walk the deck and go into the saloon where they could play cards, sew or read. Peter taught Elizabeth how to play chess, and they all had daily English-language lessons.

Some of the words were very like German, but the sentences were hard and most of the grammar made no sense at all.

Elizabeth loved the library and found many books she hadn't previously been allowed to read because they were on the banned list in East Germany. Some were adventure stories set in lands over the ocean, some were history books about life before the war, and one was a book about travel in America. It seemed extremely dangerous to her, with its ideas of the pursuit of liberty and independent thought. She was a little afraid to be caught reading these books, hiding them under her cardigan whenever an adult came near.

The passengers who spoke German gravitated towards one another and made friends. Elizabeth found one boy who was a year older than her and had come from East Berlin with his parents.

She tried to discuss home with him, but he was not a Party member and didn't approve of the lack of freedom they'd had. This surprised and perplexed her. She hadn't felt that her freedom was limited in any way, but when she discussed it with her father he explained what life was like in the rest of Germany and introduced her to the concepts of 'individuality' and 'choice'. She couldn't help thinking that if she had expressed these opinions at school she would have been severely reprimanded and given fail marks on her tests, no matter that she passed everything with ease.

When they hit rough seas, she would lie in her bunk and listen to the groans and creaks of the ship, sounds at a deeper pitch than the familiar throb of the giant steam engines. Slowly the days passed and their new beginning grew ever closer. She read and practised her English, and entered a chess competition. Just when she thought it would never happen, a buzz went through the whole ship: land! A new life!

The MS *Nelly* docked at Station Pier in Melbourne on 26 September 1950. Peter tried to find out where their hotel was, where they would stay until he found work and a house for them to live in. However, the immigration official found him impossible to understand and had to get a translator. When he heard the question, he roared with laughter.

'Tell him I'm here to issue him with an Alien Registration Card, one for each of them. They will need to register every change of address they make for the next ten years.'

Once the cards had been filled in and signed, the man waved them towards a bus. 'This will take you to your accommodation.'

With genuine relief they took their suitcases and boarded the bus. It delivered them to a train station. Again, Peter tried to find out where the hotel was. Again, the official found a translator.

'Tell them they will travel north on a train for a whole day to the Bonegilla Migrant Reception and Training Centre. Welcome to Australia.'

CHAPTER TWENTY-NINE

Bonegilla
September 1950

'What on earth is this place?'
Sabine's voice was a mixture of despair and horrified astonishment. They had put their bags down in the middle of a small cubicle in a concrete-and-fibrolite shack. It had three single beds.

'Your first stop, a migrant-holding facility,' said the man who was holding the door open.

'Where do we use the bathroom?' Peter asked.

The man pointed across the courtyard to a larger building made of the same material. 'Communal showers and lavatories,' he said.

'How long do we stay here?' Sabine asked.

The man shrugged. 'Sometimes the men go away to work on farms in the area, picking tomatoes and asparagus and the like. The women and children stay here until the men find permanent jobs and appropriate accommodation. Or you may all be sent somewhere farther afield together.'

'Is there work?' Peter asked.

The man nodded. 'Plenty. Your papers say you're a bricklayer.'

It was Peter's turn to nod. The man smiled and stretched out his hand. 'Learn English fast, my friend, and you could all be out of here in a matter of weeks.'

Peter shook the hand. 'Many thanks,' he said.

'You're welcome.'

The man turned to go, and stopped at the door. Elizabeth was staring at him, her eyes big, round and frightened.

'Welcome to Australia, little one. You'll like it here,' he said.

The facilities at Bonegilla were very basic, but adequate. The displaced persons had been given canvas sheets and a blanket, and put into long dormitories, to sleep on wire camp beds with no mattresses.

The smaller huts, divided into cubicles for families like the Gunthers who had paid their own way, were corrugated and unlined, and there were huge gaps in the floor boards. Sabine told her husband that it would be terribly cold in the winter so he had to find them a home before the end of summer.

They mingled with the other families and practised speaking English whenever they could. Every day there were lessons about the country, the culture, the animals and the language. And as the summer wore on she was amazed at how hot it became. Her mother made her a swimming costume, and she went swimming with other children at a nearby natural pool.

Christmas came and went, feeling very strange on such a hot day. They all had a barbeque by the water hole, and the locals played cricket. It was baffling! Then the men took a football and had a kick-around. Elizabeth sat beside her father and held his hand as they watched.

'When I was your age, I played football,' he said.

'Were you good?' she asked.

'I was brilliant! I scored goals.'

Sabine sat down and wiggled her finger at Peter. 'English!' she scolded.

'Father played … football,' Elizabeth said in English.

'I was … gut, *good* at running,' Sabine said.

'Thanks to Herr Hitler, I can't do either of those things,' Peter said.

Sabine patted his shoulder. 'Maybe not, but you can speak English!'

Finally Peter was placed as a bricklayer on a construction site in Melbourne. He promised to find them accommodation as soon as he could afford it and left by train. Elizabeth cried all the way back to the camp in the bus, and would not be consoled no matter what her mother said.

That night they sat outside under a tree and waited for the sun to set. The air was filled with the sounds of animals, birds, insects and frogs.

'I wonder what my school friends are doing,' Elizabeth said suddenly.

Her mother brushed her hair off her face. 'Where?' she asked.

'At home.'

'This is home now. You tell me, in English, what you think the children at your old school are doing.'

Elizabeth frowned and gathered her thoughts. 'It is the day after ... Monday. It is ... Tuesday.'

'So what is time in Berlin?' Sabine asked in English.

'The time,' Elizabeth corrected her. 'What is *the* time in Berlin?'

'Very good.'

She smiled up at her mother. 'We are in front of Berlin. It is Tuesday morning. My friends are at ...'

She screwed her face up, trying to remember the word. 'School. I do not know what they are studying.'

'Good girl! Remember what Father said: we are to speak English whenever we can. It is the only way to learn.'

Elizabeth sighed. 'It gives me a headache,' she said in German.

Peter wrote to them about the boarding house he lived in and all the different nationalities that surrounded him. They all tried to speak English because that was the only way they could communicate, and he even practised with his two German friends. The building site was in the west of Melbourne. The standards were higher than at home; everything was reinforced and measured to make sure it was compliant, and the bosses double-checked that you weren't going to have an accident when you were working at height.

He was very impressed with the way people weren't allowed to take unofficial breaks. Unlike in East Germany no one was slowing them down to make sure the job lasted as long as possible; they were encouraged to work efficiently and quickly. The work was long and hot in the summer sun, but he liked it and the boss seemed pleased with how much he got done. He was saving his money and had looked at houses in the neighbouring suburb, so he knew how much he needed. He sent them all his love and missed them very much.

Elizabeth wrote back, telling him about her lessons, and how she had graduated from reading picture books in English to reading books with fewer pictures and more words. She made lists of words she didn't know, and looked them up in her English-to-German dictionary. In two weeks she would turn nine and had made her birthday wish: for them all to be reunited.

Three days before Elizabeth's birthday, one of the camp officials called Sabine into the reception area to take a telephone call. It was Peter. He had just paid his rent in advance and his bond and taken possession of the keys to their new house. Sabine and Elizabeth were to catch the train from Bonegilla tomorrow to Flinders Street Station, and he would be there to meet them. Sabine wept with joy.

When Sabine told her the news, Elizabeth too burst into tears and they hugged each other tight. The dream was coming true: very soon they would have their own house, with their own bathroom and bedrooms and a kitchen. It had been four long years since Sabine had lived in a full-sized house and had no restrictions on the food she could feed her family. This, at last, was freedom.

CHAPTER THIRTY

Yarraville
The 1950s

The house was a wooden single-storey bungalow with a tile roof. It was painted white with blue wooden windowsills. There was beautifully carved fretwork around the front veranda that reminded them of some of the houses in Germany.

It was dry and clean and fully furnished. Elizabeth's room was on the left of the front door, and the sitting room was on the right. She had a comfy bed and a dressing table with a mirror and a built-in wardrobe. It was bliss, and she went around examining everything and counting the rooms. She had absolutely no idea how hard it had been for her father to find someone prepared to rent a house to a German and with neighbours who also didn't object.

Sabine got a job at a knitwear factory, where she worked for a year before buying her own machine and setting up work in their third bedroom. She earned more as an outworker, and was there for Elizabeth when she got home from school. Nothing would have persuaded her to share with her family how intimidated she had been by some of her fellow factory workers. One woman had lost her husband during the fighting in North Africa, and her favourite trick was to put a harmless, but enormous, spider in Sabine's wool box.

Within six months of the machine's purchase, she was working with three different designers, taking their instructions and turning them into patterns for knitting machines. As the years passed she became an expert in her field and was earning three times the average weekly wage of a machinist. Sometimes she stopped and said a silent prayer of thanks to the bully and the spider.

Peter worked hard as a bricklayer, was promoted to foreman and then site manager. Eventually, he left the company and started his own business, project-managing the construction of houses and small commercial buildings. His reputation for excellent work, attention to detail, fair prices and flexibility spread, and he was booked up for months in advance. He was the planner and his 2-I-C managed the men; they made a good team and ran a successful business.

They spoke German at home, especially when Sabine wasn't there, and English only when they had guests or were outside the house. Over time their diet adapted to the lack of spice, as Sabine found it hard to get garlic, paprika or any of the Italian herbs she was used to cooking with. Meat was boiled, roasted or fried with little additional flavouring, and vegetables were boiled excessively.

The range of sweets was more limited than Elizabeth remembered from the stores in Berlin, but the chocolate was very good, made with rich cow's milk and flavoured with nuts. The children she met at school drank Coca-Cola rather than apple juice. Peter told Elizabeth she was lucky to have two cultures, but her experiences made her doubt this.

In fact, school was the only part of Elizabeth's new life that she found a struggle. She had just turned nine and was actually ahead of her new classmates in many subjects, but she was used to being schooled in her mother tongue. Hearing, translating and understanding took time and energy, and to start with she came home absolutely exhausted.

But it didn't take long, and within months she was a fluent English-speaker and could cope with most written texts. Because of her years under the Soviet education system, her concept of the world, how the natural world worked, and the creative brilliance of mankind was light years ahead of her Australian schoolmates.

The first time she heard her teacher criticise a government policy she was astonished and afraid. The idea of complete freedom of speech and thought was totally alien to her, and no amount of reassurance from teachers and her parents could convince her that official spies wouldn't come and arrest her if she transgressed. When the teacher told her that there was, indeed, more than one political party and her parents had a choice of whom to vote for, she wanted to know how the government got the outcome it required.

It was all very confusing and, even though everyone told her it was a better system than Socialism, she wasn't sure. The first time she repeated phrases from the Socialist pioneers, maxims to live by which she had gladly memorised, the other children laughed at her.

With her new understanding of the idioms of the English language, she realised what the local kids were saying. It started when she was waylaid by a group of girls from the class a year above her. They circled her and stared.

'What's the matter?' she asked and tried to smile encouragingly.

'Vot. What sort of word is "Vot"? Can't you say your "W"?' one asked.

'Does your house smell?' Another pointed at her. 'I bet it does. I bet it smells of cabbage and vinegar and potatoes.'

She scowled back. 'Does yours smell of boiled mince?' she retorted.

'Ohhh, look here, she has claws. You're one of *them*. Of course you'd be nasty.'

'One of who?' she asked, genuinely surprised.

'You're a Nazi. My dad says most of the Krauts who have come here are Nazis. Running away from justice.'

Elizabeth glared at her. 'Well, your dad is an idiot.'

The girl raised her fist, but another caught her arm. 'We're only saying what everyone else thinks but are too polite to say.'

Elizabeth swung around and faced the girl who had made the comment. She could feel heat rising in her face. 'Actually, we had a farm and we gave extra milk to feed people who were hiding from the Nazis, and we hid people in our barn. Jews. It was very dangerous — if we had got caught we would have been sent to the camps.'

There was a moment's silence. 'So you didn't get caught?' one of them asked.

She shook her head. 'No, but we did have to run away to Berlin and we lived in a pokey apartment there.'

The girl who had spoken first turned her back and started to walk away. 'Come on, leave her alone,' she said.

Some of them glowered at her, and one hissed 'Na-ZI' as she reluctantly turned away. Elizabeth watched them run off. She was shaking and her body felt as if every fibre was tingling. On her way home she decided not to say anything to her parents.

For the rest of her school life she was intermittently bullied. Months would pass and nothing would happen, and then someone would start a campaign. Classmates would whisper 'Jew murderer' at her as they passed by, or when she went to the toilet a group would stare at her and someone would say, 'You let them get away with the small things and they think you're fair game, those bloody Krauts.'

Sometimes she made friends, and then parents intervened and she was told that 'Mum says you're one of them.' When she asked what 'one of them' meant, the child had no idea but further friendship was forbidden.

Once she reached high school she got used to taking the long way home, sometimes two buses out of her way, to avoid the gangs of bullies who looked for kids to pick on. The worst were those who had lost a parent or a close relation during the war. They hated her with a vengeance she could not comprehend. One of these kids was responsible for covering her locker with swastikas. When her father's photograph appeared in the paper after he won an industry award, another child covered copies with a Hitler moustache and swastikas and the caption *Wanted: A Nazi, for war atrocities*, and posted them around the school. The principal offered to apologise to her parents, but she declined; she didn't want them to know what she put up with.

Elizabeth wasn't the only German child, and there were Italians and a few Russians, but their homelands had fought the Germans, too. The children of those who had fought the Allies suffered far more abuse than the children of those who had fled the Nazis, children who were Polish, Czech, French or British immigrants.

No matter what she tried, she was an outsider, and the accompanying guilt and shame never left her. Her parents had both Australian and German friends but she restricted her circle to a few of her parents' friends' children; they seemed to understand her. When she reached the age where World War II was part of the history curriculum she was asked whether she wanted to attend those lessons, and when she said she did, the teacher asked for comments from the children who had lived through the recent events. She said nothing. Experience had taught her to keep her mouth shut.

On more than one occasion people painted swastikas and the words 'Nazi' or 'Kraut go Home' on the house. She would come home to find her mother scrubbing the paint off, and without a word she would get changed and join in the task.

By the time she left school she had grown into a studious, quiet, reserved teenager with blue eyes and deep auburn-coloured hair that hung to her waist. She was five foot eight, long-limbed and graceful, but her height made her feel conspicuous, so she would try to minimise her size by wearing flat shoes and stooping slightly. Her mother was forever telling her to stand up straight and be proud of her body, but it didn't help.

After graduation she worked in a local café for a few months while she decided what she wanted to do with her life. Her father was keen for her to train as a teacher, but the thought of spending any more time in an educational institution filled her with dread. Then again, if she went to a secretarial college and learned to be a secretary, she could help him in the business.

One day in early 1960 she got a call from her mother. Her father had been taken to the Royal Melbourne Hospital in an ambulance. It took her a while to find the hospital in Parkville, and then find out where her father had been taken. Her mother was sitting in a large waiting room and rushed to embrace Elizabeth.

'What's happened to him?' Elizabeth asked.

Sabine's face was tear-stained and pale. 'He had a heart attack, on the site. They called an ambulance, and they revived him and brought him here.'

The shock hit her like a blow to the stomach. A heart attack? Her strong, fit father who could still lift her off the ground?

'How ... Have ... Do you know how he is?'

Sabine shook her head. 'No. They said to wait here and they would come and see me when they could. That was an hour ago.'

Elizabeth put her arm around her mother's shoulders. 'Come on, let's sit down. Do you want a cup of tea?' she asked.

'Yes please, dear, that would be lovely.'

She found the cafeteria and got two teas. Time passed. They sat in silence, occasionally comforting each other with the squeeze of a hand or a pat on the arm.

The swing door at the end of the room opened and a doctor in scrubs came striding towards them.

Sabine jumped to her feet. 'How is he?' she demanded.

The doctor didn't answer until he reached her. 'He's still alive, but he's had a major myocardial infarction. We've done all we can for the moment.'

'A what?' Sabine sounded confused.

Elizabeth put her hand on her mother's arm. 'A heart attack. Can we see him?' she asked the doctor.

He nodded. 'He's in cardiac intensive care. You can sit with him for a while if you like. He's not conscious.'

Her heart fell at those last words. Would he know they were there?

'This way,' the doctor gestured towards the doors.

The nurses worked around the two women who sat by Peter Gunther's bed. There wasn't much they could do for him. He didn't regain consciousness. Just after midnight, the alarm sounded and they rushed Sabine and Elizabeth away. Some moments later, the doctor joined them in the corridor.

'I'm sorry, Mrs Gunther, there was nothing we could do. He's had another massive heart attack, and he passed away five minutes ago.'

Sabine collapsed into her daughter's arms, sobbing. Elizabeth felt numb. Mother and daughter went in to farewell Peter separately, and when it was Elizabeth's turn she brushed the grey hair off his face and kissed the lined forehead.

'Thank you,' she whispered. He had never allowed her to call him anything other than 'Father', the title he thought proper. But now she could do what she liked and those rules fell away. 'You were so brave. I love you, Daddy, and I always will. I'll take care of Mother,' she said quietly in German.

* * *

The days passed in a blur. German and Australian friends came to see them and brought food, flowers and cards of condolence. The funeral was in the local Lutheran church where her parents had worshipped for nine years. People were very kind, and she was amazed to hear the words her father's employees said about him. He had built a new life, a good life, and he had worked extremely hard. Many people told her she should be proud to be his daughter, and she assured them that she was.

It helped to crystallise another thing in her mind. A week after her father was buried, Elizabeth told her mother that she had decided she wanted to be a nurse. So she applied to the Royal Melbourne Hospital and was accepted in the next intake as an undergraduate nurse.

CHAPTER THIRTY-ONE

Yarraville
The 1960s

Sabine was terrified of her grief; it felt like a deep hole of black water she couldn't even begin to dip her toe into. Their experience as an immigrant family had caused them to lean very heavily on each other, and, even though she had made friends, Peter was still the centre of her world.

Eventually, Elizabeth found being at home depressing, so she spent more and more time with new acquaintances, socialising close to the hospital and studying in groups. She missed her father a great deal, but she was used to keeping things to herself, so it was just another part of life to be parked in a compartment with the door firmly closed. When one of her best friends went flatting, she took the plunge and joined the household of five nurses living together. Sabine didn't seem to miss her company; she was too busy working.

Two years after her father died, Elizabeth met a cousin of one of her flatmates at a party. He was twenty-three and had transferred to Melbourne from Sydney for a promotion. He worked for a large finance company and his name was Karl Voight.

'Are you German?' she asked.

He was her height, with dark hair and brown eyes and he

wore metal-rimmed glasses. He had a serious face, but when he smiled he looked handsome in a way she didn't expect.

'No, I was born in Sydney.'

'It's a German-sounding name. Are your parents German?'

'Does it matter?' he asked.

He sounded defensive. She sipped her drink and gave a shake of her head. 'No, not at all. I'm German-born, although I've been here since I was eight.'

He smiled. 'My parents came out from Munich before the war. Dad's an architect and he was brought out to work on a particular project, and he liked it so much that he persuaded Mum to join him. They stayed.'

'Do you have brothers and sisters?' she asked.

'I was perfect, so they stopped at me.'

'We came from Berlin, East Berlin.'

Suddenly he was interested. 'So, what do you think of this wall?'

The massive wall had been erected a year earlier. The news reports and pictures of people escaping and the standoffs had made Elizabeth cry.

'I think it's sad,' she said.

'And unnecessary,' he added.

She frowned. 'Why do you say that? It's to protect the citizens of East Berlin from the remnants of the Nazis. The State calls it an Anti-Fascist Protection Rampart.'

He gave a scornful chuckle. 'You mean that Socialist bunch of élitist thugs who rule from Moscow? It's actually to stop the people from fleeing to the West for a better life.'

His words startled her; she hadn't discussed German politics for a very long time. Memories of her early schooling and the phrases she had repeated every day came flooding back.

'The aim of the State is to raise well-rounded and loyal citizens who would defend the motherland to the death,' she said.

He backed away. 'Wow! How many years did you have in the system?'

She hesitated. 'We left our farm when I was five, and we left Berlin for Australia when I was eight.'

'Why did you leave a farm to live in a bombed-out shell of a city?' he asked. He sounded intrigued.

'We helped some groups during the war, extra milk for starving children and the people in hiding. The local Resistance used our barn as part of their underground route. I can only assume that we were in danger of being arrested. We left quickly.'

He moved closer towards her. 'Now that *is* impressive. My parents were very anti-National Socialism, but they were out here by the time war was declared. I think that if they had stayed they would have actively resisted Hitler and quite possibly have died for it.'

She nodded thoughtfully. 'Do they miss it?' she asked.

'I think they did at first. I was born in 1939. The war years were hard for all of us. Officially Mum and Dad were "enemy aliens" but many people just called them "Nazi". No radios or telephones and they had the windows of their home smashed. Usual story, when they caught the bastards, the jury found them not guilty. My father protested and was interned for a while.'

She looked at him, and she knew he could see the sadness in her eyes. 'That's unfair. It's not easy being German in this country.'

He took her hand. 'I know what will cheer you up: dance with me.'

At the end of the night she gave him her telephone number and he called and asked her out on a date. They went to see *Lawrence of Arabia* at the local cinema. The next date was dinner and dancing, and then a picnic on Phillip Island.

She was cautious. He was her first real boyfriend and she didn't know how to handle the situation: she wanted to keep him at arm's length so that she wouldn't be hurt, but not so far away that she scared him off. She turned to some of her more experienced flatmates.

'He's lovely, Beth. You should encourage him!'

She laughed and gave Dorothy, her best friend, a light punch on the arm.

'And how do I do that?' she asked.

'Has he kissed you yet?'

She blushed. 'On the cheek. He's a gentleman.'

Dorothy scoffed. 'Well, you should definitely tell him that you would like a proper kiss, thank you very much!'

'I couldn't do that!'

'Oh for goodness' sake, Beth, it's 1962! Don't you listen to the music? Everyone is into free love and having a good time. Doesn't mean you let him go all the way, but it's time you knew whether he's a good kisser!'

Two nights later they walked hand-in-hand to Elizabeth's front door. She dug in her purse for her key.

'Beth?'

He took her hand. She looked at him and smiled. 'Yes?'

'Can I ask you a question?' he asked.

She frowned. 'I guess, so long as it's not too serious.'

'Are we … I mean … do you consider yourself to be my girlfriend?'

It was a hard sentence for him to get out, and she felt a sudden urge to burst out laughing — not at him, but for him. 'Yes, I do … Is that okay?'

His relief was tangible. 'It most certainly is!'

'Well then,' she put her hand out and touched his face, 'can I ask you a question?'

'Of course.'

'Would you like to kiss me, Mr Karl Voight?'

He smiled and she could see a slight blush. 'Very much, Miss Elizabeth Gunther.'

'Then go ahead.'

He took his time, gentle to start with, then pulling her into his arms and kissing her with more urgency. Finally, they stepped apart. He was embarrassed and ran his hand through his hair.

'Well, that's that settled,' she said. 'Please feel free to do that whenever you fancy.'

He laughed. 'You are funny, my Bethy Bunny.'

Over the next few weeks Karl became a regular at dinner with Sabine on a Monday night, and she decided that she liked him. He was sensible and ambitious and had a plan for his life, which appeared to include her daughter.

When they had some time off, Karl took Elizabeth by train to Sydney and introduced her to his parents, Greta and Karl senior. It took her about a minute to realise that Karl had grown up in a very different environment from hers. They seemed absolutely delighted that she was German.

The front room had two cuckoo clocks on the wall and numerous miniature and full-sized beer steins on the shelves. There was a bookshelf of German books above a stereogram, and a collection of German music records.

'Karl said you are more comfortable in English?' Greta asked as they took tea. Elizabeth nodded.

'Yes, please. I don't even speak German with my mother anymore.'

'That's sad. Does she miss it?'

'No. Life in Germany was a long time ago. She's very Australian.'

'Do you dance? Maybe the folk dances of the old country?' Greta asked, her eyes alight with possibilities.

Elizabeth shook her head. 'No. I do dance, but I've never done German dancing.'

The woman didn't seem to be listening to what she was saying.

'Come with me.'

Greta took her into their bedroom and showed her the wardrobe of costumes, genuine leather lederhosen and white blouses and embroidered dresses. The thought of them dressed this way nearly made her laugh out loud.

'There's a German society here and we go every week. They have wonderful meals of schnitzel and *spätzle* and proper German beer and dancing. You and Karl will have to come with us.'

Elizabeth felt her heart sinking. Obviously their negative experiences during the war hadn't put them off their heritage.

'That would be lovely,' she said.

Greta beamed. 'Karl said you spent your early years in East Berlin.'

'Yes, from the age of five until we left Germany when I was eight.'

Greta nodded. 'We have found what has happened to Germany very sad, watching from this distance,' she said.

Elizabeth felt as though she was being tested. Did she mean Hitler or East Germany, or both? Better to just agree, which for the most part she did. 'Yes, my parents helped the Resistance during the war, as much as they could.'

'Karl told us that! I must say it is very impressive, such brave people who did that. Tell me, my dear, do they believe in God, your parents?'

Aha, so this is where she's leading.

'My father died in 1960, but he did, very much. He read the Bible out loud at night, and my mother and I still go to our local Lutheran church.'

Greta stiffened ever so slightly. 'That's good. Ourselves, we are Catholic and our faith is important to us.'

But not so much to your son, Elizabeth thought to herself as she smiled dutifully.

* * *

The world was still reeling from the assassination of John Fitzgerald Kennedy when Karl Voight married Elizabeth Gunther in her local Lutheran church. His parents had wanted a Catholic service, but Sabine insisted that if it was to be a church wedding, it would be in Elizabeth's church. As a compromise, Elizabeth suggested that a Catholic priest be present and bless the couple. After considerable discussion, Sabine agreed to that.

It was a lovely day, with some concessions made during the reception to the German heritage, but not as many as Greta and Karl senior would have liked. Karl's parents suggested a honeymoon in West Germany, but it was cold there in December and Elizabeth used the weather as her excuse to request somewhere warm, so they went to Tahiti.

Karl had put a deposit down on a house just two streets away from the house Elizabeth grew up in. It was a modern home, brick and tile, with two storeys, three bedrooms, two bathrooms and a kitchen full of new appliances. Sabine gave them furniture as a wedding present and made new curtains for the windows. Greta and Karl senior gave them a very fine cuckoo clock and a fondue set. The week after her honeymoon Elizabeth walked around her house and realised that for the first time in many years she felt as though she truly belonged somewhere.

Karl was adamant that she didn't have to work and, as they planned to have a family, she should prepare herself for motherhood. She was going to argue with him but nature intervened and their first son was born a little under a year later. They named him Andrew Karl. Elizabeth knew that her in-laws were hoping for a more German Christian name — perhaps three generations of Karl — and were certainly hoping he would be brought up a Catholic, but neither of those things was going to happen. Elizabeth promised her husband that if they had more children, he could name the next one.

He was made a branch manager the same day she discovered that she was pregnant again, in 1968. This time it was a girl, and Karl lost no time reminding her of her promise. He announced his daughter would be Lisle Sabine. Everyone seemed thrilled with the choice, so Elizabeth smiled and agreed, vowing she would call her 'Sabby' when no one was listening.

Married life suited Elizabeth: she had a kind, generous husband who made her laugh, adored his family and earned a good wage; a home she could only have dreamed of as a child; two beautiful, healthy children; and the support of her husband in keeping the German mementoes her in-laws kept giving her in a box unless they were visiting. She couldn't imagine life being better or anything happening to cast a shadow over her world.

Then in 1970 Sabine became ill. It started with digestive problems and then pain, fatigue and weight loss, and when she finally went to a doctor it was quickly diagnosed as advanced pancreatic cancer. There was little that could be done except to keep her comfortable. Karl was happy to look after the children and give Elizabeth extra time to be with her mother, shop for her, clean her house, and sit and talk.

Elizabeth asked questions about the farm and their flight to Berlin. It was, as she had supposed, to keep a step ahead of the people who had wished Peter dead. And they reminisced about the apartments in East Berlin and the Sundays spent in the western sector; the sea voyage and the weeks at the camp in Bonegilla. Soon there would be no one left to share these memories with; it was the end of an era.

When Sabine moved into the hospital for her last days, Elizabeth spent every moment she could with her. In many ways they had never been closer. The pain relief induced a light coma and the bedside vigil began.

'Would you like a cup of tea?' Karl asked one afternoon as they sat by Sabine's bed.

Elizabeth looked up at him; he looked tired. She smiled. 'Yes, please. Then why don't you go home for a while and get some rest before Dorothy drops the kids off?'

He returned her smile. 'I'll rest when you do. Won't be long.'

The door closed quietly behind him. Elizabeth knew he was trying to be supportive, but really she would have liked to be on her own with her mother. Suddenly Sabine stirred and opened her eyes. Elizabeth got to her feet and bent over her.

'Hello, Mother,' she said softly. 'Do you want a sip of water?'

Sabine shook her head, her gaze fixed on Elizabeth's face. She raised her thin arm and gripped Elizabeth's collar. With all the strength that she could muster she pulled her daughter closer.

'Maria Weiss,' she said in a rasping, broken whisper.

'What? Who?' Elizabeth wasn't sure she had heard correctly.

'Maria Weiss,' Sabine said again, her voice stronger this time. Then she closed her eyes, released her grip and sank back onto the pillow.

Elizabeth watched her for several minutes: her breathing was regular and she seemed to have slipped back into the coma. Who? A name she had never heard before. She was assuming it was a name; it sounded like a name. She wanted to shake her mother and wake her up and demand to know what those words meant, but she couldn't. As she sat down again, the door opened and Karl stepped in with a paper cup in each hand.

'Here we are,' he said brightly.

She took the cup from him. 'Thank you. I really need this.'

He touched her arm and sat down beside her. 'I know. But remember what the doctor said, she's not feeling any pain.'

A day later, Sabine died.

CHAPTER THIRTY-TWO

Melbourne
September 2014

'Maria Weiss.'

Rafael sat very still and repeated the name. Elizabeth said nothing, but nodded her head.

'Did you ever try to find out who she was?' he asked.

'No. I didn't even know if she was a person.'

'Did you share it with Karl?'

She shook her head. 'I thought he might suggest we go back to Germany and try to find her, that she might be a relation of Mother's. You have to remember there was no internet, no Google, no easy way of finding anyone.'

'Who did you think she was?' he asked.

'Why would I have any idea? I just forgot all about it. And by then I had three young children, life was very busy.'

'The fact that your mother knew her name ties her to the letters, yes?'

Elizabeth said nothing.

'She must have brought them with her from Germany. That could have been difficult to explain, might have meant trouble. And yet she kept them.'

Still, Elizabeth said nothing.

Eventually, Rafael gave a sigh. 'Thank you for telling me

your story, and I can see by your son's face that he has heard much for the first time, yes?'

Kobi was slumped back in his chair, studying his hands. Elizabeth smiled at him, but he didn't look up.

'Yes,' she said.

'You have suffered, and some of that has to do with being German. But we live in a much more enlightened society now, you know; those attitudes are largely gone.'

'Have they? My husband died in 1996, of cancer. After the Berlin Wall came down and the country was reunified, he desperately wanted to see Germany and I told him to go on his own and experience it for himself. But he wouldn't, and then it was too late. The third time I visited his grave someone had painted a swastika on it.'

Kobi looked up sharply. 'You never told me that!'

She smiled at him. 'There was no need for you to know. I cleaned it off. All my life, being German has brought me nothing but heartache.'

'I had an uncle — you never told me that either!' His tone was defiant and she looked crestfallen.

'He was killed because we lived in a divided city. It was too painful to talk about.'

Rafael watched her for a long moment, and then he rubbed his face with his hand. 'I want to leave you with one more thought, Mrs Voight. Your mother, your biological mother, died in a gas chamber. She suffocated, she was murdered. The last thought she had was of you. You were the child she didn't abandon, you know; she put you somewhere to keep you safe. You are her legacy. If you reject that, reject her, then everything she believed in, lived and died for, is meaningless.'

The silence hung across the room like a blanket, weighed down by history, separating them from each other.

'She chose to stay with them, with my father, and not go with me,' Elizabeth said quietly.

Kobi shook his head. 'Read the letters again and study what happened to the circle. If she had gone with you to the farm, the Gestapo would have hunted her down. Someone in the circle would have given her name up under torture, and they would have come for her. Not only you, but the Gunthers would have died as well. She sacrificed her role as a mother to ensure that you would grow up.'

Elizabeth frowned. She seemed to be digesting his explanation.

Kobi moved in his seat. 'You do understand, Mother, that there was a point in 1947 when your life could have changed completely, don't you?' he asked gently.

'What do you mean?' She looked tired — more than that, exhausted.

'You do understand why Grandfather and Grandmother fled to Berlin now, don't you?'

For a moment she looked confused, and then a smile crossed her face as if the relevant fact had clicked into place. 'Of course. Mother told me, years later. There were men who wanted my father dead, because we had helped during the war. We supplied milk and a safe place to hide. We left because we had to.'

He shook his head and knelt down beside her. 'No. You left because they realised that you had blood relations still alive. I told you: Maria Weiss took Simon and Levi Horowitz out to the farm, and Peter Gunther told them that you were dead. If they hadn't believed him, had come back to check, they would have found you and taken you with them to America. Into your real family. Grandmother remembered Maria Weiss when she was dying because she had outwitted Maria and kept you for herself.'

It was obviously a shock. It was a piece of the puzzle she hadn't connected.

'No ...' Her voice trailed off.

Kobi put his hand on her arm. 'It's okay. They were doing what they thought was right, to make sure you stayed with them. I don't know for sure, but I suspect the person they saw that Sunday, when you went to the big department store, was Maria Weiss. She didn't see them, but the fact that they could bump into her at any time meant they had to leave Berlin.'

Her blue eyes were racked with pain and bright with tears. 'But I loved them!' she said.

'Of course you did, and they loved you. No one is asking you not to love them anymore,' he said.

Rafael stood up. 'Mrs Voight, you have much to think about, and I will leave your son and you to discuss this, yes? One suggestion I would make is that you don't have to accept the Horowitzs as family in order to go and meet them. They will understand that you loved your parents and that you don't consider yourself German anymore. You would have the right to walk away and come home whenever you chose.'

Kobi put his arms around her and hugged her.

'He's right, you know, it could just be a trip to DC and New York and Vermont, and to meet some people who could be friends.'

She hugged back tightly, and he held her until she felt ready to let go. Then she looked up at him and smiled. 'Now that, gentlemen, is a plan I could agree to!'

CHAPTER THIRTY-THREE

Vermont
Early October 2014

T he letter arrived from Nuremberg just before Kobi, Lisle
and Elizabeth were due to depart for the United States.
The crest was impressive. The writer was Philip von Hoch.

Dear Dr Voight
Thank you for your enquiry regarding the Albrecht
Dürer painting of my ancestor. The subject of the
painting was Paul von Hoch and it was painted in 1520.
Paul's grandson, Charles von Hoch, sold the painting
in 1585 to an Aaron Silverman, a cloth merchant in
Nuremberg. It was purchased because it was a Dürer,
and because the sitter reminded Mr Silverman of his
young grandson.
It is my understanding that the painting was passed
down through the Silverman family and was last
known in the possession of Levi Silverman's only child,
a daughter, Elizabeth, who married Benjamin Horowitz
and resided in Berlin. It was appropriated by the
Third Reich in 1939 and nothing has been heard of the
painting since.
I hope this helps with your research, and if you do
happen to come across any reliable information on the

*whereabouts of the painting, I would be most interested
to hear about it. Our family has no claim to it, but if
it were to come onto the market we would certainly
consider purchasing the painting.*

This confirmed what Kobi had suspected: the portrait was
painted for one of the great Catholic families of Bavaria, and
the sitter had no direct connection to the Jewish family who
had owned it when it was looted. He wondered how Simon
and Levi would react to this news. He certainly had every
intention of telling them.

After four gentle days of sightseeing and shopping around
New York and one Broadway show, they decided they were
over the jetlag and were ready to meet the Horowitzs. Kobi
rang Rafael, and he came back to them and said he would pick
them up early the next morning.

'He does understand, doesn't he, Jakob?' Elizabeth asked
anxiously.

'Yes, Mother, he does. He'll take you away anytime you
want to leave. He has a local motel booked in case you don't
want to stay with them, and then the next day he will bring
you back to New York.'

'And you will come with me?' She looked from Kobi to
Lisle.

'Yes, Mother, we will,' Lisle said, in as reassuring a voice as
she could muster. 'If you don't want to stay with them, we will
come with you.'

'Because I'm not going to see them as relations, just friends
because I happened to have had the letters their sister wrote.'
It was obvious she was talking to herself as much as to them.

'Everyone has accepted the conditions, Mother.'

She had brought a framed double picture of her parents, and
kept it on the table beside her hotel bed. Kobi knew she had

girded herself with as much emotional armour as she could, and he was determined to support her.

Rafael did everything he could to relax Elizabeth during the seven-hour drive north. Over lunch he extolled the virtues of classical music, and when they were on the road again he argued with Elizabeth over the correct order for a list of the top-ten best ever tenors and conceded defeat to her, entertained them with anecdotes from his 'what happens backstage, stays backstage' collection, and delighted Lisle with his knowledge of folk music.

Eventually, he pulled onto the side of the road, stopped the car and turned towards Elizabeth. She was in the front seat and her two children were in the back.

'We are nearly there and there is something I wanted to say to you. About Simon mainly. I know that experts will say our memories make us who we are and we can be defined by the past. But, you know, we must not forget to evolve and grow because some memories are very strong. So powerful that we can get stuck inside them and become frozen in that time. Simon will try very hard not to be overcome with his memories of the past, of Rachel, but it will be hard for him. So we will understand, yes?'

'Absolutely,' Kobi said.

Rafael was looking at Elizabeth.

She smiled at him. 'Understood, yes,' she said.

It was David and Daniel who greeted the guests when the car pulled into the driveway.

'Forgive my father and Feter Levi, they want to meet you inside,' David said to Elizabeth.

They all shook hands or exchanged hugs, and then followed father and son up the path and through the front door. Kobi and Lisle went in first and were warmly greeted by the two old men.

'Oh, dear girl,' Simon said when he took Lisle's hands in his, 'you have my chin. Look, Dan! You see he has it, too. How wonderful!'

Lisle laughed with delight and kissed him gently on the cheek. 'Simon, Levi, this is my mother, Elizabeth Voight,' she said.

Elizabeth stood in the doorway and looked at them, while they looked at her.

'Mama!' Simon exclaimed.

Levi walked forward and took both of her hands in his. 'You do look remarkably like our mama. Welcome to our home, Elizabeth. May we call you Elizabeth?'

Words failed her. He kissed her cheek and stood aside.

Simon took her hands. Then he reached up and touched her face with the palm of his hand. '*Shalom, toda raba, toda raba*,' he said softly.

Elizabeth looked confused. 'I ... I'm sorry, I don't speak Hebrew,' she said.

'He's saying welcome and thank you,' David explained, smiling at her, 'for coming.'

She leaned down and kissed Simon on each cheek. 'It's lovely to meet you, Mr Horowitz.'

His dark eyes flashed with amusement. 'Ha! None of this Mr Horowitz nonsense. I am your uncle, you call me Feter Simon. And this is your Feter Levi.'

Lisle tapped Kobi on the shoulder. 'So much for not mentioning the family relationship,' she whispered to him.

'Watch them take her over,' he replied.

And so they did. They led her to a sofa by the window and sat her down. Daniel brought her a cup of tea, and then David suggested that everyone else have a look around the garden. Kobi very nearly asked if they could see the painting instead, but decided that it was too soon. He hesitated at the door and wondered whether he should ask his mother if she was happy to be left, but Simon had fetched a shoebox and they were showing her the contents.

Elizabeth had built a formidable wall around her heart. She had spent time remembering her parents and her childhood in Australia, and had prayed that God would protect her from being hurt by these new forces that threatened to tear apart what she knew about herself. She had planned to sit to one side and listen and watch and let her children take the major part of the discussion, then thank the old men politely and take her leave.

All of that evaporated in a single second when her uncle touched her face and thanked her. Then he told her to call him '*Feter*' — Yiddish for uncle. She could actually feel the warmth spreading from her heart to her limbs, a sensation she had never felt before. It seemed as though a black cloud had rolled away and the sun poured down on her. She just didn't have the words to express what was happening.

They took her to the sofa and sat her down between them. Daniel brought her tea, just with milk as she liked it, without even asking her. Then Simon brought an old, battered shoebox from a cupboard and they showed her what was inside it. She held two miniature portraits of her grandparents, and couldn't get over her grandmother's hair. It was the same colour and texture as her own. Looking at her grandfather was like looking at her son, Andrew, in 1930s period dress. She grasped her grandfather's tortoiseshell comb and stroked it, then stared at photographs of her uncles as teenagers, no older than her grandsons, each holding a violin. There was a list of possessions written in German but the ink was so faded she couldn't read it, and two pencil drawings.

One drawing showed a tall man seated at the piano, and the other a younger, shorter man playing the violin. She turned over the first drawing and there was a poem written in her mother's handwriting, the same as the letters, but written in German. It talked about being free and singing prayers in a joyful voice and all being together in the Promised Land. Without warning, Elizabeth burst into tears.

CHAPTER THIRTY-FOUR

Vermont
October 2014

There was so much to say. The housekeeper had prepared a meal of schnitzel, bratwurst sausage, potato and sauerkraut, and Simon opened a bottle of Rhine Valley wine. Kobi told them all about what he knew of the 'Red Orchestra', the spy network Rachel had joined and his theory about Harro Schulze-Boysen being Elizabeth's father. Simon and Levi told Elizabeth what they remembered about Maria Weiss and some of the memories they had of her mother.

Then, as a special treat, Daniel got the Amati violin out of its case and played for them. The music was spellbinding. He played Bach, the allegro from the *Concerto in E*, and then told Elizabeth it was her grandfather's favourite piece of music and that Benjamin had played it for the guards in Dachau. This made her cry again.

Eventually, Kobi and Rafael took their leave and went to stay at the motel, David and Daniel retired for the night, and Lisle went to bed in the room she would share with her mother. Simon, Levi and Elizabeth sat up beside the fire and continued to talk. At some point the conversation changed from English into German.

258 • JULIE THOMAS

A few miles down the road, Kobi and Rafael had a last nightcap and reflected on the day.

'I didn't expect her to react like that,' Kobi said. 'I am surprised, I have to admit.'

Rafael smiled and sipped his scotch. 'She was determined to repel any emotional overtures, but in the end the power of family ties triumphed.'

'Were you surprised?' Kobi asked.

Rafael shook his head. 'Not really. It was what I had hoped would happen, but you can never tell with human nature. She is a strong woman.'

'Her rejection would have hurt them and she would have been upset by that; she's basically a kind person. She doesn't like causing people pain.'

Rafael sighed. 'So, who are we, Kobi? Are we the product of the people who bring us up and the things they teach us? Or are we, you know, pre-programmed to react like your mama did when we meet people who share our genes?'

'A very good question,' Kobi said.

'Someone should write a book about it — about Simon and Levi and finding your mama, yes?'

Kobi smiled at him. 'I do intend to write a book, but not about that.'

Rafael raised his eyebrows. 'Really? You went to Germany to start a book, I remember you saying that.'

Kobi took a long slug of his drink and didn't answer for a moment. 'Tell me, what do you think Simon would say if I told him that I want to write a book about his Dürer painting?'

Rafael frowned. 'I think he would say he would rather you didn't.'

'He knows it's the Paul von Hoch, so he knows how precious it is. What the art world would say if it becomes public knowledge.'

'And he sees that as a very good reason to keep it where it is —'

'But that's wrong! It's one of the cultural treasures of the world and it deserves to be displayed. The current von Hoch family would love to see it.'

'His reasoning is driven by fear. The fear of losing it again. When they look at it, they see their mama —'

'Well, they shouldn't.'

Rafael looked at him sharply. 'Why not?'

'She wasn't related to the sitter at all. Paul von Hoch's grandson sold it to a Nuremberg cloth merchant in 1585. Elizabeth Horowitz was a Silverman by birth. Simon and Levi are the direct descendants of the man who bought the painting.'

'He ... doesn't know this.'

'I have a letter from the von Hoch family, verifying the story behind the painting. They don't know that Simon and Levi have it, but they do know that the last authenticated owners were Elizabeth and Benjamin Horowitz. They think the family are all dead.'

'Are you going to tell them?' There was concern in Rafael's voice.

Kobi hesitated. 'That depends.'

'On what?'

'On what they say when we discuss the painting. I know that David is Simon's legitimate heir and that my mother is Rachel's illegitimate heir, and maybe that makes David's claim stronger, but surely we have some say in what happens to it?'

Kobi looked at Rafael. He was staring into his glass and swirling the liquid around inside it.

'It's not as if I want to sell it,' Kobi added. 'I just want to share it.'

Rafael looked up at him and smiled. For some reason Kobi thought he could see sadness in the older man's expression.

'I'm sure something can be worked out.'

* * *

The secret weighed heavily on Rafael's mind. He lay in the motel bed and wondered what to do. He wanted to pick up the phone and call Mags, tell her about his dilemma and ask her advice. But he couldn't do that. This was a very private matter. Kobi had said, *I know that David is Simon's legitimate heir and that my mother is Rachel's illegitimate heir, and maybe that makes David's claim stronger ...* But David wasn't Simon's legitimate heir; he was Levi's illegitimate son. Did that make his claim no greater than Elizabeth's, or was the fact that he was born in wedlock, just not conceived from Simon, enough?

If Rafael said nothing, everyone would assume that David had a stronger case. He wouldn't hurt Simon for the world, and this truth would devastate him. But then did Levi have a right to know? And David? Would it change David's relationship with Levi? He knew the answer to that; he had seen it today when Elizabeth met the people she was genetically linked to. All the conditioning in the world couldn't overcome the biological pull. Here he was, once again, playing God with the lives of these people who meant so much to him. Was it fair? Or was keeping quiet the greater sin?

The next day Rafael and Daniel returned to Washington DC. They would be back in a week, and would bring Cindy with them. David stayed to get to know his first cousin and to drive the car, much to Simon's disgust as he announced himself perfectly capable of driving long distances.

Before they left, Simon ushered everyone into the locked room to see the Dürer portrait. They took it in turns to stand in front of the masterpiece and gaze at it.

Elizabeth had dutifully looked at the portraits in Kobi's books for years. She appreciated the finer points of Old

Masters' art but had never felt particularly moved by it. But this was different, this time her hand covered her mouth and tears sprang into her eyes.

'It's magnificent,' she whispered.

'He is our pride and joy,' Simon said, beaming at her, 'a nobleman from our mother's family. You look like him!'

Kobi and Rafael exchanged glances. Elizabeth stood aside and Lisle stepped up. She sighed. 'You gorgeous, gorgeous man,' she said. 'Look at your clothing — how awesome is that cloak?'

'The hairs in the fur are individually painted.' It was Levi's turned to smile with joy. 'Every hair on the collar and the cuff, with a single stroke of a tiny brush. And the light falling on the pattern of the silk damask. I can look at that for hours,' he continued.

Kobi said nothing. He stood there and wrote the opening sentence of his book in his mind as he felt a familiar quickening of his pulse.

Over the next few days the three Horowitz men took their new relations to events across the state: a train trip to see the fall foliage up close; a jazz festival in Burlington; an Oktoberfest in Stowe, where an entire field was transformed into a Bavarian village and the Voight children couldn't help laughing at how much their paternal grandparents would have loved it.

Elizabeth regaled them with tales about her in-laws and the endless stream of 'German' gifts that had found their way into boxes in the garage. After both of her in-laws passed away, she had donated everything to the local Lions club and they had been able to have a 'German-themed charity sale'.

When Kobi and Lisle caught the odd phrase in German passing between their mother and their great-uncles, they exchanged looks of astonishment. Their mother hadn't spoken the language for years, and yet she had no trouble with it — more amazingly, she seemed happy to share a private joke in a language she had ignored for fifty years.

They found many connection points. Levi and Elizabeth discussed fabrics, design, embroidery and the skills she had learned from Sabine. All three shared beloved pieces of classical music, and Kobi joined in the conversations about opera and favourite singers.

Lisle discovered that her Great-uncle Levi had dabbled in pottery, and they retreated to the shed to explore his work and debate the virtues of different glazes and clays.

All too quickly the week was over. The night before Rafael, Daniel and Cindy were due back, Kobi sat with his mother and watched the stars in the crystal-clear night sky.

'I haven't asked you: are you glad you came?' he asked as he squeezed her hand.

She smiled at him. 'Of course I am. They're wonderful men.'

'They're family.'

'Yes, they are.'

For a moment they sat in contented silence.

'Have they said anything about wanting you to move here? Or anything about converting to Judaism?' Kobi asked.

She hesitated, and he wondered if she was deciding what to share with him. 'On the first night I told them that Australia is my home and I would miss it too much if I left now. Simon told me that he considered me to be Jewish and the letters left him in no doubt that it had been Rachel's wish to bring me up in their religion, had she lived.'

'But she didn't and you were brought up a Lutheran.'

'That's what I said to him. I've been a Lutheran for over seventy years. Some of my earliest memories of my father are of him reading the gospels to me. I believe in the same God that Simon and Levi do, but I also believe in the new covenant and that Jesus came to Earth, lived, died for me and rose from the dead. I believe he was the Messiah and I can't just change my mind because someone I've known for a few days tells me I'm Jewish.'

Kobi nodded. 'That's logical. I have no desire to be Jewish. Lisle might have a different approach.'

'I know, she's told me she wants to investigate Judaism when she gets home. I've told her I have no problem with that, although her husband might. Rachel has become very important to her.'

Again a silence descended.

'So, have you forgiven me for giving you the letters to read?' Kobi asked eventually.

She turned to him, genuine surprise in her eyes. 'Forgiven? My dear boy, there's nothing to forgive. I'm very glad you did.'

'Good. So who do you consider to be your parents?'

'It's a complicated thing and I'm still working through the language. Grandma and Grandpa are the people who brought me up, so yes, they were my parents. But I acknowledge that Rachel Horowitz was my birth mother, and I understand why she did what she did and I am very proud of her. From what Feter Simon and Feter Levi say, she was an extraordinarily gifted girl, let alone what she achieved in her short life.'

He leaned over and kissed her softly on the cheek. 'And I am proud of you. What you have done is a brave thing, and I know it would have made your biological mother so happy. You've given us new family, too. Lisle adores Feter Levi.'

Elizabeth nodded. 'I can see that. She's going to find it hard to leave him and, realistically, she may not see him again.'

'That's true for all of us,' he said.

'I was thinking today that I really wish Andrew had come with us. It would do him good to expand his world view.'

Kobi concealed his smile. His mother sometimes surprised him with her perception. 'Work, immediate family and money,' he said.

'Indeed. The artistic gene bypassed dear old Andrew,' she said with a sigh.

He couldn't help but laugh. 'He should have done what Dad did: marry into a truly gifted and creative family.'

CHAPTER THIRTY-FIVE

Vermont
October 2014

Cindy Horowitz had grown up in a large family and had always been labelled the 'pretty one'. Not much was expected of her intellectually; her job was to smile and win the Homecoming Queen title. She had married her childhood sweetheart and they'd had one son. Her father-in-law had been a New York banker, and he had financed his son into a hardware store and lumber yard. When she had learned what the family had once owned and lost to the Nazis, she had told herself not to be disappointed over a fortune that was not hers to have.

David worked hard and made a success of his business. By a stroke of great good fortune, and because she had nurtured his talent, their son turned out to be a violin virtuoso. This fact had had a cause and effect. It had brought them into the orbit of Rafael Gomez, and he had taken on the role of mentor to Dan. He had also helped them recover some of the lost treasures of the Horowitz family.

Not just the odd piece of silver or gold, but two priceless violins and a priceless painting. When her father-in-law and her husband's uncle died, the riches would come to her husband, and she had no intention of allowing them to sit in a vault — she was determined to realise their value. At last the final strands in her plan would come together and she would be beautiful, the mother of a phenomenally talented son ... and extremely rich.

Cindy had expected that she would need to console her father-in-law and her husband's uncle after the visit of Elizabeth Voight and her children. These people from Australia would arrive, Elizabeth would find it all too hard, and they would leave. No damage done to her plan and the old men would get over it.

When her son rang from DC and told her that it had all gone brilliantly and everyone was behaving like family, she was astonished — and furious.

A week after the Voights arrived, she flew from Chicago to DC, met Maestro Gomez and Daniel and flew up to Burlington Airport. David picked them up, and filled them in on the week's activity. He said that Simon and Levi were tired but very happy, and bonds had been quickly formed. Cindy kept her mouth shut, but was conscious of the loaded glances she was getting from her husband. The car swung into the driveway and they climbed out. Daniel took his mother's arm as she passed him.

'You'll like them, Mom, they're lovely.'

Cindy gave him an indulgent smile.

'I'm sure I will, darling.'

She squared her shoulders and followed her husband into the house. David drew Elizabeth towards her.

'Elizabeth, this is my wife, Cindy.'

She shook the woman's hand and smiled at her. Tall, elegant, well-groomed and confident. She could see the family likeness to Levi and her husband.

'Lovely to meet you, Mrs Voight.'

'Likewise. I have to compliment you on your son: he is such a delightful young man.'

Cindy nodded. 'Thank you.'

'Kobi Voight you've met before and this is Lisle Spencer, they're my second cousins,' David added.

She shook both hands and sized the woman up. Lisle looked like a Horowitz, with her dark colouring and the cleft in her chin.

They had their feet firmly under the table and seemed very comfortable. It was irritating but for the moment the best strategy was to say nothing and watch. Their behaviour might reveal their true motives before they left; if not, she would have more chance to talk her family around once the happy gathering was over.

After lunch, Simon asked whether he and Levi could talk to Elizabeth, Kobi and Lisle, suggesting that maybe the others would like to rug up for a walk along the nearby hiking trail. Once they were alone, Simon sat the Voights down at the dining-room table.

'I felt we should talk about this now and get it out of the way,' he said. The others nodded and watched expectantly. With the exception of Levi, they had no idea what he was going to say.

'I get a monthly pension from the German government to help with medical expenses arising from my internment in Dachau. It's not much, but it helps.'

Again there was some nodding.

'Last year, Levi and I joined a class action suing the German government over Jewish-owned banks unlawfully acquired by the Third Reich. The gold and money in the bank owned by our father and our uncle was transferred into a Swiss account in early 1940. That transaction has been established and the amount confirmed. As a result, we stand to gain a substantial amount of compensation. None of my uncle's family survived, so the money comes to us, as Benjamin's heirs. We have discussed this with our lawyer, and we would like to add you, Elizabeth, as Rachel's sole heir, to this claim. The money will be split three ways. When we die we will leave two-thirds of our shares to David and one-third to you.'

There was a moment of silence.

'I'm very flattered, Feter Simon, but I've done nothing to deserve this,' Elizabeth said.

Simon smiled at her. 'Maybe not, but your mother did much. She was the only one who actively resisted the horror. I know it would have been her dearest wish for you to benefit from any compensation she would have received.'

Kobi cleared his throat. 'I have a question.'

Simon turned to look at him. 'Ask away, my son,' he said.

'If Mother is entitled to some compensation for the loss of the bank, is she not also entitled to part-ownership of the painting?'

Elizabeth frowned at him. 'I don't feel in a position —'

'No, no, Kobi has a point,' Simon cut across her. 'The painting is a part of the estate our parents would have left, and Rachel would have shared in that. She was the artist among us, after all. I strongly suspect that the musical instruments would have come to us and the art would have gone to her.'

'What do you want to do with it?' Levi asked.

Kobi hesitated.

'For instance, should it spend half its life in Melbourne?' Levi continued. The concern in his voice was obvious to all.

'No, no, I'm not suggesting that. But I do think that it should have a life outside of your vault. It is a very important piece of the Dürer story, and at the moment it is missing.'

'Missing from where? It is in the right place, with the people who have always owned it.' Simon frowned, his small body tense with concern.

Kobi chose his words carefully. 'I believe that when it comes to old masterpieces and the heritage of great art, there is a case that transcends private ownership. This painting is missing from the collective artistic consciousness of the world.

In other words, everyone should have the right to see it and appreciate it.'

Simon raised his eyebrows. 'Everyone?'

Kobi nodded vigorously. 'Yes, sir, everyone who wants to, who appreciates the artist and his work. It's one of the very best examples of Dürer's ability as a painter and —'

'It belongs to us,' Levi said firmly.

'Of course it does and it always should, and to your heirs. But that doesn't mean that it should be hidden away.'

'Why not, if that's what we want to do with it? It has special significance to our family.'

Kobi sighed then looked at Levi. There was defiance in his eyes. 'Why?' he asked.

'What do you mean, *why*?' Simon said impatiently.

'Why does it have special significance to your — our — family?'

'I thought I had explained this to you! Paul von Hoch was an ancestor of my mother's, Elizabeth's grandmother, your great-grandmother.'

'Why do you say that?' Kobi asked.

Levi and Simon looked at each other in confusion.

'We have always known that. Mama told us when we were children; you only need to look at it.' Simon's tone was defensive.

Kobi reached into his jacket pocket and took out a piece of paper. He unfolded it and passed it, without comment, to Simon. Simon read it and passed it to Levi.

'That is a lie,' Simon said.

Kobi shook his head. 'No, it's not. I have checked the records and the purchase is listed in the provenance of the painting. It has been sold once in its history, from the von Hoch family to the Silverman family in 1585.'

At that moment the double doors to the lounge swung open and Daniel, David, Cindy and Rafael came into the room.

There was silence. Levi held the letter in his hand. David looked at the figures seated around the table.

'What's going on here?' he asked brightly.

Simon turned and looked up at him. 'Kobi has just informed us that our painting is not a family heirloom.'

'Yes, it is,' Kobi said hurriedly. 'You have owned it for over four hundred years, surely that makes it an heirloom?'

'But the subject is not an ancestor of our mother,' Levi said. His voice was flat and hoarse.

'Does that matter?' asked Cindy.

Simon nodded. 'To me, it matters a great deal,' he said.

'I'm sorry, Feter Simon, I didn't mean to hurt you. I'm just trying to prove that you could let the painting out into the world and it wouldn't be breaking some precious family story,' Kobi said.

Cindy circled the table and stopped opposite Kobi so she could look him full in the face. 'What exactly do you want to do with *our* painting?' she asked.

He returned her gaze with equal fire. 'I want to write a book about it and I want to tour it around the world.'

She smiled, but there was no warmth, just triumph. 'In other words, you just want to make money.'

'No! Not at all —'

'It looks that way to us,' Simon said.

Elizabeth opened her mouth to say something, but closed it again. Kobi could defend himself.

'I am more than happy to donate any proceeds from a book and a tour to any charity you nominate. A Holocaust survival charity maybe. I'm not the slightest bit int —'

Cindy snorted with disgust. 'I'm sorry, I don't believe that. You've had your eyes on the painting from the moment you first came here. It's worth millions.'

Kobi stood up. 'Of course I have! But not because of any monetary value. Albrecht Dürer is my life's work. But it is *nothing* compared to what the letters have given to my mother, your father-in-law, our whole family. Possessions mean very little when your family has been torn apart.'

They faced each other. David moved swiftly and took his wife's arm. 'And if we're not careful this subject will tear us all apart again. There's plenty of time —'

Cindy pulled away. She walked back around the table and pulled up very close to Kobi. As she spoke, she spat in his face. 'No, there isn't! Don't you dare lecture me about the Holocaust; I've lived with it all my married life.' She turned towards the others. 'There's too much at stake here — money, violins, a priceless painting. The Horowitz family history. How can we let these people — people we have known for five minutes — muscle their way into our lives and take our possessions? Gentiles, claiming our possessions, *again*.'

Levi rose to his feet and bashed the table with his clenched fist. 'Enough!' he roared.

Everyone stopped and turned towards him. He was glaring at Cindy. 'How dare *you* come here and insult our family!'

He pointed to Elizabeth. 'You married into it; Elizabeth was born into it. She is the daughter of my sister. I loved my sister so much that it still hurts. In all my years I have not felt the joy that I have felt in the past few days, and you come here with your poison and try ...'

His voice broke into a cough that turned into a choke and trailed off. He stood very still, his eyes bulging with sudden pain, then his face crumpled and he clutched his chest with his hand, and fell sideways to the ground.

Rafael reacted swiftly and reached him before anyone else. 'Levi!'

He rolled Levi onto his back. The old man's eyes were open but lifeless. Rafael felt his neck for a pulse; there was nothing. 'Call an ambulance,' he yelled.

Simon went down on his knees beside his brother and picked up the top half of Levi's body in his arms. He started to wail.

David tapped Rafael on the shoulder. 'He has a DNR notice,' he said quietly. 'He didn't want to be resuscitated when his heart gave out.'

Rafael stumbled backwards and got to his feet. Everyone was staring at Simon, holding his brother, stroking his hair and keening.

'Feter Levi,' Lisle said softly. Tears ran down her face. Kobi went to her and embraced her.

Cindy sank down onto a seat, her face white. Daniel wrapped his arms around her from behind and kissed the top of her head. Elizabeth drew herself up and walked over to where Levi lay. She knelt down and took one of his hands in hers. Simon looked across at her.

'*Baruch Dayan Ha'emet*,' he said.

'*Baruch Dayan Ha'emet*,' Daniel replied.

'*Baruch Dayan Ha'emet*,' David and Cindy both followed suit.

Rafael drew Kobi and Lisle to a far corner.

'They're saying "Blessed is the True Judge",' he whispered to them.

Cindy left the room, returning with a white cloth and candles. Simon took the cloth from her and gave one side of it to Elizabeth. He closed Levi's eyes and mouth with his hand, then gestured to Elizabeth. She followed his lead and together they laid the cloth across Levi's face. Simon and David lit candles and placed them around his head. Elizabeth joined Kobi and Lisle and took one of their hands in each of hers.

The Horowitz family gathered around Levi and began to recite Psalm 23, verse 17 of Psalm 90, and the whole of Psalm 91 in Hebrew.

CHAPTER THIRTY-SIX

Vermont
October 2014

They buried Levi the next day. It was a simple service, but eloquent and moving. Afterwards they all returned home and had a first meal together.

During their absence, friends had prepared the house for Shiva. The mirrors were covered, a water pitcher, bowl and paper towels were placed by the front door, and the kitchen was full of food. The family would sit Shiva for seven days, sitting on low, uncomfortable stools and benches and receiving friends to share in their mourning.

Simon was devastated. The last person who understood his past, who had known the family they had lost, was gone. Levi's health had deteriorated over the past year but Simon had secretly believed that Levi would live to be a hundred, outliving his younger brother.

Towards the end of the first day a small woman dressed in black came to the house. The front door was left unlocked for the mourning period, so she slipped in without anyone noticing. She picked up a framed photograph of Levi from a sideboard and studied it.

'How did you know Levi?' The questioner wore glasses and a *yarmulke* and he looked like Levi. She put down the photograph and looked up at him.

'Who are you?' she asked, her voice barely above a whisper. Her accent was East European, blunted by years in America.

'I'm David Horowitz. Levi was my Feter.'

'I want to see his brother,' she said.

'Come with me.'

David led her into the main room and over to where Simon sat on a low bench. 'This woman wants to give you her condolences,' he said.

'*Baruch Dayan Ha'emet,*' the woman said. She was elderly, and a black shawl covered her head.

Simon nodded. She sat down beside him and he looked sharply at her and moved a little down the bench.

'So, you are Wolfie's younger brother. He talked about you. He called you Amadeus. Amadeus Bite.'

Simon stared at her. 'Wolfgang Bach,' he said softly.

She nodded. 'I knew it wasn't his real name, but he loved music and it seemed so right.'

'They were our nicknames when we were little boys. It was our joke, no one else knew.' His voice was full of wonder. He took her hand. 'When did you know him?' he asked.

She smiled sadly. 'During the war. Did he tell you about his war?'

Simon nodded. 'Yes, he made it to England and he worked on a farm and he was interned for a while. He used to get embarrassed, because I was in Dachau and he hadn't suffered the way I had.'

She gave a soft laugh. 'Oh, he suffered. When your Shiva is over I shall come back and tell you all about Wolfie's war. You will be amazed.' She patted his hand. 'Know that he had a full life.'

Then she got up and walked across the room and out the door. Simon watched her go, a frown on his face and immense sadness in his dark eyes.

* * *

There was tension in the family. Kobi noticed that Simon spoke to Cindy as little as possible, and he wondered whether his great-uncle blamed his daughter-in-law for Levi's death. Daniel was agitated about the events leading to his great-uncle's heart attack, and he didn't seem to want to be around Cindy either. On the second day, Elizabeth, Kobi and Lisle agreed that they felt out of place in the traditional Jewish grieving process. Elizabeth called David and asked whether Simon would mind if they went to New York until the seven days were over. David confessed that his father's grief was so deep he doubted the old man would notice. So they packed their bags and got a cab to the airport.

The day before they were due to return to Vermont, Kobi sent his mother and sister off to the Metropolitan Museum of Art and took a cab to Dunblane, McGowan and Shaw, a legal firm in Brooklyn.

Rose McGowan was of Irish descent, early thirties, attractive and obviously very smart. She sat and listened to his story. He changed some of the details to keep it theoretical, including what the painting was.

'So,' she said thoughtfully, 'you want to know whether your mother can challenge your great-uncle's will. Presumably at this stage he leaves everything to his son, but some of the property could be considered family estate, having been reconstituted to the family after the war.'

'Yes.'

'And in particular you want your mother to have a say in what happens to this painting.'

'Yes.'

'Do you want a financial share, if it's sold?'

He frowned. 'It won't ever be sold. But at present it is locked away and I want it to be on public display for at least part of the time, and I'd like to write a book about it.'

'Your argument would be that your mother, as the illegitimate daughter of a member of the original family unit, has some stake in what would have been communal property?'

'Yes.'

'The son, I assume, is his father's legitimate heir?'

'Yes, of course ... Do we have a case?'

She nodded. 'You do. Whether you'll win or not could come down to the judge you get. Courts tend to care less about legitimacy now, but you can get sticklers. And it's not as though you want sole ownership, you just want a say.'

'Will you take the case, if it comes down to it?'

She hesitated. 'I'll need more information, but in principle, yes.'

That night the three Voights met Rafael for dinner in New York. The next day they would go north. Rafael had spoken to David and heard that they were all coping well but were relieved the Shiva was nearly over. They wanted to see their Australian family again, and he had agreed that they would return to say goodbye.

'I went to see a lawyer today,' Kobi announced as they were eating.

'Why?' Elizabeth asked.

'I wanted an opinion on where we stood if Simon leaves the painting to David. Solely to David.'

Rafael looked up at him. 'And what did he say?' he asked.

'It was a she, and she was very good. She said we do have a case. We could challenge the will, after the fact, and put our side to a judge. It may come down to the fact that David is Simon's legitimate heir, in that his father and mother were married, and mother is Rachel's illegitimate daughter, but she didn't seem to think that would rule us out. Not in this day and age.'

Elizabeth grimaced. 'We would do nothing until after Feter Simon dies?' she asked.

'Absolutely nothing. But I am tempted to tell him, or David, what we intend. It might make them agree to let me write the book, to share some access now.'

Rafael put his knife and fork down on his plate with measured movements. 'Kobi, can I ask a favour?'

'Of course, Maestro.'

'Don't say anything to anyone for the moment. They have just suffered a huge loss, and grief can make you lash out, yes? It would be easier if you could leave it for a while. It is not as though you are going to lose contact with them, you know. David wants to bring Cindy and Daniel out to see Melbourne and meet Andrew and his family, and Lisle's family. But they won't want to leave Simon alone at present.'

Elizabeth nodded firmly. 'Rafael is right, Jakob. Please don't raise the subject again on this trip. Out of respect for the memory of Feter Levi.'

CHAPTER THIRTY-SEVEN

Vermont
October 2014

Simon had been thinking about the elderly woman who visited on the first day of Shiva. When his new extended family were all back together, they sat down to lunch and he shared the story with them.

'What on earth could she have meant?' David asked.

Simon shrugged. 'I really have no idea. But she knew him, that much is certain. She knew my nickname and his nickname, and no one else alive knows those.'

David gave a shake of his head. 'She's going to tell you about his war. What could she tell you that you don't already know?'

'I suspect it has something to do with his journey through Switzerland and up to Sweden and across to London. He never spoke much about his hardships, and nothing about that part of it.'

'Oh well, I guess when she comes back, we'll find out,' Cindy said as she stood up and started to clear the table. 'Let's hope she didn't have his baby.'

Simon glared at her. She ignored him.

'Let me help you.' Lisle stood up at the other end.

'No, thank you, I can manage.' Cindy gave her a frosty smile, and Lisle sat back down.

As soon as Cindy had left the room, Simon reached over and patted Lisle's hand. 'Don't worry, my dear. The ice queen is going home tomorrow. It'll be a long time before she's invited back.'

'Poppa!' Daniel exclaimed.

Simon winked at him, and his grandson tried not to smile.

David sighed. 'Please forgive my dysfunctional family — or should I say, *your* dysfunctional family.'

Elizabeth laughed. 'You should have seen my children growing up: it was all I could do to stop them whacking each other.'

Kobi nodded to David and they both got up. 'Excuse us for a moment,' David said.

Kobi followed him from the room. When they got to the locked room David punched numbers into the keypad and the door slid back. He switched on the light.

'Stay for as long as you like. There's an exit button on the inside, the door will open to let you out and then close behind you. Just don't take him down or you'll set off an alarm.'

'Thanks very much.' Kobi touched his arm and stepped into the room. The door closed behind him. He stood in front of the painting.

'Hello, my beauty,' he whispered. The awe never left him. That feeling of standing in the presence of glorious ability and the link with the life of a painter centuries ago. He took his mini iPad from his inside jacket pocket, opened up the photo app and started taking photographs and a video of the painting.

Rafael couldn't sleep and the narrow motel bed didn't help. He got up, made himself a cup of coffee and sat on the edge of the sofa. When Rafael didn't know what to do, he prayed. He had sung in church choirs as a child in Madrid and loved conducting Sacred music. He didn't go to Mass or confession as often as he should, and he had been a widower and then a divorcé before marrying his beloved Mags. But he had been lucky enough to conduct a concert for Pope John Paul II, and meeting his Holy Father was among the highlights of his life.

But this current problem needed the Wisdom of Solomon. He held knowledge that could be vital to any court case, could strengthen Kobi's side and weaken David's. The truth would cause his dear friend Simon more pain than the old man could bear, and it was completely unnecessary for him to know. So what should he do? Keep silent until such time as — if — a court case arose? Or did David have a right to know more about the man he had been mourning as a much-loved uncle?

The next day they enjoyed another family lunch and then Simon went for a walk.

'Next summer's outdoor concert,' Daniel said, looking at Rafael. 'We thought it might be a nice idea to hold a concert in honour of Rachel's memory. Would that be a good one?'

Rafael stirred his coffee. 'The one in DC or the one in New York?' he asked.

'Does it matter?'

'Not really. Do you want to make it a fundraiser?'

Daniel nodded. 'A scholarship.'

'In her name to an art school for the descendant of a survivor,' Kobi added.

Rafael beamed. 'What a splendid idea! Would you come back for it?' he asked.

Kobi looked across at Elizabeth, and she smiled at him. 'Of course. We all would,' she said.

'There's your answer,' Kobi smiled back at her, 'the Voights are in. I'll design you a graphic, something that includes one of her sketches.'

'The ones of Feter Levi and Poppa,' Daniel added.

'And maybe you could play exclusively Jewish composers,' Lisle suggested.

Daniel and Rafael nodded in time with each other. 'Fritz Kreisler,' they both said at once. Everyone laughed.

'What's the world's shortest book?' Daniel asked. The others shook their heads. He winked at Rafael. 'The Book of Non-Jewish Violinists!'

Again they laughed.

'Many of the Jewish composers converted, they had to, to be allowed to play at court. Felix Mendelssohn, Gustav Mahler,' David explained.

'I'm sure we can find enough with Jewish heritage, and I suspect New York might be a better venue for a Jewish concert,' Rafael said.

When Simon came back from his stroll around the block, he found his family sitting at the table with Rafael planning a concert to honour his sister. He was delighted.

'Levi would have loved this!' he exclaimed as he sat down with them.

'Poppa,' Daniel laid his hand on the old man's arm, 'I've had an idea. Would you play a duet with me? The Guarneri and the Amati together.'

Simon frowned and looked at his grandson. 'What would we play?'

'"Hallelujah", the Leonard Cohen song, with just the Maestro on the piano accompanying us.'

Daniel looked over at Rafael, who nodded vigorously. 'It's a spark of genius, Simon. It would make the night perfect.'

Simon smiled at Daniel, who had turned back to him. The young man's dark eyes were sparkling, and his face shone with health and vitality. Suddenly he was struck by the contrast with himself at the same age. Where had he been? Playing for the guards in a concentration camp, focusing every day on staying alive. For what? For this. To see his genes passed on to such a talent, such a hope for the world to come.

'Of course, my boy, it would be an honour to play with you.'

A month later David attended an end-of-year function at the Kennedy Centre. He and Rafael arranged to have a coffee together the next day.

'Do you keep in regular contact with the Voights?' Rafael asked.

David nodded. 'Kobi and I skype about once a week, and sometimes he'll call from Elizabeth's computer so we can have a chat as well. They're fine. It's the beginning of their summer, and they're looking forward to coming back for the concert next June.'

'I love the title, *Rachel's Legacy*. It can mean so many different things,' Rafael said.

'That was Dan's idea. He sees her legacy as life, hope and love. Simon sees it as Elizabeth. I think Kobi sees it as the painting.'

Rafael laughed. 'We humans are a funny lot, yes?'

'Indeed.'

Rafael looked at him across the table. David was a quiet man, studious and thoughtful, but nothing escaped him.

'How is Cindy coping with all this?' Rafael asked.

David gave a grimace and then shrugged. 'Her relationship with Papa has been damaged, but it is her own fault. I was worried that Dan was going to blame her for Feter Levi's heart attack, but he seems to have forgiven her for the argument. She's a lioness when it comes to her family's interests. I thought Papa was very brave when he asked her if he could have Grandmama's jewellery box and some of the pieces back. Cindy was within her rights to object strongly — she knows what he wants to do with them. But the letters proved that

Grandmama wanted Rachel to have them, so he's doing what she would have wanted. I took his side — and needless to say I've had to replace them!'

Rafael chuckled. 'I'm sure Elizabeth will be deeply touched. What did you want to see me about?'

David hesitated. 'Something between you and me, is that okay?'

'Of course.'

'When you brought the DNA results to Vermont, did you bring them all?'

Rafael stirred his coffee. 'What do you mean by that?' he asked.

'We had a full range of tests, didn't we?' Rafael nodded. 'And that would have included the Male Specific Y-chromosome tests,' David continued. It wasn't a question.

Rafael leaned across the table and looked straight into the hazel eyes. David was calm and in control, his emotions deeply hidden.

'You know,' Rafael said softly.

'And now you do, too. You didn't take those results with you.'

'What good would it have done? What harm could it have done — much pain for your dear father?'

David nodded. 'I wanted to thank you for that.'

'If I may ask, how do you know?'

David shifted in his seat. 'Mama told me years ago when I was in my twenties. I'm not sure why — maybe she felt the need to confess when Daniel was born.'

'How did it make you feel?'

'Your father is the man who brings you up. We've always had a good relationship. Growing up with the shadow of the war wasn't easy. I can't tell you how much my father has suffered over the years, and I was his pride and joy. Now Dan is. Besides, mother said no one else knew —'

'Not even Levi?' Rafael looked at David quizzically.

David shrugged. 'Apparently not. Don't ask me, I don't understand this family of mine any more than you do. I always thought of him as my Feter and I have mourned him in that way.'

'Why are you asking me about this?' Rafael asked.

'Because it makes me legally the same as Elizabeth: we are both the product of liaisons our mothers had. I am as entitled as she is to the family legacy, no more, no less.'

Rafael nodded. He was stunned by David's revelation, and more than a little relieved. The decision had been taken out of his hands. 'So what are you going to do?' he asked.

David smiled. 'I'll sort it out. I just wanted you to know that there is no need to wrestle with your conscience. It is not a fact for public consumption. My father, my wife, my son, need never know. We're family.'

Rafael shook his head in awe. 'You are. A family of survivors.'

CHAPTER THIRTY-EIGHT

New York
June 2015

The morning of *Rachel's Legacy: The Rachel Horowitz Memorial Art Scholarship* concert at Damrosch Park, two members of the Horowitz family reached out to two members of the Voight family.

Simon asked his niece, Elizabeth, to come into his hotel room, sat her down on his bed and gave her a large silver jewellery box. It had *ERH* engraved on the lid among swirls executed with exquisite craftsmanship.

'This is the box your mother played with before the war. Sergei returned it to us in 2008, and now it can go where Rachel would have wanted it to go.'

Elizabeth was speechless. When she looked up at him her eyes were glistening with tears.

'Open it,' he said.

Slowly, she lifted the lid. The box was lined with red velvet, and inside sat a double string of pearls, a large sapphire ring, and a ruby-and-diamond bracelet.

'Oh my goodness, Feter Simon! It's too much,' she exclaimed.

'It is your birthright, my dear. Had your mother lived, she would have been with us when it was returned and she would have left it to you. And you can leave it to Lisle. That is what a family heirloom is all about.'

She put the box down on the bed and held out her arms. He embraced her and kissed her on each cheek.

'I so wish Feter Levi was here for this day,' she said softly.

He smiled. 'So do I, but he is here, in his own way. As are your mother, David and our parents. They watch us all with love.'

Later in the day, David took Kobi aside and asked whether they could spend a few moments together. Kobi suggested a walk in Central Park. The two men liked each other and found conversation easy. They sat on a grassy hill and talked about how Dan must feel.

'Such a weight on his shoulders,' Kobi said.

'Dan's used to it. He thrives on it. He's very comfortable with the expectations people place on him. No one really appreciates the hours of practice that go into each performance.'

'I admire his dedication immensely.'

'So do I. Proud doesn't cover how I feel when I see him on the stage. He went through a phase of not wanting to play when he was younger, and then he found his passion again. He loves that violin so much.'

'And when the Russian, Sergei, dies, he inherits it?'

David nodded. 'Yes, and we have to figure out how to store it and keep it safe when he's not travelling or playing. He's bought an apartment in DC, so eventually it will be there.'

'What will you do with the Amati? Will he play both?' Kobi asked.

'No, Papa wants it to go to the Smithsonian, and that seems a good solution. He really doesn't want us to sell it. That's not what his papa would have wanted ... Kobi, I want to talk to you about the painting.'

Kobi turned and looked at him. He had thought that might be the real reason for their conversation. But surely this was not a day for rows? 'What is there to say? We are on different sides of the fence,' he said.

'Plenty. I have persuaded Papa to change his will. The Dürer will be left to Elizabeth and myself in equal measure. When she dies, or if she predeceases Papa, her share must be left to you.'

Kobi was speechless. He felt tears pricking behind his eyes. This was completely unexpected, and the sense of relief was huge. He put his hand out and David shook it.

'Thank you, David. It seems inadequate, but I don't know what else to say,' he said eventually.

David smiled at him. 'On no account tell my father this, but I share your sentiments. I think we will be able to work together very well. Go ahead, start your book. Eventually we'll get any scientific access you need, but we already have the authentication papers. Perhaps we should get it professionally photographed? Eventually it will tour ... and maybe the proceeds can go to the Rachel Horowitz Art Scholarship?'

'Of course! I have the perfect place for it to be revealed, the Gemäldegalerie, the Old Masters Art Gallery in Berlin. Professor Kribbler will mount the perfect exhibition.'

Kobi felt a wave of joy rising within him that was akin to the first time he had laid eyes on the painting. Suddenly he could see his future and it looked like the Paul von Hoch.

'The only thing I ask is that you leave your share to Dan. After our tenure he will become the guardian, even if it is on permanent public display by then. It must never go out of Horowitz hands again,' David added.

Kobi nodded. It was a lot to take in, and his mind was full to bursting. 'It's a big gesture on your part. I had thought about going to court over it, but there is no doubt your case is far stronger than mine,' he said.

David shook his head. 'Elizabeth and I are first cousins and we share a common story: no matter how we got here, we are Horowitzs.'

The sound-shell rose like a white sail from the stage; the area before it was covered with enough chairs for a crowd of three thousand.

Elizabeth, Lisle and her husband and three children, Andrew and his wife sat in the front row with Cindy and David. A little way down the row, Sergei Valentino sat and beamed at everyone. Kobi watched from the wings. He kept his distance from Daniel as the young man did his last-minute stretching exercises. Over to his left he could see Simon sitting with the Amati on his lap, eyes closed, going over the music in his mind. The venue was full and it was the largest audience Kobi had ever addressed, but if Daniel could do it, so could he.

Rafael and the MET Orchestra opened the evening with the overture to *Orpheus in the Underworld* by Jacques Offenbach. The audience rose as one when Daniel walked onto the stage. He shook Rafael's hand and then played *Liebesleid* by Fritz Kreisler on the Guarneri. After more rapturous applause, he left the stage and Rafael stepped down from the podium to face the audience, microphone in hand.

'Welcome, ladies and gentlemen. We are here tonight for a very special reason, to raise money for a very special cause. Without any further ado, I would like to introduce the Chairman of the Rachel Horowitz Art School Scholarship, Dr Jakob Voight.'

Kobi coughed, stroked his beard and walked out into the lights of the stage. Rafael took his hand and they shared a quick half-embrace, and then Kobi stepped up to the microphone.

'Thank you, Maestro Gomez, for everything. Good evening, ladies and gentlemen, my name is Jakob Voight and I am Australian. Rachel Horowitz was my grandmother. She was a truly remarkable young woman. You can see a photo of her and read her story on the back of tonight's programme. She was a member of a group known as the Red Orchestra, Resistance fighters in World War II Berlin. She was a skilled artist and she forged papers and ration books. She also helped to hide, feed and save Jews for two years, at great risk to herself. She was a mother, giving birth in early 1942. Her child survived the war and is my mother, Elizabeth Voight.

'In recognition of my grandmother's bravery, we are going to establish a scholarship to the fine arts college at the wonderful Berlin University of the Arts. The campus of this university is in Charlottenburg, which happens to be the suburb where my grandmother lived during the war. I would like to thank you all for attending this inaugural concert and contributing to the establishment of this memorial to an exceptional woman.'

Applause broke out throughout the venue. He waited for it to die down.

'The next item on the programme is a duet. One that is seventy years in the making. Daniel Horowitz will play his Guarneri del Gesú violin, and he will be accompanied by his grandfather, Simon Horowitz, on his 1640 Amati violin, and by Maestro Rafael Gomez on the piano. They will play that classic piece of modern music by one of the great contemporary Jewish songwriters, Leonard Cohen. Here is, in memory of Rachel and Feter Levi, "Hallelujah".'

Kobi walked to the wings and stopped to shake hands with all three men as they made their way back to the stage. He could feel a tremble in Simon's body and he squeezed his hand. Rafael went to the piano. Simon and Daniel stood, side by side, on the stage.

For around eight seconds Rafael played the introduction, and then Daniel put the violin to his shoulder and began to play. The minor notes were haunting, and yet it was beautifully melodic as the familiar tune rang out across the hundreds of heads. Everyone was transfixed. At fifty-four seconds in, Simon joined him and the sound became deeper, richer and built to an aching climax. The Hallelujahs became questions and answers from each violin, the Amati underneath and the del Gesú soaring above. It was three and a half minutes of extraordinary music, with the del Gesú finishing the piece on its own.

For a second there was total silence, and then the audience roared its approval. Everyone sprang to their feet and clapped, hands above heads and feet stomping. Calls of 'Bravo' rang from every quarter. Elizabeth, Lisle and Cindy were all crying.

Daniel and Simon embraced, and then gestured to Rafael, who got up from the piano and joined them. They clasped hands and bowed in unison as the applause continued to pour forth. Eventually, Simon broke away from Daniel and Rafael and went to the microphone. The crowd could see he was waiting to speak, and little by little they stopped clapping.

'Thank you, from the bottom of my heart. Rachel was my baby sister and I am the last of the siblings. My elder brother, Levi, died last year, and Rachel's twin brother, David, died in Dachau. Until Kobi arrived with letters written by Rachel, I thought my niece, her daughter, had died in 1947. By having the courage to bring a child into a war-torn world and making sure that her story was written down, Rachel ensured that she left us Elizabeth, and Elizabeth's children and grandchildren. She left us her legacy.'

EPILOGUE

Jerusalem
November 1986

The old woman hadn't spoken for several minutes, and he wondered if she had gone to sleep, or, even worse, died. She was stretched out on a day bed on a first-floor balcony with a blanket draped over her frail body. Her hair was white, her skin remarkable for a ninety-year-old, and it was obvious that she had once been tall, statuesque. Suddenly her eyes opened and her head turned towards him.

'Where was I?' she asked.

Her accent was German, softened by many years of speaking Hebrew and English.

He smiled nervously. 'You were telling me that you had another life before the war.'

She nodded slowly. 'Yes, I did. I was the wife of a banker and we had four children. We lived a privileged and interesting life. I had servants, I had my hair done, and I wore silks and furs and diamonds and we went dancing.'

'Then the Nazis came.'

She frowned at him. 'It was all so gradual at first; we couldn't believe that our Gentile friends and neighbours would let it happen. When my Benjamin and my two younger boys were taken, I wanted to march into the camp and demand that they be released. After all, they weren't criminals!'

He could see the thin arms lying on top of the blanket, and he knew that under one wrist was a faded tattoo.

'Tell me about what happened to you, Mrs Bernstein.'

She sighed, as if remembering was too hard or too painful.

'I lived for a while as a governess. A lovely family, with lovely children. Very bright. Their father worked for the government. They thought I was a spinster, a Catholic and homeless. They took pity on me and bought me clothes — such plain dresses you never saw!'

He smiled, and she smiled back at him.

'But they fed me and I had a warm room and the Gestapo weren't going to burst in and arrest me.'

'So why didn't you stay there?'

'I felt guilty. Levi, my eldest son, was in London. Benjamin was in Dachau, and I knew he would be taking care of my boys. Rachel was living on a farm outside of Berlin and working as a maid. She was safe and Maria said she was happy. I was doing nothing, nothing to help. I thought if I could get to London I might be able to help Levi. Join the Jewish community in exile there. I longed to be able to go to the synagogue and eat kosher food again.'

He nodded. This was one of the more interesting Shoah stories he had recorded. She seemed to have forgotten that the device was on — if he could keep her on track, the most interesting was yet to come.

'So what did you do?'

'I joined a group of people wanting to go into exile. We had proper exit visas in our false names, and we were confident and happy. But we were stopped at the Swiss border. The guard said it was random; every sixth group was looked at more closely. One of our number started to get very nervous so the guard called in the Gestapo.'

She stopped and seemed lost in thought for a moment. He

had learned not to hurry his subjects; the words would come out when they were ready.

'We were arrested and taken to interrogation rooms. I just kept repeating my story, answering their questions. We had all studied the Catholic faith so we could recite whatever they asked of us. But I could tell that they were suspicious. Some of the group had been very orthodox and they found the pretence hard. They kept the bright light on, directly in our faces, and kept us awake. They threw water at me.'

Again she stopped.

'Someone broke,' he said simply.

She nodded. 'I don't know who. There were three men missing when they rounded us up and put us on a train. Micah told us they had been shot. Maybe that had prompted one of the others to confess. Who knows? It didn't matter. They believed we were all Jews and they sent us to Auschwitz.'

'When was this?'

'1941.'

'Do you remember the camp?' he asked.

Slowly she turned her head and looked at him. Her moss-green eyes were clear and piercing. 'What do other people say when you ask that? It is not something you are ever likely to forget. The memories fade slightly, but are never forgotten.'

'What do you want to tell me?'

'I was strong and fit and healthy, so I was selected for work. My hair was shaven, my wrist was tattooed with a number, and I was given a rough dress to wear. The first few weeks were a blur, not much sleep, not much food, and lots of guards shouting at me to move to roll call faster. Then something happened.'

Again she stopped, again he waited. 'God saved me.'

He leaned forward. 'How?'

'I was chosen by a man who was important, not the camp commandant, but almost. I remember his face, but I have tried very hard to forget his name and rank. He lived in a house and he wanted another worker and he chose me. His family were in Frankfurt and he lived alone. I cleaned and I cooked, and I slept in the basement with two other Jewish women. One did lots of laundry — the man was paid by other men living on their own who wanted their laundry done. The third girl was young and very beautiful, and she sometimes went upstairs at night-time. She was traumatised, so we didn't ask why. And so each of us, in our own way, survived.'

'Did he beat you?'

She frowned. 'No. The further I got away from it, from the unrelenting terror, the more I realised that he fed us and gave us blankets in the winter. When there were other guards in the house he ignored us, but they seemed to know that they weren't to mistreat us.'

'Did you stay there until the end of the war?'

She nodded. 'Many people were marched away during the last weeks, but we stayed in the house until a Russian soldier found us and took us back to the main camp. We couldn't understand the Russians and we were frightened of them. At first they thought we were collaborators, but then they realised that we were prisoners who had been given domestic duties.'

'And after the war?'

'I was sick. They put me in hospital and fed me through a tube and gave me antibiotics and I got better, but it took a long time. Then I was taken to a Red Cross camp, still in Poland. I wanted to go back to Germany and find my family, but the man said they would check for me. Weeks later he told me that my husband and my boys had died in Dachau and my daughter had been a traitor, a spy. I laughed at him and told him he was mistaken, she was a farm girl, she wouldn't have known the first thing about spying! But he had a record of her trial in Berlin in 1942, and then she had been sent to Auschwitz!

I couldn't believe it! Somewhere out there my darling girl had died and I hadn't even known.'

'So they were all gone?'

She shook her head. 'No, there was Levi in London. It took a year before they told me he had reached London, but he had not been happy to sit and watch his country torn apart. They could not tell me much because it was classified, but he had been parachuted back into Europe and joined the partisans. He had fought the Nazis. My gentle, funny, creative boy had become a soldier of freedom! I was so astonished. There was no record of him returning, so they assumed that he had died fighting ... I hope his death was quick.'

She had stopped talking to him; she was talking to herself, lost in her grief.

'When did you come to Israel, Mrs Bernstein?'

She frowned. 'No, my name is Horowitz. Elizabeth Rachel Horowitz — Oh, I forgot. I remarried, didn't I? Joshua was a good man. He had always wanted to go to Palestine, and then it became Israel, so we came out here, in 1955. It was a new country, a new beginning. Not easy, but not the hardest life I had led. He wanted to stay and we had nothing to go home for, so we stayed. We made friends and some of them had children and grandchildren, so we became honorary relations. We celebrated birthdays and Bar Mitzvahs and weddings and births as if they were our own family, but they weren't, for our families were all dead.'

An emotion he couldn't describe crossed her face — profound sorrow and yet, a sense of peace.

'I have outlived them all. I wonder sometimes what lives they would have had. Would Levi have made exquisite furniture? Would Simon have been a concert violinist, or a banker like his father? Would David have become a politician or a comedian? Would Rachel have married her true love and had beautiful babies and been a wonderful artist? And would Benjamin and I have been a happy old married couple?

'Instead they were forced to be things that were foreign to them — a partisan, a spy, a camp prisoner. And they never saw this wonderful country where I have lived for over thirty years. They come to me in my dreams sometimes and try to speak to me, but I can't understand them. I wake up in the morning … and they're still dead.'

ACKNOWLEDGEMENTS

It took some considerable time for me to realise that there was a sequel to *The Keeper of Secrets*. I knew that there were areas I had researched that weren't used as extensively as I had wanted them to be, and it was a fascination with the Red Orchestra that led to this story.

Firstly, I wish to acknowledge my 'partner in crime', my friend, research assistant and vicar, the Reverend Jan Tarrant. Jan came with me to Berlin and Munich, and we saw many of the places that Kobi sees when he is on sabbatical. We also went to London and stayed with my childhood friend, Ruth Warrens, and her family, and, no doubt, disrupted their celebration of Passover. It was a time of great learning and raw emotion, and Jan's help with the book as it developed was invaluable.

I also want to acknowledge a book called *Red Orchestra*, written by Anne Nelson and published in 2009 by Random House. It is a detailed account of the spy organisation into which I put my fictional character Rachel, and it helped bring these extraordinarily brave people to life for me.

As usual my beta reader, Reuben Aitchison, read my work before anyone else, and his comments were always very helpful — thank you, my friend. When I was staying with Reuben in Melbourne in 2014 I visited the Holocaust Centre and the Jewish Centre, and I met two lovely ladies, survivors. They shared their remarkable stories with me and I was left in awe of their bravery and their wonderful senses of humour.

There are people too numerous to mention — family, old friends, church friends, experts — who have encouraged and supported me along the way. If I had a dollar for every person who has told me that they are waiting for the sequel, I could retire to a villa in Tuscany … and keep writing.

Lastly, I am blessed with wonderful publishers in HarperCollins. To Finlay Macdonald and Sandra Noakes in the Auckland office, and to Kate Stone my editor and Nicola Robinson, my brilliant project manager: thank you so much, you all rock!!

After spending thirty years as a writer, producer, director and executive producer in the media, Julie Thomas made a life-changing decision in 2011. She sold up her Auckland home and moved south, to the lovely rural town of Cambridge. On 9 September 2011 she uploaded her novel to Amazon and Smashwords and over the next ten months it sold fifty thousand copies. In mid-2012 she was contacted by HarperCollins USA who published her novel, *The Keeper of Secrets*, in 2013.

Two years later Julie released her second book, *Blood, Wine and Chocolate*, a venture into the crime genre which features several innovative ways of despatching the 'bad guys' and plenty of glorious wine and chocolate.

Meanwhile she moved further south, to the smaller rural town of Putaruru. She is now firmly entrenched in local life, helping with a children's ministry through her church, judging short story competitions and manning the cake stall at the annual daffodil show. Her highly manipulative and intelligent cat, Chloe, is very happy in her new environment, climbing trees and catching mice.

THE ENIGMA OF LOOTED ART

In 1997, while researching the subject of art looted during World War II, I discovered a magazine article about looted musical instruments. This led to the writing of *The Keeper of Secrets*, which tracks the story of Simon Horowitz and his family's beloved Guarneri del Gesú and Amati violins. The Horowitzs' stolen treasures, as described in *The Keeper of Secrets*, included a Dürer painting, and as the subject of looted art has continued to fascinate me, I took the opportunity to further delve into it in *Rachel's Legacy*.

In recent years, the fact that the Nazis looted the possessions of the Jews before and during the war has become much more widely known; however, few understand the scale of theft. During the thirteen war trials held in Nuremburg between 1945 and 1949, thirty-nine volumes of documents about seized art and antiquities were entered as evidence.

Reichsmarschall Hermann Goering stashed as many as 1800 artworks at Carinhall, his country home outside Berlin, most of them stolen from French and Italian Jewish families. At the end of the war he attempted to hang on to his collection by loading it onto a fleet of private trains and heading for Austria. The trains were intercepted by the Allies and Goering was arrested. He committed suicide the night before his scheduled execution in 1946. About eighty per cent of his loot has since been traced and returned to the rightful owners.

Many Soviet palaces and churches were looted and destroyed by the invading Germans, a situation that was reversed when the Soviets liberated Berlin in 1945, and took truckloads of war booty back with them. It's incredibly difficult to get an accurate estimate of what may be hidden beneath Russian art galleries and palaces, although in 2005 Anatoly Vilkov, deputy-chief of the federal agency that preserves cultural heritage, said that Russia has over 249,000 works of art, and more than a million books, that were taken from Germany as war compensation.

The subject has made it to the arena of film, with movies such as *Woman in Gold* and *The Monuments Men*. Court cases have arisen between museums or art galleries and the descendants of families who had their possessions ripped from them. Many are ongoing and bitterly contested.

I chose Dürer for very personal reasons. Like Kobi, I studied Dürer in my last year at secondary school, giving birth to a lifelong passion for his work. During my first trip to Europe in 1978, with my mother in tow, I visited every gallery and church I could find. We spent days in Paris and I returned to the Louvre several times. In Florence I fell in love with the Uffizi and we went to Milan to see da Vinci's *The Last Supper*. Since then I have been to London many times and the National Gallery is one of my first stops on every visit.

Of all of Dürer's paintings my favourite is the third self-portrait painted in 1500. In 2015 I went to Germany to research *Rachel's Legacy* and I finally got to the Alte Pinakothek in magnificent Munich. There it was, smaller than I had imagined and quite dark, but breathtakingly beautiful, with intricate detail and the best depiction of hair in any portrait I know. Sitting on the bench in front of it I was struck by the fact that it was accessible to me. Six hundred and fifteen years after it was lovingly created I could travel halfway round the world and gaze upon it. It reinforced for me my belief that great art belongs to everyone and should be hung where all can see it. It is part of our cultural consciousness.

The actions of a few monsters in the 1930s and 40s means that many of the greatest pieces are lost to the world forever. They were destroyed or they sit forgotten, in a collection of war loot, hidden in dark rooms. I consider this to be a tragedy and a forgotten consequence of war. Next time you find yourself in a city with a magnificent art gallery take the time to visit and revel in the art on display — it belongs to us all.

BOOK CLUB QUESTIONS

Who, or what, are the components that make up Rachel's legacy?

What is it about the letters that draws Kobi in and makes him determined to find out what happened to the author and her child? Why does the story resonate with him?

Is Rachel aware that she is being brave or is she just doing what has to be done? Do the threats to her safety come only from the Nazi regime? What does she have to do to hide in plain sight as a Catholic maid? How can she know who to trust?

Was she right to give up Ebee? Were the adults around her right to demand that she did? What comfort did writing the letters give her? Did she have a realistic attitude to the father of her baby?

What would you have done as a Gentile German in World War II? Would you have been part of the Resistance, would you have kept out of sight, would you have collaborated or would you have been seduced by the rhetoric and the propaganda?

What role does George play in the story for Kobi? Why does Kobi react the way he does to George?

Why has Elizabeth blocked out so much of her early childhood and found accepting her German heritage so hard? Do you know immigrants who have come from war-torn countries? How do they react to their heritage? Are they bullied?

Think about the Horowitzs' reaction to Kobi. Why are they suspicious of him initially? How does he change their minds?

How important is the Dürer painting to Kobi? What does it mean to Simon and Levi? Who has the bigger claim to it? Are they right to keep it hidden and why do they do so?

Do you believe that great art belongs to all of humanity and should be shared and displayed where all can see it?

What does the discovery of Elizabeth mean to Simon and Levi? What matters more — the way she was brought up, her beliefs and image of herself, or the genes inside her? Why does she react the way she does to them when she first meets them?

What are Cindy's motivations and is she justified in feeling the way she does?

How does Rafael Gomez become involved in the Horowitzs' lives again and what role does he play in the story? Is he right in the decisions he makes and should he share all he knows?

How does the story reflect the effect of war on people and their lives? Can people like Simon ever fully recover from the experiences of war?

How did the Epilogue make you feel? Do you think there are many stories of families torn apart by war who never find their loved ones again?

The story of the Horowitz family
will continue in

Levi's War

Take a sneak peek here ...

Levi's War

I wasn't a natural soldier. I had never considered spending one second of the twenty-one years of my life in any of the Armed Forces. As the black Mercedes drew away from my family home and the forlorn group on the doorstep continued to wave goodbye, I was imagining a new life working in a bank in London.

Berlin had become an increasingly dangerous place for a Jew. The restrictions applied by our Nazi masters continued to pile up, new laws almost every day, and the night before my departure we had witnessed the biggest pogrom for a hundred years. My younger brother, Simon, and I had been caught up in the midst of the shattering glass, the acrid smoke and the vicious batons of the storm troopers, and had found refuge with a Gentile woman. We'd spent the evening in her apartment on the Handerstrasse, talking, eating and feeling grateful for warmth and safety. But this morning we'd taken our leave and made our way home. Simon had led me to the music shop of Amos Wiggenstein, a local luthier. He'd seen the violins burning in a pile on the cobbled street and Amos's assistant, Jacob, being beaten and now he wanted to see what was left. We salvaged seven complete violins, carried them home in a wooden box and hid them in the attic of our home. Violins were an integral part of our lives. Our papa and mama owned two, a 1742 Guarneri del Gesú and a 1640 Amati. Both Papa and Simon played the Guarneri and I played the huge Steinway grand piano.

And now I was being driven away from terror and towards safety. Did I feel guilty? Perhaps. I had some of our family treasures hidden in a leather pouch in my armpit and some documents in a package strapped to my chest. It felt like I was the guardian of centuries of family possessions. If we were forced to surrender them, I carried a complete inventory and some of the most precious pieces of jewellery with me to sanctuary.

I was under the impression that I would be taken south to the Swiss border but the driver informed me we were travelling north to the Danish border. Once into Denmark I would be met by a contact who would take me north to the sea and put me on a boat for Sweden. From there I would fly to London. It all sounded very exciting. The miles were gobbled up by the quiet, comfortable car and after a while I fell asleep.

'We've come to a checkpoint, Herr Horowitz.'

The voice roused me and I sat up. There were very bright lights ahead and a barrier across the road.

'They'll need your papers,' the driver added.

I fumbled inside the pocket of my papa's woollen coat and pulled out the folded exit visa Papa's friend had given him.

'I have it here,' I said.

I rolled down the window and put the paper into a gloved hand that was thrust inside the car. There was a full moment of silence. All I felt was impatience.

'Get out of the car please, sir.'

The voice was firm but neutral. I hesitated and then did as he asked. My suitcase was on the seat beside me. The speaker was a soldier in uniform.

'Bring your case and follow me.'

I had layers of clothing on under the coat so bending in

the middle was quite hard as I leaned in and picked up my suitcase.

'I won't be long,' I said to the driver.

As I followed the soldier across the stony ground towards a large hut, I heard the car engine fire. I spun round and watched the Mercedes make a wide U-turn and disappear into the blackness.

'Hey! Come back.' It was a cry of shock and anger.

'Never mind, sir, just follow me. There are plenty more cars coming.'

With reluctance, I did as he said. The wooden hut was cold and draughty. He pointed to a chair behind a table. 'Sit there, please.'

I put my suitcase on the ground beside the chair and sat down. The soldier picked up the case and took it with him. I heard a key turn on the other side of the door. The room was lit by a bright bulb hanging from the centre of the roof. Over to one side was a bench with a kettle and two cups and a bottle of milk. I got up and walked around the room. Behind the blind, the one window had a grid of iron bars across it. The door handle turned but the door was locked. I returned to the seat and slumped down. I hadn't anticipated this. The car was gone, my exit visa and suitcase were in the hands of a soldier and I was locked inside a small wooden hut on the German side of the Danish border. It felt like a good time to pray, so I bowed my head and asked G-d to intervene and set me back on my road to London. After some time the key turned in the lock and the door opened.

'Get up!'

This man was in plain clothes, a tight-fitting black leather coat and jackboots. He held my suitcase in his hand. I rose to my feet, I was over ten centimetres taller than him. He snarled. 'Where are you going?'

I swallowed hard.

'London. My papa got my exit visa from a friend in the government, it is genuine.'

He dropped the case to the ground and drew a gun from his pocket. He was Gestapo.

'Genuine?' It was a sneer.

'Yes. My papa is an influential banker —'

He gave a humourless bark of laughter.

'Your papa is a Jew. And so are you and you are trying to leave illegally. That is a crime. Punishable by death.'

He levelled the gun at me.